Maine Men Book Six

Aaron's
AWAKENING

K.C. WELLS

Aaron's Awakening
Copyright © 2022 by K.C. Wells
Cover Art by Meredith Russell
Edited by Sue Laybourn

Warning
This book contains material that is intended for a mature, adult audience. It contains graphic language, explicit sexual content, and adult situations.

Maine Men
Levi, Noah, Aaron, Ben, Dylan, Finn, Seb, and Shaun.
Eight friends who met in high school in Wells, Maine.
Different backgrounds, different paths, but one thing remains solid, even eight years after they graduated – their friendship. Holidays, weddings, funerals, birthdays, parties – any chance they get to meet up, they take it. It's an opportunity to share what's going on in their lives, especially their love lives.

Back in high school, they knew four of them were gay or bi, so maybe it was more than coincidence that they gravitated to one another. Along the way, there were revelations and realizations, some more of a surprise than others. And what none of the others knew was that Levi was in love with one of them…

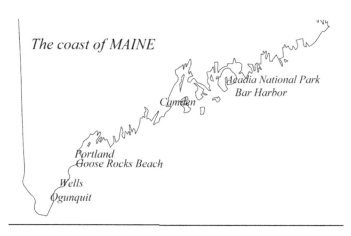

The coast of MAINE

Acadia National Park
Bar Harbor

Camden

Portland
Goose Rocks Beach
Wells
Ogunquit

K.C. WELLS

Prologue

From Shaun's Salvation

Ben cackled. "Is there ever gonna be a shindig where we just get together and *no one* springs a surprise partner on us? Dear *Lord*, this is certainly a year to remember."

Aaron scowled. "Hey, what gives? The end of the year, and I'm suddenly a minority?"

"You're not the only one," Noah complained. Then his eyes widened. "Hey, wait a minute. This means we've gone from eight to thirteen. There can't be thirteen of us. That's bad luck."

"Wait until Easter. Or Valentine's." Wade chuckled. "The way things have been going, anything could happen." His eyes sparkled. "Which of you, Aaron, and Levi, is gonna take the plunge?"

Aaron folded his arms. "Well, don't look at me, 'cause *I'm* not looking."

Levi grinned. "Oh, you've done it now. Haven't you learned anything from the past nine months?" He pointed to the couples in the room. "None of *them* were looking, but it didn't matter. Love snuck up on 'em and hit 'em over the head with a baseball bat." His gaze met Shaun's. "And I fucking *love* it."

K.C. WELLS

Chapter One

January 1, 2021

"Finn and Joel, huh? Here's to the happy couple." Aaron raised his glass, and the punch made an attempt to escape. "Oops." He drank half of it, a little too quickly, and the back of his throat caught fire. Once he'd finished coughing, he wiped his lips. "Christ, what does Grammy put in this stuff?"

Levi let out a drunken chuckle. "Trus' me, you don't wanna know. An' after three or four glasses, you're too numb to care."

Aaron did his best to focus on Levi. "Is it me, or is your beard tryin' to eat your face?"

"'S you. Drink some more. You won't notice it then."

Aaron had a feeling he'd drunk enough. He couldn't remember the last time he'd been this wasted. Then he grinned. Sure he could. That would have been the *last* New Year's Eve party. Not that he was all that wasted. He could probably walk in a straight line, if he really put his mind to it. "Looks like you, me, an' Noah are gonna be confirmed bachelors."

Levi narrowed his gaze. "Hey, wait a sec. Who says I *want* to be a fuckin' bachelor?"

Aaron widened his eyes and tried to press a single finger to his lips, but he missed his mouth. "Sshh. Grammy'll hear ya."

"Grammy's in bed, an' everyone's gone 'cept you an' me."

It was three in the morning, and he and Levi had been putting the world to rights. It was the same discussion they had after every New Year's Eve party, except the more punch they'd drunk, the more difficult it became to propose solutions to stop world hunger in its tracks, bring a halt to climate change, and deliver peace to all nations.

Aaron squinted at him. "Since when do *you* drink so much?" He couldn't recollect *ever* seeing Levi drunk.

"We're celebratin', aren't we? Finn an' Joel, gettin' hitched. Congratulations to 'em."

The uncharacteristic note of sadness in Levi's voice made it through the fog of alcohol enveloping Aaron's brain. "What's eatin' you?"

Levi gazed at him with wide eyes. "Me? Not a goddamn thing. I'm happy for them. They found each other, didn't they?"

Aaron wasn't buying it. "Let's get back to you not wanting to be a bachelor."

Levi swallowed. "No, let's *not*, okay?" He raised his glass of punch. "To Finn and Joel. May life bring them everything they desire. It's already brought them love."

The warm fuzziness produced by the punch had dissipated. "Levi, what's wrong?"

Levi sagged against the seat cushions. "We don't all get to be with the one we love, all right? Sometimes, the one we love is out of reach." He locked gazes with Aaron. "He doesn't have a clue, you know? Not a fucking clue. And it's gonna stay that way." Sadness had given way to an edge of frustration in his voice.

A horrible suspicion grew in Aaron's mind. "Levi, you... you're not in love with Finn, are you?" That might account for the state he was in.

Levi's eyes widened. "God, no! I mean, I love Finn like a brother, always have, but... no." He sighed heavily. "No, I had to go and fall for someone who... who doesn't want me. At least, he's never given a *sign* that he wants me. Sometimes, I think he cares more about his goddamn *trains* than he—" He clammed up, his eyes huge. "Fuck. You didn't hear that, okay? Because I didn't say it."

Aaron gaped at him. "Oh my God," he said in a soft voice.

Levi's gaze hardened. "I mean it, Aaron. Forget I said it. You got that? And we're not gonna mention it, *ever* again."

Aaron couldn't let it go, not like that. "How long, Levi? How long have you been in love with Noah?"

Levi crumpled before his eyes. "Oh, not long. Since I was fourteen, maybe?" He finished the last of his punch. "You want another?"

"I've had enough, and so have you." *Fourteen years old? Oh man.*

Levi stared at him. "Let it go, okay?" He placed his empty glass on the table beside the couch. "And maybe we need to find someone for you. What's your type?"

Aaron didn't want to let it go, but he knew Levi was resolute. "Don't think I have one. And like I said earlier, I'm not looking for anyone either."

"But if you were?"

Aaron rolled his eyes. "Okay, okay..." He

stroked his bearded chin. "She'd be younger than me—not *too* much younger, maybe in her early twenties. She'd be pretty. And she'd be like me."

"How exactly like you?"

"Neither of us would be looking for a soul mate."

Levi blinked. "Okay," he enunciated.

"Hey, I'm making this up as I go along, all right?" Aaron drank the last of his punch. "Not that any of this matters, because like I keep saying, I'm not looking. And no girl is suddenly gonna materialize out of nowhere and grab my attention. I'm not gonna be lying awake nights, 'cause I can't get her out of my head. I'm happy the way I am." When Levi didn't respond, Aaron narrowed his gaze. "Well? Nothing to say?"

Levi bit his lip. "Nothing I haven't already said tonight. And when the moment comes, remember it was me who told you so."

"Told me what?"

"About love sneaking up on you with a baseball bat."

Aaron smiled. "Don't worry. Nothing and nobody is gonna sneak up on *me*." He glanced at their surroundings. "Don't look now, but someone made a mess." The floor was barely visible through bits of colored paper. "Who let off a confetti cannon in here?" They'd done the party popper thing when Shaun had arrived, but to Aaron's mind, there was a whole load more of the stuff.

Levi chuckled. "That was Ben. He brought a couple of those air-compressed party poppers. Huge tubes." He squinted. "You didn't see him and Wade set them off?"

"I was too busy watching the fireworks." Except that wasn't entirely true. He'd kept his gaze focused on the display because that way, he didn't have to watch the couples around him exchanging kisses at midnight.

He hadn't lied to Levi—well, not exactly. He wasn't looking for someone, that much was true. But maybe he was getting a little tired of his own company.

Am I lonely?

Aaron wouldn't have thought it possible to be lonely with so many friends, but he did feel kind of isolated up there in Bar Harbor. And he had seen less of them the past year.

Is it any wonder, when five of them went and found themselves boyfriends?

Not that he begrudged any of them their happiness. Shit, some of them had been *way* overdue for a little of that.

Then he realized the room had gone quiet.

He glanced at Levi, and smiled. Levi's eyes were closed, and his breathing had become deeper, more regular. *I guess the punch finally knocked him out.* Well, either that, or something else far stronger. *I had no idea about Noah.* Then he recalled the barbecue at his house late that summer, when Noah had finally told them he was ace. *If I'd loved someone since I was fourteen, and then they came out with a revelation like that, I'm not sure how I would feel.* Not that there was anything wrong with being asexual, but if Aaron had been in love with someone for as long as Levi had, he figured somewhere along the line, the thought of making love to them might have crossed his mind. Then again, Noah had said something about having sex, just not being sexually attracted to someone.

Shit, what do I know about this stuff? He was too tired and too muddleheaded to contemplate his *own* situation, let alone Levi's.

Aaron got to his feet, a little unsteady, and squeezed Levi's shoulder. "Hey, wake up, sleepyhead. It's time to go to bed."

Levi opened his eyes. "Can't," he murmured drowsily. "Gotta clean all this up before Grammy sees it and pitches a fit."

"Hate to break it to you, but it usually looks like this after New Year's." Aaron helped him to stand. "Grammy will leave it all for you to get rid of. And me, seeing as I'm staying over." He smiled. "What does she always say?" In perfect synchronization, they intoned, "Clean up your own damn mess."

"You don't have to sleep on the folding bed," Levi said as Aaron guided him to his room. "Too late to be setting it up. You can sleep in my bed, if you promise not to hog the comforter. Or snore."

"You sure? And I don't snore."

Levi waved his hand. "Noah always shares my bed when he stays over."

Now he was in full possession of the facts, Aaron guessed that would amount to torture.

They paused at the bedroom door, and Levi glanced toward Grammy's room. "Sometimes I think she knows every thought that goes through my head."

Aaron stifled a chuckle, for fear of waking her. "That's probably because she does. She knows you, balls to bones."

Levi shivered. "What a scary thought." Aaron pushed the door open and ushered Levi into the large bedroom that had been his all his life. He sat Levi on the bed and helped him to undress. "'M not that drunk," Levi protested.

"If you say so."

"*You're* more drunk than me."

"Mm-hm."

"Aaron?"

He paused in his task. "What?"

Levi gazed at him, his blue eyes suddenly more alert. "You won't tell anyone, will you?"

Aaron didn't have to ask what he was talking about. "I won't. I promise." He dragged a finger across his chest. "Cross my heart."

A shudder rippled through Levi. "Thank you."

On impulse, Aaron kissed his forehead. "You're a sweet guy, you know that?"

Levi narrowed his gaze. "I'm not your type, remember? For one thing…" He cupped his pecs. "I'm missing some important equipment."

Aaron pulled back the sheets and Levi clambered in, wearing only his briefs. "Something I've always wanted to ask. Boobs do nothing for you?"

Levi managed a shrug. "They're pretty, but that's as far as I'd go." He grinned. "Now, a nice long dick? That's a different story."

Aaron laughed, and it sounded way too loud. He hushed instantly. "So you're what Seb calls a size queen?" *The things I'm learning tonight…*

"Long enough to reach all the right places. Not that I have any actual experience, you understand." He sighed. "I can look, though… and dream."

Aaron froze. "Are you saying you're a—"

"Yes, I am, and that's something else I don't want spread around, okay?" Levi propped himself up on his elbows. "I mean it."

"But…" Aaron got into bed and lay on his side facing Levi. "You're gorgeous, dude."

Levi smiled. "Aw, you're a pretty sweet guy too. Thing is, I was kinda… saving myself." His face tightened. "Except I'm starting to realize I've been saving myself for the wrong guy. Maybe I need to follow the guys' example and find a man. Any man'll do."

I have a feeling there's only one man for you.

Aaron turned the light off, plunging the room into darkness. "Goodnight, Levi."

"Night." A moment later, he sighed heavily. "Did you hear him tonight? When you said something about being in a minority, and he agreed with you? Why should he care? He doesn't want… anyone."

Aaron didn't have to be a mind reader to know what Levi really wanted to say. *You mean, he doesn't want you.* Christ, the pain in Levi's voice just about broke Aaron's heart. He reached over to where Levi lay, and encountered a bare shoulder. Aaron tugged the comforter higher until it covered him, then lay on his back, fingers laced beneath his head.

Another year. The last one had brought so many changes. Who knew what the new one had in store—for any of them?

If I did make a New Year's resolution, what would it be? To work harder on my personal life than I do on my job? While he hated to admit it, his earlier realization was on the money.

I'm lonely.

Maybe it was time to put himself out there

and meet someone who *completed* him. Because much as he loved his job, his house, his friends, he wasn't complete. And seeing his friends find someone who completed *them* only confirmed his suspicions that he was missing out on something vital.

Something life-altering.

Aaron was ready for a little life alteration.

Chapter Two

It didn't matter that he'd gone to bed at a ridiculous hour—Aaron always woke as soon as the birds started singing. One look at his phone told him it was just past seven o'clock. He'd take a nap once he got home, provided he stayed awake long enough for the drive back to Bar Harbor.

That's assuming there hasn't been a lot of snow overnight. It was almost a four-hour drive, but if it had snowed? Yeah, no. If that was the case, he might be staying one more night.

Levi was dead to the world, only his dark hair visible above the comforter. Aaron snuck out of the bed, grabbed his jeans from the chair where he'd left them, wriggled into them, and pulled on his sweater. He knew from past experience Grammy would be up too, and that meant one thing—good coffee.

Aaron opened the door quietly, closed it behind him, and padded barefoot to the kitchen. The enticing aroma hit him with full force before he'd taken one step into the kitchen, and he sniffed.

Grammy was standing next to the coffee pot. "I figured you'd be the first to climb out of bed. Want some?" Aaron regarded her with a pained expression, and she cackled. "Dumb question." She grabbed a cup from the cabinet, then grinned. "This big enough for ya?" She held up a huge *I heart Maine* mug that had to hold twenty ounces.

"*Now* you're talking."

Grammy inclined her head toward the living room. "Get your butt in there. It's the best room for when the sun comes up." She glanced at the wall clock. "And that'll be in about five minutes."

"Thanks, Grammy." He went over and kissed her cheek.

She flushed. "Get away with you."

Aaron headed for the living room, steeling himself for how bad the mess really was—and stopped dead at the threshold. No confetti, no bottles... The only indication there had been a party at all was the birthday banner strung over the fireplace, and Aaron figured that was because Grammy couldn't reach. Levi wasn't happy to have her climbing steps.

God bless Grammy.

He removed the tacks and took down the brightly colored banner, revealing the painting that had sat above the mantelpiece for as long as Aaron had been coming to the house. He folded the banner, then took a step back to appreciate the painting in all its serenity and beauty. It was a landscape, except half the image was of the ocean. The artist had captured the early morning light: what clouds there were in the expanse of sky were tinged with orange and gold, reflected in the calm waters. A rocky outcrop stood to the right, topped with trees dark against the brightening sky. The beach below was a rich copper color, lying in the shade of the rock. One lone fishing boat sat out there, a figure standing in it with a rod, too small for Aaron to see any features.

"So peaceful," he murmured. He had a feeling he'd been there.

His nostrils caught the smell of coffee, and Grammy joined him, handing him the mug. "You always do that, y'know."

"Do what?"

"Stare at that painting."

Aaron took a step closer to peer at the signature. *DD 2002.* "When did you get it?" It had been there since the first time he'd visited Levi's house, back when they were in high school.

"About fifteen years ago, so only four years after it was painted."

"Who's DD?" he asked.

"No idea. I just saw it in a gallery in Portland one day, when I was shoppin' for clothes for Levi."

Aaron stood still, letting his gaze wander across the varnished surface. "I've never asked, but do you know where this is?"

"Ayuh. It's Owl's Head."

"Ah. I think I went there when I was a kid. Mom was the one who got me into hiking. Near Thomaston, right?" He smiled. "I love it. Kinda reminds me of early mornings in Bar Harbor." He sipped his coffee. "Damn." That hit the spot.

Grammy chuckled. "I know you like it strong. I guess you're gonna be busy now, with all them morons arrivin' to heave 'emselves down a hillside, riskin' life 'n' limb."

He laughed. "It's called skiing? Snowboarding?" She waved a hand. "But you're right. It gets busy in the park in the winter." He returned his attention to the painting. "Did he do any others?"

Grammy snorted. "How in the Sam Hill would I know? I don't even know his name. Could be a her, of course. There *are* female artists, y'know."

"My bad."

"And I only bought it because it caught my eye." She gestured to the living room. "Just like the rest of the stuff in here." She raised her eyes to the ceiling. "Levi still asleep?" When he nodded, she pointed to the two-seater couch that sat under the front window. "Let's sit. My bones complain if I stand too long."

He joined her on the comfy couch, leaning back against the plump cushions. Grammy settled, her hands wrapped around her cup. Outside, the morning sun was slowly creeping over the landscape.

"You cleaned," he said in a mock accusatory tone.

"As Levi is so fond of sayin'… Bite me. You boys stayed up late last night. I wasn't about to wait for ya to clean up the mess."

"Did we wake you?"

She cackled. "Boy, do you really think at my age I fall asleep as soon as my head hits the pillow? Or that I sleep the whole night through? So no, you didn't wake me. I guessed it was one of those conversations fueled by my punch. I'm surprised you lasted as long as you did." Her eyes twinkled. "How's the head this mornin'?"

He chuckled. "My head is just fine, thank you."

A comfortable silence fell, broken by the birds chirping and the ticking of the grandfather clock in the hallway.

"Is he all right?"

Aaron blinked. "Sure. Why do you ask?"

"Nothing I can put my finger on. He just seems… I don't know… outta sorts lately." Her dark brown eyes met his. "I did think he might confide in you. If there *was* something botherin' him."

"He's okay." Aaron wasn't about to share Levi's involuntary revelation.

Grammy stared out at the front yard, the morning sun showing up every line and wrinkle. "I worry about him."

"That's 'cause you love him."

She sighed. "I know he has all of you, and you're the best bunch of friends he could have. God knows I thank Him every day for every last one of you. But… I think he's lonely."

Aaron said nothing.

"Seems like lately, every time we have a party, one of you turns up with a fella on your arm. And Levi? He sits up there on the shelf, twiddlin' his thumbs and waitin'."

"There's a lot of it going around," Aaron murmured. When Grammy gave him a quizzical glance, he smiled. "Loneliness."

Grammy widened her eyes. "Seriously? You gotta have girls linin' up for your number." She grinned. "Of course, there's one thing about you that might put 'em off."

"And what's that?"

She snorted. "You're a redhead."

"Hey! My hair's not *that* red." Not something he could say when it caught the light.

"Child, have you looked at your beard in a mirror? And you know what they say about redheads."

He drank a little more. "Please, enlighten me." Dylan and Noah were usually the ones who teased Aaron about his coloring.

"Well, there's that hot temper you're s'posed to have… skin that frazzles in the sun so you end up lookin' like a lobster fresh from the pot. Redheads can be clowns too."

Aaron laughed. "I spend most of my days outside. I haven't frazzled yet. And as for a temper…"

Grammy smiled. "Yeah, I know. Hardly anything ruffles *your* feathers. I've always thought of you as the calm one of the bunch, although Noah comes a close second. But there *is* one thing they say about redheads that you can't deny."

"And what's that?"

Her eyes glinted. "You're all weird."

He laughed out loud, reining it in at the last minute for fear of waking Levi. "Not gonna argue with that one. You have to be weird to hang around with these guys. But I was reading some article the other day that paints us gingers in a *very* different light." He buffed his fingernails on his sweater. "According to scientists, we have weird genetic superpowers."

"Is that right?" Grammy arched her barely there eyebrows. "This I gotta hear."

"We have a higher pain threshold, for one thing."

She smirked. "Didn't notice that when I was wallopin' you with my broom, that time I caught you stealin' apples off of my tree."

"We know when it's getting cold."

She laughed. "So do I. It's called goosebumps."

"We love getting busy."

Grammy nodded. "Okay, you got me with

that one. You're always busy."

"We're funnier."

Another raise of her eyebrows. "This, from a kid who could never remember the punchline of a joke?" She shook her head.

"When I was little, my mom used to tell me redheads were sunshine mixed with a little hurricane."

Grammy set her cup down on the coffee table. "What did Lucille Ball say? 'Once in his life, every man is entitled to fall madly in love with a gorgeous redhead.'"

Aaron started to laugh, but then came to an abrupt stop. "Wait a minute. Does that mean I'm gonna find another redhead? Or that some *guy* is gonna fall for me?"

Grammy shrugged. "Well, you *are* gorgeous." She cackled. "Go with the flow, I always say." She smoothed her hair. "If some good-lookin' woman in her fifties took a shine to me, I wouldn't say no. Never too late to change lanes, right?"

He burst into laughter. "Grammy, you're awesome."

The door opened and Levi walked in, running his hand through his tousled hair. "You two are awful noisy this morning."

Grammy stood. "Us early birds gotta get our day started with coffee 'n' good conversation. And now you've rejoined the land of the livin', I'll make breakfast. Blueberry pancakes okay?"

Aaron mimed wiping away drool.

Levi glanced at the room with a frown. "Grammy…"

"You hush. And before you start yellin' about me and heights, Aaron took down the banner."

He walked over to her and kissed her cheek. "You know I worry about you."

"I do, but I can take care of myself. Mostly. Now go pour yourself some coffee, then keep Aaron company while I cook. I'll call you both when the pancakes are done." She returned his kiss. "Love ya, boy." Then she left the room.

Aaron waited till she was out of earshot. "She worries about you," he said in a low voice. "I do too—now."

Levi sighed. "I knew I should've kept my big mouth shut. And no, I'm not going to discuss this again. Change the subject. Tell me what you'll be doing when you go back to the park."

"I'll be watching and helping all those people who don't let a little snow stop their fun, just like I do every winter." The park would welcome an influx of cross-country skiers, snowshoers, snowmobilers, ice fishermen, and birdwatchers. Plus, there'd be people out for a scenic drive: a small section of the Park Loop Road closest to the ocean would be open for driving. That didn't mean Aaron wouldn't have his share of assholes to deal with, the folks who seemed to leave their brains at home when they ventured into spots where the snow was way too deep.

He'd be busy as a mule for the next twelve weeks, then spring would arrive—and he'd be even busier.

Maybe I could find time to go on a date? It had been a while, that was for damn sure. Aaron couldn't remember the last occasion someone had shared his bed.

"Aaron?"

He blinked. "Sorry. Must've zoned out. Did

you say something?"

"I said, maybe I should throw a party for Valentine's Day, except then I thought better of it." His face fell. "Not sure I want to be surrounded by a group of loved-up guys. And you *know* all the talk will be about Finn and Joel's wedding. So maybe I'll leave it for a while—until Easter."

Recalling his own reaction to kisses at midnight, Aaron was with Levi on that issue.

I said I wasn't looking. Maybe I need to rethink that.

Chapter Three

January 15

Dean Durrell was ready for coffee. In fact, he'd been ready an hour ago.

He surveyed the living room floor. There weren't that many boxes—a lot of his stuff was still in storage—but he knew the log house didn't come with a whole lot of closet space. There was always the basement, but he'd brought things he wanted around him, not packed away in a basement. The slim case containing his paints and brushes sat in one of the bedrooms, his easel leaning against the wall, and in another box were his cleaning fluids, rags, mediums and pencils.

The fact that he'd brought them at all was a positive sign.

"Where do you want this one?" Ash staggered through the front door, weighed down by a large cardboard box.

Dean smirked. "What does it say on it?"

Ash peered at the side. "Kitchen."

"Well, there's a clue for you right there."

Ash rolled his eyes and veered to the left where the kitchen stood behind a partition wall. "Feels like your pans are made of concrete, it's so heavy."

"They're cast iron, so you were close. And be careful with that box. It's got my Le Creuset skillet in it."

"What's wrong with an ordinary skillet? You know, one that's lighter?" Dean caught an *oof* as Ash deposited his burden on the kitchen floor. He reappeared, flexing his fingers. "Man, they've gone numb."

Dean laughed. "Quit exaggerating."

"That was the last of the boxes." Ash closed the front door and shivered. "*Now* can we light that stove? I'm freezing my ass off here. I'll even go back outside for the logs."

"There are logs in that basket. Knock yourself out."

Ash hurried over to the wood stove in the living room. "What kind of idiot moves to Downeast Maine in the middle of winter?" he grumbled as he stacked kindling in the oven's belly. "Oh yeah—my brother, that's who. I swear, all these trips back and forth to the truck? My toes have developed frostbite."

"You are *such* a drama queen."

Ash glanced at him over his shoulder. "Er, excuse me? The only queen I see around here is you." Then he went back to his task. "Couldn't you have rented a place with a view?"

Dean pointed to the snow-laden trees at the front of the property. "That's a view."

"I meant a view of the water. You move to an island, and you choose a place that faces inland. I swear, the only things to look at on this road are freakin' trees. Wasn't there a house somewhere closer to the ocean?"

"Sure there was—if I happened to have three thousand dollars a month to spend on rent. Have you even *looked* at rental prices recently? Bar Harbor is a popular place."

"I still think you've been cheated. Bay View Drive kinda implies there's a view, don't you think? Doesn't this come under 'false advertising?'" Ash grinned.

Dean had liked the house well enough when he'd seen it online. Seeing it in the flesh, as it were, had only cemented his opinion. It had that in-the-middle-of-nowhere vibe going on. The wraparound porch would be great for sitting out when the weather got warmer—and before the mosquitos took over.

"I'm the one who's living here. If I like the view, that's all that matters."

"But why here?" Ash aimed the gas lighter at the crumpled paper beneath the kindling. It caught, and soon flames were licking at the kindling.

"Why not here? I loved Maine when I was a kid. Hated that we had to move." Dad's job had taken him to Ohio, and Dean had never warmed to the place. When he'd finished college, he'd moved to Pennsylvania, followed by a stint in New York, ending up in Massachusetts. It wasn't until the last few months that he'd figured out he'd been moving inexorably along a straight line toward the coast—and Maine in particular.

Maine felt like coming home.

He'd taken a trip to Mount Desert Island the previous fall, to check the place out and had come to a final decision. He liked Bar Harbor, and a drive through Acadia National Park had his fingers itching for a pencil. For the first time in a long while, he pictured himself standing in front of his easel, capturing the beauty of the landscape before him.

What surprised him was, the idea felt good.

"Besides," he added. "Some of my earliest work was views of Maine." For his tenth birthday, Mom had given him a camera, and Dean had spent many happy hours capturing the natural beauty all around him. In his teens, those photos had inspired him to pick up a paintbrush, and the rest was history. He didn't have any of his early pieces: he'd given them away, to neighbors, relatives, friends of his parents...

"Before you discovered how much people would pay to have their portrait painted?" Ash shook his head. "Dad was forever telling people about you. 'My son, the prodigy.' And then the photo album would come out."

"Does he still do that?"

Ash snorted. "Are you kidding? Every time you finished a painting, he'd find a photo of it and stick it in there." His gaze met Dean's. "Until you stopped painting, of course."

Dean had figured the subject would come up. What shocked him was how long it had taken Ash to broach the subject. His younger brother wasn't known for being reticent. "Thanks for coming all this way to help me move my stuff."

"Do I get the five-cent tour now?"

Dean smiled. "There's not that much more to see, but sure." He led Ash toward the rear of the house, through a pine-clad hallway.

"They really like their pine in Maine, I guess," Ash quipped. Then he chuckled. "What was it Dad used to say? 'I hate pine trees. All they do is drip sap on the frickin' car.'"

"You have his voice down perfectly," Dean observed. "It was like he was in the room." He guessed the cladding on the walls had been there a while: it had lost its youthful pallor, developing a darker patina that in turn made the internal hallway a little gloomy. He opened one door. "This will be my bedroom." It was a large square room, with another door connecting to the bathroom. Two windows, one at each corner, let in the bright light that bounced off the snow outside. The closet was small, but it wasn't as if Dean had a lot of clothing to fill it.

"Where am I sleeping tonight?" Ash demanded. "I haven't shared a room with you in almost twenty years, and I don't intend to revisit that experience."

"Hey, you have nothing to complain about. I was the neat one—*you* were the slob."

"I know! You were always making me look bad."

"And that was somehow my fault?" Dean went back into the hallway and opened another door. "This is where you're sleeping."

Ash studied the corner room. "Nice. Lots of light in here. You know, it'd be perfect for a studio."

"Subtle, Ash. Very subtle."

Ash folded his arms. "Unless you want to continue with your obviously satisfying career in book illustrations?" He met Dean's gaze. "How long has it been since you painted? And I don't count the illustrations."

Dean's stomach clenched. "You already know the answer to that. Five years."

Ash walked over to one of the windows and stared out at the snow-covered yard, his back stiff. "I get that he was your muse, okay? He inspired you. But Christ, Dean… He was the one who dumped *you*.

Why give him so much power?"

"Excuse me?"

Ash turned to face him. "Sorry, but it's how I see it. He's stopped you from painting these past five years. That's giving way too much power to someone who wasn't worth it, especially since he broke up with you. He lost the right to have any influence over you."

Dean walked over to him and gave him a hug. "You're a pain in the ass, but you have moments when I'm reminded of what an awesome brother you are." He released him. "And I know you're right."

Ash gaped. "Then you'll start painting again?" He beamed. "Damn, I'm good."

Dean laughed out loud. "I hate to burst your bubble, but one of the reasons why I rented this place? I saw this bedroom and had the same thought as you."

"Oh. So you're going back to landscapes?

Dean nodded. "You're right, by the way. About giving him too much power. I'd reached the same conclusion."

Ash grinned. "Does this mean the world is gonna be seeing Dean Durrell masterpieces in galleries once more?"

"I don't know about masterpieces. Let me get back into my stride before I start planning what I'm going to paint." The plan was to sketch the views around Mount Desert, to get his eye in again. And when he was ready, he'd begin working.

"Hey, Dean? There isn't a bed in here."

"I've got one of those mattress toppers. You can sleep on that."

Ash glanced at his painting paraphernalia.

"Okay, step one is painting again. What about step two?"

"I didn't know there was a step two."

"Sure there is." Ash's eyes twinkled. "Getting back on the horse."

"I thought I was doing that with the painting." Then Ash's meaning sank in. "Oh. I see."

Ash nodded slowly. "Man cannot live by painting alone. Occasionally he needs a little… company. Especially if he's been on his own for five years." He speared Dean with a look. "And you have, haven't you?"

Dean raised his eyebrows. "Do I ask *you* questions about your sex life?"

"No, but yours isn't exactly a secret. Not since I came home from school that day when I was fifteen, came up to the attic, and found you and Steve Burnett pashing on the couch."

"Pashing? What the hell is pashing?"

"Sorry. Something I picked up from watching shows from Australia and the UK." He smiled sweetly. "How about necking? You know what *that* means, right?"

"We were not necking. I was painting."

Ash rolled his eyes. "Dude, his tongue was down your throat. Kinda difficult to paint like that."

What Dean recalled about that day? Ash hadn't said a word about what he'd seen to their parents. It had been the impetus Dean needed to come out to them, not that he'd been concerned about their reaction. Only, once he'd done that, Mom had insisted he didn't take any more boys up to the attic—or his bedroom. When he'd complained, she told him she'd have had the same rule if he'd brought girls home.

Popping his cherry had to wait until college.

"I'm not looking, okay?"

"But if a good-looking dude crosses your path…"

Dean chuckled. "Will you just quit?"

Ash's smile faded. "I want you to be happy, that's all. And… I think you've been lonely. You're not meant to be alone, bro. You need that… connection with someone."

Dean's throat tightened. "You really do know me, don't you?"

"Man, I fucking *love* you. I want you to find some sweet, sexy guy who makes you happy, because you are *way* overdue for some of that." There was a glint in his eye. "And besides, you're three years shy of forty. If you don't find someone soon, you'll end up as one of those confirmed bachelors everyone whispers about. You know, the ones who have romantic relations with their stamp collections." Dean gave him a quizzical glance, and Ash waggled his eyebrows. "*You* know… lots of licking?" He cleared his throat. "Now, is it too much to hope there's somewhere on this rock that does really good pizza?"

He laughed. "Pat's Pizza in Bar Harbor. Great pepperoni, and breadsticks to die for."

"Now you're talking." Ash's face lit up. "Grab your keys. And you're buying."

"I was going to anyway, as a thank you."

"And can we get enough pizza so there's leftovers for breakfast tomorrow?"

He grimaced. "You still do that?"

Ash stared at him. "Dude. That's the best part." That twinkle was back. "You never know. Our

server might be a sexy guy who has the hots for you."
He frowned. "On second thoughts? Scrap that idea. I
don't wanna be in here trying to sleep while you
bump uglies with him."

"You don't have a filter, do you?"

Ash huffed. "I think I've been remarkably
restrained. Now feed me."

As they locked the door and headed down the
porch steps, Dean replayed Ash's words in his head.

You're not meant to be alone.

Damn it. He'd been that for far too long.

K.C. WELLS

Chapter Four

March 27

Aaron drove into the parking lot for the Bass Harbor campground and pulled into a space. There were a few cars—not as many as there would be when May arrived, although not *that* many because it was still freaking cold—and he spied a couple of RVs. Still too damn cold for camping out in tents. It was a beautiful cool day, and he was carrying out his usual inspection, checking no one had lit any huge fires, and that campers were following the rules.

He liked the start of spring. The first of the hikers made their appearance, though not all that many of them, and his schedule was less frantic than it would be within six or so weeks. By the end of May, he'd be conducting guided tours from a boat cruise five days a week, albeit bundled up, and by early summer that would increase to every day. Some of his coworkers were already taking part in a virtual program of events.

Aaron got out of the car and strolled through the campground, nodding cheerfully at campers. When he was happy all was well, he got back into the car and drove along Lighthouse Road, which ended at the Bass Harbor Head Light. It was one of his favorite hiking spots, walking along the trail that led down to the water, then looking up at the white lighthouse on the cliff. By the time the season was in full swing, there would be a lot of tourists heading that way. Little wonder there were so many photos of the lighthouse online—it had to be one of the most popular sights in the park. Right then, only one truck sat in the lot, and he stopped next to it. Aaron got out and walked toward the beginning of the trail. From his vantage point, he spotted a lone figure on the rocky outcrop below.

Are they painting? There was certainly something that could have been an artist's easel in front of them, but Aaron imagined such an item might be precariously balanced. His natural curiosity won the day.

He wanted to investigate further.

Aaron followed the trail to the beach, enjoying the warmth of the sun on his face. As he drew closer, he saw the figure was a man, alternating his stares between the view of the lighthouse and the sketching pad balanced on the easel. He wore a brown wool beanie, but the long hair protruding from beneath it curled slightly at the ends, reaching his bearded chin. His cheeks were dusted with light freckles. And then Aaron got a little closer.

Well, what do you know? I'm not the only blue-eyed redhead on this island.

Aaron paused a few feet away, waiting for the artist to acknowledge him. He seemed lost in concentration.

Finally, the man looked in Aaron's direction. "Is there a problem? I *am* allowed to be down here, right?"

"Not a problem," Aaron assured him. "This gets to be one of the busiest spots in the park in the summer. You picked the right time to come." He peered at the easel. "Are you sure that thing is steady?" He had visions of it falling into the water, and the artist tumbling after it in an effort to save his precious work.

"I've jammed the back leg into a crevice between two rocks," the man told him.

Aaron nodded toward the sketching book. "Can I see?"

The artist smiled. "Sure. Not that there's a lot to see right now. I'm just making preliminary sketches for a painting."

Aaron stepped onto the rocky bluff, and walked over to stand next to him. The white sheet of paper was filled with a detailed drawing of the cliff to the right, the lighthouse perched on top, and the ocean to the left. The composition reminded him of Grammy's painting.

"Will you paint it down here too?"

He laughed, a sound full of good humor. "Managing an easel, pencils and paper is one thing. Tubes of oil paints, rags, and brushes is another. So no, that wouldn't be my first choice. I'll make a lot of notes, take photos... But I will come back here once in a while, just to make sure I'm on the right track."

"Are you staying on the island?" Return visits indicated a lengthy stay.

"I've rented a house long-term, on the north end of the island. Been there since January."

"I can understand why you'd come here to paint. There are some beautiful views around here."

The man nodded. "I've been making a list. I think Jordan Pond might be my next project. Newport Cove is looking like a good prospect too."

Aaron indicated the sketch. "Will this be a big

canvas?"

"Possibly."

He studied the drawing. "You're very good."
There was something familiar about his style.

"Thank you. I think I've been drawing since I
could hold a pencil." The artist cocked his head. "Will
this be a daily visit? I mean, do you usually hike down
to this point?"

Aaron chuckled. "No. It was the sight of the
easel that brought me here. That, and the fact I was
intrigued to see what you were doing."

His eyes glittered. "Ah. I get it. You thought I
was about to fall in, so you hurried down here to
rescue me."

Aaron laughed. "I don't think you need
rescuing. It was good to meet you."

"You too, Mr. Park Ranger. That *is* a ranger's
uniform, isn't it?"

"It is." On impulse, Aaron held out his hand.
"And the name's Aaron."

The man blinked, then took his hand. "I'm
Dean."

"And if you're going to be sketching around
the island, I'll probably run into you again."

"Very possibly. Mount Desert isn't that big.
Thanks for stopping by."

Aaron tipped his hat. "You're welcome."
Then he turned back to head up the trail. He was
used to seeing hikers in groups, couples, families,
tourists armed with a multitude of cameras... Dean
was his first artist, and judging by what Aaron had
seen, he was obviously talented.

I'll keep a lookout for him.

Dean watched as Aaron retreated up the trail, taking full advantage of the opportunity to take a long look at that firm ass.

Damn. There goes one fine-looking man. Maybe it was the uniform. Aaron suited the gray shirt and green pants, but the broad-brimmed flat hat hid his eyes, and Dean hoped he hadn't been staring as he tried to catch sight of them. Beneath his shirt, Aaron wore a round-necked black tee. Dean's one regret was that the olive-green jacket disguised Aaron's body shape.

If I'd known I was going to have such a handsome visitor, I'd have worn something other than my bulky coat. Then he smiled. *Whoa there.* It was not cool to be lusting after the first good-looking guy to cross his path in months.

He glanced at his pad. He'd done enough sketching, so he wouldn't be returning to this spot for a while. Aaron was already out of sight.

What are the chances of running into him again?

With all his duties, and getting trails and facilities ready for the season, Dean imagined they'd be pretty slim.

Pity.

Aaron reached his car and got behind the wheel. As he was fastening his seatbelt, his phone vibrated, and he smiled when he saw Noah's name. "Hey. How are you?"

"I'm good. Actually…I was thinking about heading up to your neck of the woods, and I wondered if we could get together."

"Why're you coming all the way up here?"

"Well…" After a brief pause, Aaron caught Noah's sigh. "I've moved out."

"Seriously?" Aaron was surprised Noah had stuck it out so long. Living with parents had to cramp his style. "So where are you living now?"

"You know Wellington Manor?"

Aaron frowned. "The rental place near Levi?" The complex of condos was vacation accommodation, usually brimming with tourists come June and July.

"Yeah, that's it. You remember I worked there a couple of summers? Cleaning the pool, the units…"

Aaron remembered, all right. Noah had complained at how much dirt some vacationers had managed to create. "You're living in one of the units?"

"Yeah. The guy who runs the place said I could stay there. He's not charging me the full rental though. And it's only until the end of August. I'm hoping by then I've found something more permanent."

Aaron fell silent. Things had to be pretty bad at home to force Noah to take such a step.

"Aaron? You still there?"

"Wanna tell me what's going on?"

"Not over the phone."

"Are you okay?"

Another sigh. "I've been better. I just need something to take my mind off of stuff. I was planning a visit to Bar Harbor to take pictures. I figured my next train layout could be based on places on the island."

Aaron had an idea that was an excuse. "Dude, you can come visit me whenever you want, you know that."

"Thanks. I didn't want to wait until the next cookout. It's still too cold for that." Another pause. "I was hoping you'd be doing your Easter thing again. But Easter is a week away, and so far, you haven't said anything about it."

Aaron frowned. *Easter thing?* Then it came to him. "You mean, that time I bought a chocolate fountain, and we all made ourselves sick by eating way too much of it?" Man, they'd dipped everything they could think of in that fountain—and a few food items that had no business being covered in chocolate.

Aaron drew the line at vegetables, but *someone* had tried it.

A party? Why not? He hadn't seen any of the guys since New Year's. He wouldn't be doing his boat tours yet. And the idea of getting together with his friends really appealed. He'd have to check his schedule was clear, but…

"Lemme make sure I've got that Sunday clear."

"Really?"

"Sure, why not? If any of the guys want to drive up Saturday and stay over, it might be kinda crowded, but I can squeeze you all in. Knowing Seb, if he and Marcus are coming, they'll want to stay in a hotel anyway."

"Can I bring anything?"

Aaron laughed. "Let's make sure it's gonna happen first. *Then* I'll message everyone, and we can decide on the menu. Only, this time? Let's not make chocolate the only thing we eat, okay?"

Noah chuckled. "Between us, I'm sure we can rustle up something. You sure you don't mind?"

"I wouldn't be doing this if I minded. Now, let me go check."

"Thanks, Aaron. Meeting up with you would've been great, but having the others there too… Okay, I'll let you get off the phone. Talk soon?"

"You know it." Aaron ended the call. He pulled up his work schedule on his phone. Sunday April 4 was looking good. He sent Noah a text.

Okay, NOW you can invite them. Tell them about staying Sat night too, and about bringing food. I'll get going on the chocolate for the fountain, and stuff to dip.

Seconds later, Noah's reply pinged back. *No sprouts this time, okay? I swear I almost heaved when Seb suggested that.*

Aaron laughed out loud, his thumbs sliding over the screen. *Absolutely no sprouts.* It wasn't until he'd added the event to his calendar that a thought occurred to him.

Noah now lives even closer to Levi.

Was that a deliberate move on Noah's part? Of all of his friends, Levi and Noah had been in each other's pockets for years. At least now, Aaron had an idea about Levi's motivation.

What if Noah felt the same about him?

Then he pushed such ideas aside. It sounded as if Noah had problems.

I hope we can help him.

Movement caught his eye, and he looked up. Dean was walking toward the truck, a folded easel under one arm, and his sketching pad under the other. He glanced at Aaron, and then did a double take.

"I thought you left?"

Aaron wound down the window. "Yeah, that was the plan, but I had to take a call. You done for today?"

Dean nodded. "Back to the house to prepare a canvas, I think."

"You do that yourself? Can't you buy those things ready-made?"

"Sure, but this way, I get to choose the size. And besides, I don't think there's an artists' supply store around here."

"Yeah, you have a point." He smiled. "Have a great day, and good luck with the painting."

"Thank you." Dean hesitated. "I hate to admit it, but you're the first person I've had a decent conversation with since I came to live here. Apart from the mail man, and the nice lady at Hannaford's, but do you think 'sign here, please' and 'have a nice day' count?"

Aaron chuckled. "Not really. In that case, I hope we run into each other again."

Dean's eyes gleamed. "I look forward to that." He opened the door to the truck, and stowed his easel and pad. Then he gave Aaron a cheery wave and climbed into the truck. The engine growled into life, and he backed out of the space and drove away.

Aaron had the vaguest suspicion he'd just been flirted with.

Chapter Five

March 31

Dean liked Hannaford's. As supermarkets went, it was well-stocked, and even managed a few surprises. He was looking at one of those.

Coffee-flavored brandy?

"That's just *wrong*," came a voice from behind him. Dean turned, and smiled when he saw Aaron, dressed in jeans, his upper body hidden beneath a coat. His red shopping basket sat at his feet. Aaron pointed to the brandy. "Why ruin the taste of perfectly good coffee by adding brandy?"

He chuckled. "I was thinking pretty much the same thing." He looked Aaron up and down. "Not working today?" The lack of uniform was a bit of a giveaway.

"This is my day off. Except it's already full—groceries, laundry… I was hoping to find time for a walk later. How's the painting going?" Aaron's eyes twinkled. "You've finished it, right? I mean, you've had five days."

Dean loved a guy with a sense of humor.

"The canvas is ready, I've primed it, and—"

"What does that entail?"

He put his basket down, and counted off on his fingers. "First, put a wooden frame together, stretch the canvas over it, and staple it. You size it with rabbit skin glue. Then—"

Aaron gaped. "Tell me you buy that stuff. 'Cause I have visions of you boiling innocent little bunnies."

Dean laughed out loud. "Yes, I buy it. You can use PVA too. It helps to stop fluid from leaking through, and it stiffens the fabric. I usually apply a couple of coats of it. Then I add the acrylic primer. If you don't, the oil from the paints sinks into the canvas and leaves dull patches on the surface."

Aaron cleared his throat. "I'm thinking ordering from Amazon sounds like a lot less hassle." He cocked his head. "So is that what you paint in? Oils?"

Dean nodded. "I tried acrylics, but I'm far happier with oils." He smiled. "And here we are, having another conversation." An unexpected but pleasurable one.

Aaron peered into his basket. "Are you done shopping? Because if you are, we could continue this over coffee." He grinned. "I can recognize a fellow caffeine addict when I see one."

The abruptness of the invitation took him by surprise. *Why not?* "Can you recommend a place?" Dean wasn't averse to coffee and chat with a handsome park ranger.

"Sure. There's a great coffee shop right around the corner from my house. And they have the most amazing pastries too. Apple coffee cake, banana bread, scones, chocolate peanut butter cake—"

"Stop right there. You had me at coffee, but then you went and said the two magic words. Chocolate peanut butter cake exists? How did I not know this?"

Aaron beamed. "A guy who loves coffee, chocolate, and peanut butter? Then let me take you to heaven."

Just *looking* at Aaron got him halfway there.

Dean glanced at his groceries. "It might have to wait. I've got frozen stuff in here. I should really take all this home first."

"Hey, not a problem. You in your truck?" Dean nodded. "Then follow me. I live real close. It's just down Cross Street, a right onto Main Street, then a left. If you want to put your frozen stuff in my freezer, there's plenty of room."

Maybe it was Aaron's job that made him so helpful. Whatever it was, it was charming.

"Okay. I can do that. I just have to find a couple more things, then I'm done."

"I'll meet you in the parking lot. Take your time, I'm in no hurry. Anything to put off doing laundry." Aaron lifted his basket. "I'll go pay for this." Then he headed for the checkout.

Dean consulted his list. He had to smile when he saw the last item. Coffee…

Once he'd paid, he walked out of the store and through the parking lot to his truck. Aaron waved from his truck, and he waved back. Dean stowed his shopping bags, started the engine, and waited as Aaron pulled out of his space.

He hadn't been kidding about how close he lived to the store. Dean reckoned they were outside Aaron's house in under four minutes. He parked behind Aaron's truck, and glanced at their destination. It was a town house, its exterior walls covered in cream cedar shakes, with buff-colored tiles on the roof over the front porch, and a patch containing flower beds in the center of the plot. Steps lined with white railings led up to two front doors, a pair of octagonal windows between them.

Aaron took the steps in long strides, which wasn't surprising—he had to have four inches on Dean. Aaron led him into the kitchen, and pointed to the freezer.

"The bottom drawer is empty. And if you've got anything that needs to be refrigerated, there's room in the fridge too." Aaron placed his shopping bags on the square table in the middle of the room, and proceeded to unpack his groceries. Dean tried not to get in his way, and before long, all the food was out of sight, and the non-food items were in a bag under the table.

"You have a nice place," Dean offered. The living room was long, but not cluttered, and at the end of it French doors opened out onto the yard.

Aaron smiled. "It's small enough that I don't rattle around in it, and big enough that I can have all my friends stay over." He bit his lip. "Well, a year ago, I could. Things have changed since then." Before Dean could ask what he meant, Aaron inclined his head toward the front door. "Okay. Coffee and cake time."

The coffee shop sat on a street corner. Inside, pale blue chairs surrounded wooden tables. Mugs hung from hooks on one wall, and on another were small rectangular frames containing books. The walls were salmon-pink, and covered with photos of Bar Harbor in years gone by. Dean grabbed a table in the window while Aaron went to order. The view of the street outside was perfect. Dean loved to watch the world go by.

Aaron joined him. "I ordered regular coffee, and two pieces of chocolate peanut butter cake. I figured that was a safe bet."

"Hey, if you hadn't, you'd have gotten me here under false pretenses."

"So…" Aaron put his elbows on the table and steepled his fingers. "How long have you been painting?"

"Since I was a teenager. We used to live in Maine. I was born here."

Aaron widened his eyes. "Really? Where?"

"Thomaston. But my dad had to move for his job, and we ended up in Ohio. I was twelve then." Dean smiled. "I was always taking photos, every place we visited. And I kept them all. So when I started painting, I copied the landscapes in my pictures. It was a way of reminding myself of a place where I was happy."

"A place you came back to." Aaron shook his head. "You're the second or third guy I've met who's done that. They came home too."

Dean stilled. "That's it. That's it *exactly*. I've come home."

The server brought their coffee and cake, and Dean didn't hesitate. As soon as she'd walked away, he forked off the sharp end of the cake and tasted it. He was pretty sure the sounds coming out of his mouth were almost orgasmic, but Aaron was nodding, his eyes bright, so he couldn't have been *that* bad.

"That is awesome." Then he realized Aaron was gazing at him inquiringly.

Maybe his noises had been more noticeable than he'd thought.

"Dean," Aaron murmured. "But Dean what?"

"Durrell."

Aaron stared at him. "You didn't do a painting of Owl's Head, did you? In 2002?"

It was Dean's turn to stare. "How did you know that?" Talk about spooky.

"One of my closest friends, Levi... He lives with his grandmother, and for as long as I've known him, that painting has been hanging over the fireplace. She says she bought it fifteen years ago in a gallery in Portland. It was signed DD 2002."

Dean was flabbergasted. "Okay, this is weirding me out. I gave that painting to Mrs. Solomon."

"Who was she? And when was this?"

"She was our babysitter in Ohio—she babysat me and my younger brother, Ash. That painting was one of my first. How in hell did it end up in a gallery in Portland? Did she give it away? Maybe she didn't like it." She'd seemed pretty pleased with it at the time.

"Or maybe she sold it," Aaron suggested.

Dean considered that idea. "I was eighteen when I painted it."

Aaron's mouth fell open. "Oh my God. It's an *amazing* painting. You did that at eighteen? And you gave it away?"

He shrugged. "She'd been a wonderful babysitter. I was going off to college, and Mom made me clear out my room. There had to have been four or five canvases, and I made gifts of them to Mrs. Solomon, relatives... By the time I graduated, I had a whole lot more of them. My dad had a business card made up for me, and Mom produced a flier with photos of my work. Painting was all I ever wanted to do, and my parents wanted to support me."

"Must have been tough though. How many stories are there of starving artists? Don't they say an artist doesn't get popular until they're dead?"

Dean laughed. "Then I guess I was lucky. When I came home from college, I sent my fliers to several galleries, and one in Pennsylvania wanted to exhibit my work. So… I crated up my paintings and off they went to Pennsylvania. That was the start of a great business relationship. I painted all day, and I was happy as a clam. The gallery sold my stuff as fast as they got it. When I reached twenty-four, I got tired of crating up stuff, and I decided to move to Philadelphia, to a place near the gallery. By then, I could afford it."

Aaron got out his phone, and Dean frowned, until Aaron glanced at him with a sheepish grin. "Sorry. I'm Googling you."

Dean laughed. "How long have you got? I spent ten years producing a lot of work." Then Aaron's eyebrows scrunched up. "What have you just read?"

Aaron raised his gaze. "It's an article from the *New York Times*'s arts page. 'Whatever happened to Dean Durrell?' It's dated three years ago."

His stomach clenched. "That's another story, and only to be told if I get to know you a whole lot better."

He did *not* want to talk about Lyle.

Aaron scrolled. "Wait a sec. You painted portraits too?"

He nodded. "I wanted a new challenge. So many people—gallery owners, art critics, art professors—told me artists painted landscapes or portraits, but not both. I figured that was dumb." Dean grinned. "So I started painting portraits. A totally different experience, but I loved it."

Aaron was still scrolling. "Wow. You painted all these people? But there are some really famous faces here."

Dean gave a shrug. "What can I say? Word got around, mostly due to the owner of one of the galleries that exhibited my work. He was friends with Raymond Wyatt, and—"

"Raymond Wyatt, the movie actor? The one who starred in *Empire of Glass*? *The Winds of Forever*?"

Dean smiled. "The same. Anyway, he suggested to Raymond that I paint his portrait. Raymond liked the idea. We had two sittings, I worked from photos in between, and he absolutely loved the end result. Suddenly, I had celebrities filling up my voice mail, asking if I'd paint them." Aaron's gaze grew thoughtful, and Dean had a sinking feeling he'd want to know what happened to bring a halt to ten years of productivity. Time to steer the conversation in another direction. "But I've talked enough about me. Tell me about Aaron, Park Ranger."

"Not much to tell. I was born in Wells, went to school there, did my training to be a ranger…"

"You always knew that was what you wanted to do?"

Aaron nodded. "My mom brought me to Acadia all the time when I was a kid. I spent so many summers here. Not to mention any vacation time when I could persuade Mom we really needed an Acadia fix."

Dean chuckled. "I like that. Maybe that was what I needed too—a Maine fix." He'd picked the perfect place. Acadia fueled something deep within him, inspiring him. Then he recalled Aaron's earlier words that had intrigued him. He took a drink of his coffee. "You were talking about having your friends over... and then... I don't know... your expression changed." Aaron's breathing hitched, and Dean hastened to backpedal. "Hey, you know what? It's none of my business. You've known me for all of five minutes, right?"

Aaron smiled. "You painted something I've loved looking at for years. That feels like more than five minutes." He ate a little more of his cake, then followed it with a mouthful of coffee. "When I was in high school, I made some really good friends. We didn't all meet at once—some gravitated toward us at different stages—but the thing is, we *stayed* friends. There are eight of us. Well... there were. That started to change last summer." He held up his hands. "Not a bad change, I have to say. Just... unexpected." He paused to drink, and Dean remained silent. "Finn was the first. He turned up to Grammy's birthday party with a boyfriend, Joel."

"Finn's gay?"

Aaron grinned. "Finn, Seb, Levi, Ben, Shaun... Ben only figured himself out a few years ago, and we didn't have a clue about Shaun, but that was understandable, given the circumstances, which I'm not gonna go into. Dylan is bi, Noah is ace, and it seems I'm the only one who's dated women exclusively."

Dean blinked. "That's a pretty diverse group." *And you're straight. Damn.* What surprised him was the

K.C. WELLS

depth of his disappointment. "But... you said Finn was the first."

Aaron nodded. "At the end of August, I had a barbecue at my place. Ben turned up with his new boyfriend—which was a bit of a shocker for some of us, because wow, talk about history—and then Seb, the one we thought was our happy-go-lucky, one-night-stand-kinda-guy, *he* turned up with a guy, and from the look of things, Seb is smitten."

"I see what you mean. Three of them found partners in a short space of time. What's in the water supply around here?" he quipped.

Aaron shook his head. "Uh-uh. It didn't stop there. Dylan showed up at Levi's Halloween party with a guy in tow. And boy, did *he* cause a stir." Aaron leaned in. "Mark is a gay porn star. Okay, he *was* a porn star. Sounds as if he's made a career move."

Dean couldn't resist. "Mark who? I might know the name."

Aaron blinked. "You follow gay porn?"

He figured he'd gone this far. "Well duh. I'm gay." Aaron stared at him, and Dean chuckled. "What? You've never heard of an artist being gay? And you still haven't told me his last name."

"Mark Roman."

Dean's mouth fell open. "Oh my. Your friend Dylan has extremely good taste. He's a lucky man. So was that it? Four new partners?"

Aaron shook his head once more. "Five. Shaun came to Levi's New Year's Eve party with the guy who'd been his dad's in-home nurse. I think it was a very recent development, but they seem like a good fit." He sighed. "And they're all coming to my house on Sunday."

"Is it a special occasion? Or just an excuse to get together?"

"It's my version of an Easter party. Everyone's bringing a dish of something, and there'll be a chocolate fountain with yummy stuff to dip into it for dessert."

Dean licked his lips. "Oh God. I'm drooling."

Aaron stilled. "Why don't you come too?"

What the hell? "I couldn't. I don't know these people. And they don't know me. Besides, wouldn't it look odd? 'Hey guys, here's a painter I met a week ago.' I'd feel as if I were intruding."

Aaron widened his eyes. "But if you don't, there'll be thirteen of us. That's bad luck."

"You're superstitious?"

"Me? Not so much, but Noah is. He's the kind of guy who will go miles out of his way to avoid walking under a ladder, he doesn't put shoes on the table, 'cause it's bad luck, he'll throw spilled salt over his shoulder—I know, 'cause some of it hit me in the eye once. So you see, you *have* to come."

Dean wasn't convinced. "I wouldn't want to feel awkward."

Aaron expelled a breath. "Okay, I'll come clean. You'd be doing me a huge favor if you came."

"How so?"

"Because…" He looked Dean in the eye. "*I'm* the one who's gonna be feeling awkward, okay?"

Dean frowned. "But why? These guys are your friends."

"Sure, but it's not the same. I had my first taste of that at New Year's. Midnight came, and all of a sudden, I'm in the middle of ten guys all sharing lingering romantic kisses."

Dean saw the light. "You want me to be a buffer."

Aaron nodded. "Except that makes it sound as if I'm inviting you to *use* you, and that's not right. I know I've only met you twice, but I… I feel like we've made a…"

"Connection?" Dean suggested.

Aaron's smile lit up his face. "Yes. Exactly."

"And you're sure neither of the other unattached guys is going to turn up with a new partner? Negating the need for me to make the number up to fourteen?"

"Trust me, not gonna happen. So… will you?" He gave a hopeful smile. "Do I need to remind you there'll be chocolate?"

Dean laughed. "Okay, I'm sold. I'll come. Just give me an idea of what I should bring."

"You don't need to do that."

"Yes, I do," he replied in a firm voice. "So let me know by Friday, and I'll rustle something up for Sunday." He picked up his fork. "Now… can I finish my cake?"

Aaron chuckled. "Be my guest. And thank you."

Dean ate another mouthful.

Talk about ironic.

Ash said he needed to get back on the horse, and Dean could quite willingly have done so with Aaron.

Except he's straight.
Been there, done that, got the scars to prove it.

Chapter Six

Saturday, April 3

Dean took a step back, studying the canvas. The first layers of color covered the burnt umber underpainting, and he could see the scene emerging. It was the biggest canvas he'd worked on for quite a while, and the prospect excited him.

It feels good to be painting again. Something had drawn him back to Maine, and he thanked God for it.

His phone buzzed on the windowsill, and he smiled when he saw Ash's face. "Hey," he said when they connected.

"This isn't a bad time, is it?"

"Not at all. I literally just put down my brush."

"You're painting? Then you shouldn't be talking to me."

Dean chuckled. "Will you relax? You haven't called in weeks. And you're not interrupting."

"What's the painting of?"

"A lighthouse. Beautiful spot." Dean ambled toward the kitchen in search of coffee. He'd planned on stopping soon anyway. He'd decided to make a lasagna for Aaron's get-together.

"So how is Bar Harbor in the spring?"

"Slightly warmer than it was in the winter, but not by much." Dean poured himself a cup.

Ash let out a wry chuckle. "Well, you wanted to live there. Have you met any of the natives yet?"

"'Natives'?"

"You know what I mean."

Dean knew exactly what he meant. "Yes, I have—one of them, at least—but I hesitate to tell you about him, because you'll get the wrong idea."

"'Him'? Ooh, color me intrigued."

"See? You already did."

"Just tell me about him, for Christ's sake."

Their interactions brought back memories of when they were teenagers, squabbling and bickering over the slightest thing. Happy days. "Last week, I was doing some sketching for the piece I'm working on, and I met a park ranger."

"Was he wearing one of those cute Stetsons? Was he in uniform?"

Dean almost choked on his coffee. "Ash, if I didn't know you and Claire were pretty much joined at the hip, I'd swear you were gay."

Ash laughed. "One of Claire's besties, Jon, is gay. He claims it's never a black-and-white thing, more like shades of gray. Hey, didn't someone make a movie about that?"

Dean smiled to himself. "Yeah, and there were a few books too."

"Anyway, Jon says no one is a hundred percent gay or straight. We're all at some point on a sliding scale."

"It's not so much of a sliding scale, more like a spectrum," Dean protested.

"Hey, it works for me. Then again, I might just be spending too much time with Jon, and he's rubbing off on me." Dean spluttered coffee over his countertop, and Ash snorted. "Not like that, you pervert. Christ, talk about a dirty mind." He paused. "So... back to our conversation... why would I get the wrong idea about you and Mr. Park Ranger?"

"He's having an Easter-ish get-together at his place tomorrow, and I'm invited. He played dirty to get me to accept."

"Let me guess. There'll be chocolate."

"God, it's like you know me or something," Dean quipped.

"Sounds like it might be fun. Who else is going?"

"Seven of his friends from high school—all guys—and five of them will be bringing their boyfriends."

There was a pause. "They're all gay? *Now* I understand your comment. Because it's beginning to sound less like an Easter party, and more like an orgy."

"See, I knew I shouldn't have told you. No, they're not all gay. Some of them are bi. And there's one straight guy, who happens to be the yummy park ranger."

"Ohh, so he's hot, huh? You left that part out. And didn't you listen to a word I said? You know, about no one being totally—"

"Yeah, I got that part."

"And? What's his name?"

"Aaron. He's a redhead too." Silence fell with a thud. "Ash?"

"Sorry. I was just imagining what your kids will look like."

"Ash!"

"Just kidding. So... how many times have you

met this guy?"

"Twice."

"And he's invited you to a party? I see."

"No, you don't. It's… way more complicated than that."

"But you do like him."

"Stop that."

"Stop what?" Ash couldn't do innocent to save his life.

"You know very well."

"You mean, you're not even gonna *try* to lure him over to the dark side?"

The first bubbles of panic drifted to the surface. "Ash. Will you stop your lips flapping and just think for a minute?"

Another pause, and Ash's voice softened. "Oh God. Yeah, I totally forgot. But—"

"There isn't a *but.*"

"There could be. Did you ever think about why Lyle—"

"Dumped me? Moved out? Found himself a soul mate who happened to be a woman? I try not to. I did enough ruminating on that subject at the time."

"Do you think he ever loved you?"

"I did once. Now? Not so sure." Snatches of long dead conversations filtered through his brain, and he shut the door on them. He didn't want to hear that voice again.

"Look… I'm not suggesting you find some guy and fall madly in love, okay? My ideas are on a much… baser level. Just find someone you can connect with—mentally *and* physically. Find a guy who can warm your bed on those frosty Maine nights." Ash paused. "I know you're deeper than that, but… You could always wait and see what the unattached friends are like."

"You don't think this all sounds kinda… desperate?"

"Course not."

Dean wasn't so certain. "Look… I'm painting again. For the first time in five years. I'm inspired again. I thought I'd lost this. Right now I don't want anything to distract me."

It wasn't the whole truth. The idea of a warm body in his bed sounded like heaven. There'd been no one since Lyle, but Dean had been fine with that. Now, all of a sudden, it seemed his body had come out of hibernation.

Maybe he *was* ready for more.

"I hear ya, bro. And I'm happy for you, honest. All I want is for *you* to be happy."

"Give it a few months, then come visit me again. We'll go do stuff, like when we were kids. The beach, a couple of hikes…"

"I'd love that. Is that offer just for me, or is Claire included too?"

Dean chuckled. "Bring Claire. It's been a while since the last time I saw her."

"Hey, I could bring Jon too." Before Dean could protest, Ash plowed ahead. "Except I think he's spoken for. He was dating a new guy last time we spoke. Seems it's caused friction with his gay friends. He said something about having to hand in his gay card. He was kinda pissed."

"I don't understand."

"Oh, his new boyfriend is trans, and apparently *some* members of the gay community are the teensiest bit transphobic. Jon says he's actually lost friends over it. I don't see what the problem is myself."

"That's because you're a well-rounded individual—who swishes along the spectrum more easily than I do."

"I do not swish. I slide, remember? And on that note, I'll let you get back to painting."

"I've stopped for now. I'm about to make a lasagna for tomorrow."

Ash snorted again. "How… domesticated. Have fun with the locals. Don't do anything I wouldn't do."

"That doesn't leave me a whole lot." He ended the call, then proceeded to remove the ingredients from the fridge. The prospect of spending time with a bunch of guys didn't faze him. What intrigued him was seeing Aaron interact with them.

He's grown up with these guys. He's comfortable around them. Maybe that was why he and Dean had warmed to each other so easily.

Except he knew it was more than that.

Aaron was gorgeous.

Aaron had just finished bundling yet more sheets into the washer when the doorbell rang. He opened the front door to find Noah there, a bag slung over his shoulder.

"Hey. Come on in. There's coffee if you want it."

Noah stepped into the house, dropped the bag at his feet, and gave Aaron a tight hug. That was enough to worry him right there.

"I know I said I'd be here this evening, but—"

"Stop. As if I care that you're early." Aaron smiled. "You just get to help me make up the beds and sort out the sleeping arrangements. Levi's a definite for tonight. And Seb called to say Marcus got a hotel room, so they'll be here once they've checked in. Yeah, what a shocker." They both chuckled. "Ben and Wade will be here in the morning, Finn and Joel too. Shaun and Nathan? Not sure when they'll get here. Dylan neither, for that matter. But everyone will be here by tomorrow afternoon. Oh… and there'll be an extra guest. A guy called Dean." He walked into the kitchen, Noah following, and went to grab two cups.

It was then that the silence hit him.

He turned around, just in time to see Noah's jaw drop. "No. You *haven't*."

Aaron rolled his eyes. "No, I haven't. He's an artist staying in Bar Harbor. I've only met him a couple times." He poured coffee from the pot.

"And yet you invited him."

"He's a nice guy." A *really* nice guy.

Noah bit his lip. "You sure he'll be okay with all of us? I mean, you don't think it'd sort of be like tossing someone into the lion's den? You know Seb. No filter. And Ben can be pretty snarky."

Aaron removed the creamer from the fridge. "You like this one, I remember. And Dean'll be fine.

Besides, he's gay."

Noah pushed his black-framed glasses farther up his nose. "Oh really?" His eyes sparkled. "Is he good-looking?" He added a little creamer to the inky black coffee.

Aaron frowned. "I thought you weren't interested right now."

"I'm not." He grinned. "I was thinking of you."

"Excuse me?" Aaron gave a hard stare. "Straight, remember?"

"Yeah, you keep saying that."

Aaron cleared his throat. "Hey, I have an idea. Let's forget about my sexuality, and talk about what's going on with you. Starting with you moving out."

For a moment, Noah said nothing, so Aaron took a drink. Finally, Noah sighed. "I guess it was my fault. I should've said something." He sipped the coffee. "This is good."

Aaron waited.

Noah leaned against the countertop. "You remember back in August, when I said Mom and I had had a conversation?"

He nodded. "When you told her you weren't gay."

"Yeah. I just didn't tell her the rest. You know, about being ace? To be honest, I didn't think she'd understand, and I thought it might provoke a whole lotta questions I didn't want to answer. So… I kept my mouth shut, and hoped that would be the end of it. Yeah, right."

"What happened?"

Noah swallowed. "She started asking me to go to church with her. At first, I said no, but then I thought, why not? It wasn't a big deal. So I went. Turned out to be okay. Kinda… peaceful. Well, it *was*—until the service ended. And then suddenly, everything became clear. Mom brought over this girl…"

"Oh God."

Noah nodded. "Yup. She did the introductions, I was polite, so was… Candy, I think her name was… and then Mom appeared with *another* girl. There had to have been three or four by the time she'd finished, all of them hanging around me, each trying to get a word in. Talk about awkward. I felt as if she'd shoved me into a harem and was just standing there, waiting for me to pick one of 'em."

"What did you do?"

He snorted. "I made my excuses and fled to the restroom. When I got back, they were gone, and Mom had obviously moved onto Plan B."

Aaron winced. "Why do I think this wasn't any better than Plan A?"

He sighed. "She introduced me to the guy who was in charge of the music. Florian."

Aaron tried not to smile. "He wouldn't be gay, by any chance?"

"You got it. Okay, he's cute, but… She clearly didn't believe the whole 'I'm not gay' thing. I guess me being surrounded by pretty girls and not asking one of them out on a date was all the proof she needed."

"How did you get out of that one?"

"Actually? That was easy. Florian has a boyfriend, and he was just as embarrassed as I was. But since then… it seemed like every day, the subject would crop up in conversation." Noah expelled a breath. "I was done."

"So you moved out."

He nodded. "I was lucky Walt had an empty unit. And it's so pretty. I've got a patio door that opens out onto a cute little balcony, with two chairs. Okay, the view is of the other units across the way, but it'll be good to get a little sun. It's got a small stove top, a microwave, a toaster oven—and of course, a coffee machine. The couch gets the afternoon sun. The bathroom is small, and the tub is tiny, but there's a shower, thank God. And it's just me, for Christ's sake."

"I'm guessing the trains stayed above your parents' garage."

Noah's face tightened. "Yeah." Then his expression grew brighter. "Grammy said I can move my trains to her summer house if I want. It has power and light." He shrugged. "It'd be a place to store them. I couldn't run them though. Not nearly enough room for that. But at least they'd be someplace I could get at them."

"It's good you found a place so close to Levi's." Aaron had been wondering about that ever since Noah had told him. *Was that a deliberate choice?* God knew, the two of them had been like brothers most of their lives, living in each other's pockets.

Except Levi didn't want Noah for a brother, did he?

"Okay, enough about my life. You never did answer my question about whether this Dean is good-looking. He is, isn't he?" That familiar twinkle was back, and Aaron was so damned happy to see it. He hated when his friends were hurting.

"He's a redhead."

Noah grinned. "This gets better and better. And you do like him, don't you?"

"Did you miss the part where I said he's a nice guy? Or that I'm—"

"Straight, yeah, got the memo. All I'm saying is… I always felt you were more… fluid than that."

"What do you mean?"

"I know lots of straight guys, all right? And most of 'em wouldn't be caught dead hanging around with a lot of gay guys. You, on the other hand…."

Aaron got where Noah was going. He'd always been comfortable with them. It had only been that one time at New Year's when he'd felt…

What did *I feel? Awkward? Jealous?*

But jealous of what? His friends who'd found partners? Aaron was happy for them, sure, but…

"There's a whole lotta stuff going on inside that head of yours, isn't there?" Aaron blinked, and Noah regarded him with a keen glance. "Can I give you a word of advice?"

"I think you're going to, whether I want you to or not."

Noah smiled. "Don't get stuck on labels. Go with the flow. Be open to new experiences." His eyes twinkled. "You might surprise yourself. Because when it comes down to it? No one is a hundred percent gay or a hundred percent straight." He locked gazes with Aaron. "Not even you."

Aaron stared at him. "Says you, who has a label—asexual."

"Sure, but that's also subject to change. Ace is only part of a huge umbrella of sexuality. So what if right now I'm not sexually attracted to anyone? What if I found myself deeply, emotionally connected to someone, and them to me? That would change things. Granted, I wouldn't be diving into bed with them right away—that was more Seb's arena, before Marcus—but eventually, yeah, it might lead to something. I'm not gonna close myself off to new experiences. And neither should you."

And what if there already is someone out there with a deep emotional bond to you? Maybe Levi was right. Maybe Noah didn't have a clue how Levi felt about him.

And maybe I shouldn't get so hung up about being straight.

Aaron thought back to his tipsy New Year's conversation with Levi. *I told him I wasn't interested in finding a soul mate. I told him I was happy. What if I was wrong on both counts?*

Going with the flow was starting to look like good advice.

Chapter Seven

Sunday April 4

The last time Aaron's kitchen had been this cluttered, it had been the cookout in August. Now, the countertops were hidden beneath dishes: macaroni and cheese, tuna casserole, fried chicken, garlic bread… He wasn't sure they'd all fit in the oven, so he'd decided to heat them in batches. No one would be going hungry, that was for damn sure.

On the small table, he'd assembled toothpicks, bamboo skewers, and all the stuff for dipping into the chocolate fountain. He thought he'd covered all tastes; there were marshmallows, fudge, strawberries, grapes, pineapple, brownies, cookies, watermelon, pretzels, chips, and donuts. He'd even made churros for the first time, and the kitchen was filled with the heavenly aroma of fried dough. Noah had brought a box of crystallized ginger, and Aaron couldn't wait to try it.

"When's feeding time?" Seb yelled from the living room. "We're all here, right?"

Not quite. Dean was due in about ten minutes, and before everyone started eating, Aaron wanted to make sure they understood the situation. The conversation with Noah had been proof enough that explanations would be required.

He went into the living room, where everyone

was sitting on the couches, floor cushions, and dining chairs. The room had never been so full.

"Guys?" Aaron went over to his stereo and turned down the volume.

"You gonna tell us the Easter story?" Ben quipped. "Because I think we already know that one. Some of us had to go to Sunday school."

"Look, there's one more guest to arrive, and I wanted to tell you about him before he gets here."

Aaron might as well have dropped a bomb.

Heads jerked in his direction, eyes lit up, and several mouths fell open. Seb wore a huge shit-eating grin. "A*ha.* Whatever happened to 'I'm straight'?"

Aaron snorted. "Whatever happened to 'I'm never gonna settle down'?" He let out a growl. "See? This is exactly why I wanted to have this out before he arrives. It is *not* what you think, okay?"

"But it could be," Noah added with an evil glint in his eyes.

Aaron ignored him. "He's an artist I met a week ago. He's staying here to paint. And believe it or not, you've all seen his work. You know that painting over the fireplace at Levi's? He did it."

"What's his name?" Shaun reached for his phone.

"Dean Durrell. And I think he's kinda famous. I mean, there was an article about him in the *New York Times,* for God's sake. All *you* need to know is, he's a nice guy, he's a coffee, chocolate and peanut butter addict, and he is *not* my boyfriend. You got that? So don't go scaring him."

"We'll be on our best behavior," Seb murmured, crossing his heart. Next to him, Marcus almost choked on his soda.

"Sweetheart, whoever told you that you could do innocent? They lied." Then he winced as Seb dug his elbow into Marcus's ribs.

"Wow, guys. You should see some of his work." Shaun held up his phone. "He's really good."

Nathan peered at the screen. "You're not kidding."

Next to Nathan, Mark leaned closer to get a better look. "Aaron, I'm impressed. You've got yourself a very talented friend."

"Hey, Aaron," Noah called out. "You missed out one vital piece of information."

No, he really hadn't.

"What's he keeping from us?" Finn demanded.

Noah beamed. "Dean's gay."

And there was that look again.

"Guys, he'll be here any minute. Please, don't embarrass me—or him. Okay?" Aaron wasn't above begging.

To his relief, his friends were all smiles.

"Don't panic. We can play nice," Dylan said with a sweet smile.

"Sure we can. What did you think we were gonna do?" Seb's eyes glittered. "Try a little matchmaking?"

"Seb…." Aaron and Marcus intoned simultaneously.

The doorbell rang, and Aaron gave one last hard stare.

Yeah, none of them could do innocent, if it came down to it.

He went to the door, opened it, and Dean held out a covered dish. "One lasagna."

Aaron took it. "Smells amazing. Come on in, and I'll make the introductions. Be warned—I have a houseful." He stepped aside to let Dean enter, then inclined his head toward the overburdened hooks beside the door. "You can leave your coat and scarf there."

Dean peered at the rack of shoes, and toed off his boots. "Can I admit to being a little nervous?"

Aaron thought that was adorable. "They don't bite… much. And I think you'll find you have a new set of fans." He took the dish into the kitchen, then pushed open the door to the living room. "Everyone? This is Dean."

A chorus of 'Hi Dean' filled the air, accompanied by friendly waves and warm smiles. Shaun had moved to the floor on a cushion at Nathan's feet, leaving a space on the couch.

"Dean, you can sit here."

"Thanks." Dean picked his away across the floor and sat.

Noah got up from his chair. "Can I get you something to drink? There's beer, white wine, red wine, soda, coffee, water…"

"A soda would be good. Whatever you have. Thank you." Dean glanced at the faces turned in his direction. "Aaron said he'd do introductions, but I feel I should take notes to remember all your names."

"That'll be easy. None of us have weird names," Ben said with a smile, which morphed into a grin. "Aaron's name might not be weird, but *he* sure is."

Aaron gave him a mock glare. "Insult me, and there'll be no chocolate for you." Ben pouted. "It's going to be a grab-what-you-want lunch," Aaron informed Dean. "There's plenty to eat. When it's ready, just go into the kitchen and fill a plate with whatever looks good."

Dean pointed to the chocolate fountain sitting on the coffee table. "That looks good. I'll take that."

Ben hooted. "Okay, I like him." Chuckles broke out and rippled around the room.

Aaron relaxed a little. *This might be better than I thought.* Then he reconsidered. Dean had only just gotten there. They had a few hours to go yet.

It had taken Dean about an hour of paying attention and concentrating, but he thought he had all the names down. He was pleasantly full and awaiting dessert, content to sit back and listen to the conversations. He didn't understand everything, but then he didn't need to.

I might never meet these guys ever again.

They were a mixed bunch. Wade and Ben were the same age, but Joel, Marcus, Nathan, and Mark were all older than their partners. Nathan was a gorgeous black guy, and what Dean liked most was his manner with Shaun. Nathan treated him as if he were something precious and fragile.

"Guys?" That was Finn. "Expect something from us in the mail soon." He beamed, his face glowing. "We've set a date. The wedding's in July." Next to him, Joel laced their fingers together.

"Awesome!" Dylan's eyes shone. "Where are you getting married?

"The Barn at Walnut Hill, in North Yarmouth. We went to check it out a few months ago." Joel squeezed Finn's hand. "We were on a waiting list, but they had a cancellation. We haven't written out the invites yet."

"Joel's daughter Laura wants to be a flower girl, and his son Nate wants to be his best man," Finn added. "Oh, and Nate's bringing his boyfriend, so you'll get to meet the whole family."

Dean loved the surge of genuine warmth and affection shown to the couple.

"Hey, we have news too," Wade announced. "We broke ground last week. We've finally started work on the new house." He grinned. "Except it's not ours." He exchanged glances with Joel and Finn. "These two came in with us when we bought the land in Lincolnville. They're going to be our neighbors, but when they told us about the wedding, Ben and I decided their house should be built first. That way, they can start married life in their new home."

"That's fantastic," Levi declared.

"Plus, I got myself a new laborer," Finn announced. He pointed to Shaun. "And he's sitting right there. I'm gonna teach him everything I know."

Shaun grinned. "So Finn and Joel's house might take a little longer to build than Finn anticipates. Especially when he realizes I'm a slow learner."

"You'll be amazing." Nathan leaned forward and kissed the top of Shaun's head. "And when you

AARON'S AWAKENING

come home, I'll run you a hot bath and give you a massage."

Seb blinked. "Something you guys wanna tell us?"

Shaun smiled. "We were going to leave things as they were, until last month. Nathan got a change of landlord, and the new one brought in a new rule—no pets."

"And I am *not* getting rid of Cat," Nathan added.

Shaun's eyes blazed. "Hell no. So I asked Nathan to move in with me. Cat already loves me," he said with a grin.

"Only because you bribe him with that catnip-filled mouse," Nathan declared.

"You're not working at the restaurant anymore?" Noah asked.

"I *was* going to go part-time, but Finn says he'd rather have me work full-time from the get-go." Shaun sighed. "The only negative? It's a two-hour drive. Nathan's gonna be seeing less of me. God bless weekends."

"What about you, Marcus?" Levi demanded. "You still living in Cape Porpoise?"

Marcus nodded. "Yes. And still looking for a place. Seb is there every weekend. Most nights too." He grinned. "In fact, I think he spends more time at my place than he does in his own."

"So what happens when you find a place?" Ben asked. "Will it be just you, or will Seb be changing addresses too?"

"I've told Seb I'm looking for a place for us both. A permanent place. Preferably closer to the ocean." Seb leaned in and kissed him, and Dean loved

77

how at ease they were.

Of course they are. They were with people who accepted and loved them.

"Hey, did I tell you? We've got new neighbors," Levi declared. His eyes gleamed. "Not sure about them yet."

Dylan laughed. "I was gonna tell everyone. Mark inherited his grandfather's house—and it's the one next door to Grammy's."

"No shit." Aaron gaped. "Seriously? The dark blue one?"

"Yup. And I moved in with him last month. It's an easy commute to the hotel."

Seb made puppy dog eyes at Mark. "Tell me you're gonna be making content there."

Mark sighed. "Sorry. The only content will be the stuff I'm promoting for other porn stars. My new career. Well, one of them. Finn is going to renovate the house, and one of the rooms will be for my massage therapy clients." He gave Seb a hard stare. "And before you ask, we're talking massages that *don't* come with happy endings, okay?"

Seb pouted. "Damn. You had me going for a minute there."

Dean glanced at Aaron, who was watching his friends with an expression that bordered on wistful. *Oh my God. He wants what they have.* It couldn't have been plainer. Then Aaron caught him looking, and schooled his features.

"Having fun?"

Dean nodded. "I'll have even more fun when you start up that chocolate fountain."

"Yeah, what's the holdup?" Ben gave Aaron a mock glare. "You promised chocolate, so deliver."

There were vehement nods, and noises of agreement.

Aaron stood. "Okay. I'll bring in all the stuff for dipping."

"I'll help." Dean followed him into the kitchen. Aaron handed him a tray full of fruit.

"Thanks for coming."

Dean smiled. "Thanks for the invitation. I like your friends. They seem like good people."

"They're the best. But they're being much more reserved than usual, thank God."

"Oh really? And why is that?"

Aaron snorted. "Because I threatened them with no chocolate if they came out with their usual shit."

"What's the worst they could come up with?"

Aaron flushed. "How about Seb dropping heavy hints that you really need a new boyfriend— namely, me."

"But… they know you're not into guys."

That earned him another snort. "As if *that's* gonna stop 'em. In fact, the more I think about it, the more convinced I am someone's gonna say *something* before this shindig is over."

"Let them." Dean gave him a warm smile. "It takes a lot to embarrass me."

Aaron chuckled. "You've met Seb, right?"

"Hey, are you two making out in there?"

Aaron rolled his eyes. "Right on cue." He picked up another tray and pushed open the door. "In case I forget to tell you, I'm really sorry."

"For what?"

He inclined his head toward the living room. "Whatever's about to happen. I'm covering all bases."

Dean followed him into the living room. "I've

got your back," he whispered. "And I can give as good as I get."

What surprised him was his reaction to the idea of making out with Aaron. Far from shocking him, it sent a surge of warmth through him.

It's not going to happen.
Damn.

Chapter Eight

Dean couldn't remember the last time he'd laughed so much. Aaron's friends all seemed blessed with a sense of humor. Aaron had told stories about what visitors got up to in the park, and Seb had countless anecdotes about the kids in his class. Shaun appeared to be the quiet one of the bunch, and Dean liked his thoughtful comments. He asked questions about Dean's work, and Dean was happy to talk.

They were in the living room. The chocolate fountain had been a great success, and the guys were still eating. He doubted there would be a smidge of food remaining.

Dean shook his head at the sight of Seb mopping up the last traces of lasagna with a piece of garlic bread, and Finn doing the same with the tuna casserole. "Now I know what a horde of locusts looks like."

Seb grinned. "Can't let this go to waste. It's delicious. Who made it?"

"That would be me," Dean admitted.

Seb's eyes gleamed. "Dean, you're gonna make some lucky man very happy one day. They say the way to a man's heart is through his stomach. Isn't that right—Aaron?"

Dean bit back a smile. *He's about as subtle as a train wreck.*

Aaron glared at him, but said nothing.

"Whoever wrote that line was obviously talking about Finn." Joel grinned. "You should see him when my ex brings her beef casserole. She barely has time to set down the dish before he attacks."

"Hey! I am *not* that bad," Finn remonstrated.

"How many slices of Carrie's meatloaf did you have last week when she and Eric came over? Think carefully now." Dean loved the twinkle in Joel's eyes.

"Two?"

Joel snorted. "And the rest. Not that I'm worried. You're real good at working it off."

Dean had a feeling he wasn't talking about Finn's occupation, and the implication sent warmth through him.

It's been way too long since I burnt off some calories between the sheets.

Five years too long. The abstinence hadn't bothered him—until recently.

"Is there anything you need for your new place, Noah?" Levi asked.

Noah shook his head. "I only took what I had space for. And it's temporary, until I find a place of my own. I mean, you're all doing it, right?"

"Dude, what a personal remark," Seb quipped.

Noah gave him a superior eye-roll. "I *meant*, Finn and Joel will have their own place, so will Ben and Wade. Shaun's got his dad's place with Nathan, Mark's got his house with Dylan, Marcus is hunting for a place for you two, Aaron has his own space…"

"Not *all* of us are doing that," Levi commented in a low voice.

"Hey, Aaron, if you like Dean's paintings,

there's an exhibition coming up at the Farnsworth museum in Rockland that might interest you." Shaun pulled his phone from his pocket. "The works of three Wyeths."

"There's more than one of them? The only Wyeth I've heard of is Andrew."

Dean smiled. "They're an artistic family. His dad was also a painter, and his son Jamie too."

Aaron peered at Shaun's phone. "Wow. These are amazing. Rockland's a bit of a trek though."

"Then stay with me," Ben suggested. "Rockland's real close to Camden. The number of times we've all slept over here? My floor is your floor. Just don't listen to my bitch of a landlady when she grouses about me having a guest."

"She's not that bad," Wade countered.

Ben snorted. "With you, no. But you go out of your way to butter her up. I mean, you bought her flowers last week."

Wade smiled. "If it's a choice between you staying over at my place, with Mom and Gramps just down the hallway, or buttering up your landlady so I get to be alone with you, it's a no-brainer."

"Thanks for the offer," Aaron said. "When does the exhibition open?"

"Early May," Shaun replied.

"And seeing as we're all here, can I point out that there'll be a party in June?" Levi's eyes twinkled. "Since she hit seventy, Grammy has decided she's not gonna wait for more milestone birthdays—she wants to celebrate every year. So you're all invited." He glanced at Dean. "And that includes you."

"I'm not sure about—"

Levi narrowed his gaze. "But *I* am. Any friend

of Aaron's is a friend of ours."

"Plus, you made us lasagna," Seb added. "That makes you family."

"Hardly," Dean said with a smile.

"Look, here's the deal." Levi met his gaze. "When June comes around, if you and Aaron are still buddies, then you're coming. End of discussion."

"And who knows what will happen before then?" Seb gave a sweet smile.

Aaron coughed. "Okay, maybe it's time to wrap up this shindig. Some of you have a long drive home."

"We should help you clean up first," Finn suggested.

"I'll stay to do that," Dean interjected. "After all, I only live fifteen minutes away. It makes more sense."

"He cleans, he cooks…" Seb's eyes held a wicked glint. "Hey, Aaron? This one's a keeper."

Dean burst into laughter. "You don't have a whole lot of use for subtlety, do you, Seb?"

Seb grinned. "*And* he's a fast learner."

Marcus got up. "I'm getting you out of here, before that mouth of yours gets you into trouble."

Noah cackled. "Way too late for that."

Dean went into the kitchen and started loading the dishwasher, while Aaron sorted out coats. One by one, all the guys poked their heads through the door to say goodbye to him, and that they hoped to see him in June. Finally, the house was quiet.

Aaron came into the kitchen. "I think this is where I apologize."

Dean chuckled. "Are we talking about Seb? That mouth has no filters."

"You noticed, huh?"

"And there's no need to apologize. It was kind of sweet." Not to mention amusing. "They care for you. That much was obvious. They just want you to be happy."

Aaron gave him an incredulous stare. "So setting me up with a guy is gonna do that?"

Maybe it was the feel-good atmosphere of the afternoon, the camaraderie, or even Seb's hints that led to the impulse. Dean just rolled with it. "Hey, don't knock what you haven't tried," he said in a teasing tone. "You don't know what you're missing."

"Have you ever been with a woman?" Aaron demanded.

"Nope."

"Then neither do you."

Dean shrugged. "Possibly. But I've watched het porn. That told me all I needed to know." He cocked his head. "Something I have to ask. You have all these friends who are gay, bi... Did it ever make you the tiniest bit curious? You know, to see how things are done on the other team?" He didn't think anyone was *that* straight.

Aaron opened his mouth, then closed it again.

Interesting. Or at least, it was, until Dean remembered he had good reason not to be going down this path again. *If he's happy, leave him be.*

Time for a change of subject.

"That Wyeth exhibition Shaun was talking about... If you do go, how would you feel about some company?"

"Seriously?"

"Hey, I love looking at art. Any excuse. How far is Rockland, anyway?"

"A couple of hours. No biggie."

"Well, think about it. And it's okay if it's something you'd rather do on your own." Dean didn't want to impose. Then he realized why he'd made the suggestion.

I want to spend more time with you.

Okay, the terrain had suddenly gotten a little rocky.

I am not going to fall for the smoking hot ranger, okay?

Aaron spooned coffee into the filter. "You want some?"

Dean snorted. "You have to ask?"

"I guess tomorrow you'll be back at work on the painting."

He'd been thinking about that. "The forecast is good. I might give painting a miss and go for a hike." He smirked. "My brother Ash says I'm really a vampire because I stay inside all the time."

Aaron cackled. "Hey, I saw you at the lighthouse. I could set him straight. And can you afford to take time off? I mean, don't you have a deadline? Or an exhibition you're working toward?"

"No, not really. I'm just getting back into painting." The road that had brought him to his present situation had been hard enough, and he was thankful to be on the right path again. His surroundings were inspiring, and he'd made a new friend.

A very attractive new friend.

AARON'S AWAKENING

Ever since he'd read the article in the *New York Times*, Aaron had been dying to ask about the gap. As far as he could make out, Dean hadn't painted a thing in the last five years, and Aaron burned to know why. There was a reason why Mom's nickname for him had been Curious George: when he was a kid, he'd wanted to know the ins and outs of *everything*.

Dean's question was still there in his head. *Didn't it make you the tiniest bit curious?* Oh yeah. More than once, he'd caught himself wondering if kissing a guy would be so different to kissing a girl. And then there was the whole... technical side. Not that he supposed there was a lot of difference, when it came down to it. And then there had been the night of his barbecue in August, when sounds had drifted through his open bedroom window, and he'd hastened to close it, because listening to his friends making love should *not* have been such a turn-on. It had been sexier than any porn he'd ever watched, and that had disturbed him, until he realized what set him on fire was not the knowledge that it was Ben and Wade out there.

It was the intimate connection between two men, the noises they made speaking of desire and need and want...

"Aaron?"

He snapped back into the present. "Will you go back to painting portraits again?" It was the first thing that came to mind, and the furthest from the direction his thoughts had taken him.

"I haven't done one of those for a while."

Light bulb.

"How long does it take to finish one?"

"Depends."

"Can you work just from photos? If that was all you had, and sittings weren't possible?"

Dean arched his eyebrows. "Why do I think this is leading somewhere specific?"

The coffee pot beeped, and Aaron filled two cups. "You know it's Grammy's birthday in June. Well, I was thinking…"

"You want me to paint her portrait?"

Aaron nodded. "But it's already April."

Dean stroked his chin. "If you got hold of photos ASAP it could be done. Did you want it to be a surprise?"

"Yes."

"Then Levi will need to get them to me soon. That's if he has suitable photos." Dean sighed. "I had a commission once. A woman wanted a portrait done of her mother, for her sixtieth birthday. Except what she gave me to work with? Her mother's ID. We are talking one *seriously* tiny photo."

"Did you do it?"

"Hell no." Dean guffawed. "I'm not a miracle worker."

Aaron thought quickly. "Actually… what if it was a double portrait?" He hurried on. "I think Levi should be in it too. We just won't tell him. And what if *you* took the photos?"

Dean blinked. "Me?"

"Sure. You told me you're into photography. What if I took you there? That way, you'd have control. You know what looks good in a portrait. You'd be able to take the photos you'd need."

Dean's eyes sparkled. "What excuse would you give Grammy?"

Aaron smiled. "You leave that to me. And I'd pay you, of course. Whatever the going rate is."

Dean's face glowed. "My first commission in a long while."

There was no way Aaron could hold it in any longer.

"What happened, Dean? Why did you stop painting?" Dean's face tightened, and Aaron regretted his impulse. "I'm sorry. You said you'd tell me when you got to know me better. And you've known me for all of five minutes."

Dean said nothing for a moment, and Aaron was positive he'd just ruined what promised to be a good friendship. Then Dean expelled a long breath. "I opened the door to that question, didn't I? I told you about coming here, seeking inspiration... And considering I've been living here since January, you're the only person I've connected with." He smiled. "I don't count the guy at Hannaford's who flirts with me in the produce section." Dean inclined his head toward the living room. "Can we at least be comfortable for this conversation?"

"Of course." Aaron led the way, wondering what on earth was coming.

Whatever it was, he wanted to know.

K.C. WELLS

Chapter Nine

Dean sat on the couch, his cup in his hand. He didn't want to let go of it. If he did that, he had the feeling his hands would tremble.

"You don't have to tell me, you know." Aaron's voice was soft.

Yeah, Aaron was one of the good guys.

"It's okay. I was reminded recently that… someone had lost the right to have power over me. Maybe telling you about him will be a sort of final exorcism."

God, he hoped so. Lyle had haunted him long enough.

Aaron settled against the cushions. "Then tell me."

Dean drank a little first. "So, after graduating from Hanover College with a degree in Art and Design, I came home with a car-load of paintings. I think I told you I moved to Philly in 2008. Then in 2010 I moved to NYC. By 2012 I was in Boston, with my work in four different galleries around the country. I painted all day, and I couldn't have been happier. I was starting to get noticed, even if some of the critics made comments such as 'why doesn't Durrell just concentrate on *one* field? Has he never heard the phrase 'Jack of all trades, master of none?'" Dean chuckled. "Because I didn't want to, that's why. Because I could paint whatever I damn well wanted."

"I think I read a comment once on Twitter, by a famous author. She was advising a new writer, and her advice was basically one line—Don't read reviews." Aaron shook his head. "I also think critics are critics because they couldn't cut it, so they try to tear down those who can." He cocked his head. "Is that where this part of your story starts? In Boston?"

Dean nodded. "In those days, I'd contact one of the galleries to arrange a date for an exhibition. Then I'd work on amassing enough paintings for it. I'd allow myself plenty of time—I didn't want to be accused of 'churning them out'," he air-quoted. "And in the fall of 2012, I had a new exhibition in Boston, which was great. Usually, I traveled to whichever gallery was showing my work, which I hated because that meant time away from the next canvas. As the gallery was local, I could show my face occasionally during the week-long exhibit, then retreat to my apartment to continue working. And it was at the gallery that I met Lyle." His stomach clenched, and he took another sip of coffee.

The memory was still crystal-clear.

Boston, October, 2012.

Opening night was always the busiest, and the constant smiling, hand-shaking, and answering questions had taken its toll. Dean had all but collapsed into his bed when it was over. The next afternoon, he popped in to talk to the owner. He couldn't resist walking through the white-walled rooms, listening to muted conversations as prospective buyers discussed his work.

Then he caught sight of a tall, slim man staring at one of his landscapes with such rapt attention that Dean was intrigued. He stood beside a pillar, unable to tear his gaze away

*from the handsome stranger, praying his scrutiny would go
unnoticed.*

"So he was handsome?"

Dean sighed. "Oh yeah. I told myself I was
watching him because he was staring at the painting,
but that wasn't true. I was ogling him because he was
gorgeous."

There had been times during the afternoon
that Dean had found himself staring at Aaron for
exactly the same reason, and praying no one—okay,
praying ~~Seb~~—didn't notice. Seb didn't need more
ammunition.

"Okay, back to the story."

*When it became clear the guy was oblivious, Dean
had to say something. He walked as nonchalantly as he could
manage toward the guy, coming to a halt at his side.*

He cleared his throat. "Have you found him yet?"

*The guy jumped. "Christ, warn a guy." He frowned.
"Did you say something?"*

*Dean nodded and pointed to the landscape. "I asked if
you'd found him yet."*

"Found who?"

*"Waldo. Because judging by the length of time you've
been studying my painting, I figured you were obviously looking
for him."*

*"Your painting? You're the artist?" Dean gave a half
bow. "It's beautiful." The guy's lips twitched. "He's behind
that tree, isn't he? Great camouflage."*

Dean let out an exaggerated sigh. "Not even close."

*For a moment, the guy studied him. He widened his
eyes. "Wait. You're not the artist who does 'Where's Waldo?'*

in all your paintings? I'm sorry. I'm clearly in the wrong gallery." Then he smiled, and Dean's heart melted just a little.

"I have to ask. What is it about the painting that fascinates you?" It was a simple seascape from Downeast Maine, typical of his work. It showed where land met ocean, lush green peppered with gray rock, and calm blue water reflecting the expanse of sky. In the distance were the purple-colored swell of land, an island, and in the shallows sat a lone boat, its mast mirrored in the bay.

"I've never been to Maine," the guy commented, "but if this is what it's like, maybe I should go. It feels like I'm there, standing on one of those rocks, the sun warm on my face, maybe a gentle breeze playing with my hair."

Dean smiled. *"Thank you. It's where I lived when I was younger."*

The guy arched his eyebrows. *"You're not exactly ancient now. What are you, twenty-five?"*

He chuckled. *"Twenty-eight."*

"Where did you study art?"

"Ohio. But I was painting before I ever went to college."

The guy's eyes gleamed. *"Do you have any of your earlier work in this exhibition? Could you point them out?"*

"No, this is all recent work. All I have is photos." He removed his phone from his pocket, scrolled through his images, until he found what he was looking for. *"That was one of them."*

The guy gazed at the screen. *"This was before you studied art? Then I doubt they taught you a single thing. You could probably have given classes."*

Dean's cheeks grew hot. *"You're very kind."*

"No, I'm merely being honest." He held out his hand. *"Lyle Brant."* After they'd shaken, he gestured to their surroundings. *"Do you have time to walk me through your*

collection? Maybe a half hour?"

The call of his canvas grew dim. "I could do that."

Except thirty minutes blossomed into almost an hour, and by the time Lyle announced he had to leave, Dean was genuinely sorry to see him go. He'd shared stories of living in Maine, painting, anything to hear Lyle's laughter, his intelligent comments, to see the light in those dark brown eyes...

"Thank you for the tour—and the conversation. And I will be buying one of your paintings," Lyle promised as he left the gallery. Dean walked over to the window to watch Lyle's progress along the street, a relaxed stroll, as if he didn't have a care in the world.

As for his promise? Dean had a lot of experience with people who said they'd buy, but never materialized again, so he wasn't holding his breath—until it was robbed from him at closing time, when he emerged from the gallery to find Lyle waiting for him, leaning against the wall, looking thoroughly edible in a black leather jacket and jeans.

"Artists have to eat, right?" Lyle said as Dean approached him. "So let me take you to dinner."

"And you went," Aaron surmised.

Dean sighed. "Yeah, I went. That night, the next, in fact every night for the week-long duration of the exhibition. I only stopped by at closing time to see how the day had gone—they didn't need me there during the day—and there he'd be."

"Wow. He *was* interested, wasn't he? Sounds as if you shared a lot of conversations."

He nodded. "And then the last night, the conversation changed."

Dinner was over. There was just the coffee remaining.

Dean knew his idyllic week was almost at an end. The exhibition had been a roaring success: the gallery owner was already asking when the next one would be. It felt as though he and Lyle had covered every topic imaginable—with one exception.

Whatever Lyle's personal circumstances were, he'd kept them to himself.

Lyle signaled the server for the check, and Dean protested. "You've bought me dinner every night. Can't I pay just this once?"

"No. Trust me, I'm good for it." Lyle stilled, the candlelight casting a warm glow over his face. "Mr. Durrell… has anyone ever told you that you have the sexiest eyes?"

What. The. Hell?

Dean recovered quickly. "Not recently."

Lyle's smile grew wicked. "Oh yeah. Definitely come-to-bed eyes."

Oh shit.

Dean coughed. "Damn. I didn't think I'd been that obvious."

"Do you live in Boston, or are you just staying here for the exhibition?"

Fuck, his body was on fire. "I live here. Not far from the gallery, actually." The words were almost a croak.

"Then why don't you take me there, so I can see if reality matches the promise in those sexy as fuck eyes?"

The server approached, and Dean swallowed. "Pay the check. We're leaving."

He broke off from his story to finish his coffee. "Not going to go into details, but… there was one more surprise to come."

"He had two dicks?"

Dean chuckled. "No, but it was just as shocking. We'd spent a while making out, undressing… and then he told me I'd have to take the lead, because he'd never been with a guy before. Considering he'd been the one to start the ball rolling, I didn't expect that."

"Was he newly out?"

"That was my guess at the time. Whatever the circumstances, he was a fast learner—and a very apt student. When morning came, and he had to leave, he asked if he could visit me again. I didn't hesitate, and for the next three months, every weekend he returned to Boston Friday night, and left Sunday night. I was smitten. We saw in 2013 together, in bed. And it was then that I asked him if he'd considered moving to Boston—and moving in with me."

"Oh wow. You really were smitten."

Dean nodded. "When he said yes, I thought my heart would burst. Two weeks after that, we were living together. Lyle worked from home, so he was there all the time. From the start, he loved watching me work. We'd go for walks, and he'd point out people he felt would be good subjects for portraits. And he was so good at that. He had a real eye for it. And whenever he wasn't working, or watching me paint, he was taking care of me. Making sure I ate. Making sure the laundry got done, the groceries bought, the apartment cleaned." Dean shuddered out a sigh. "He inspired me."

Aaron gave a slow nod. "He was your muse."

"God yes. He lit up my days." *And my nights.* "We were inseparable."

"So what went wrong?"

Dean's throat seized, and he struggled to get

the words out. "Apparently, I did."

Aaron's brows knitted. "It doesn't sound to me like you did anything wrong."

"I kept telling myself that if there'd been signs, I could've done something differently, but it came out of the blue." Dean scowled. "No. That's not true. I'm lying to myself. There *were* signs—I either chose not to see them, or I ignored them. But I see them now, all too clearly. He was increasingly distracted, for one thing, and that wasn't like him. And then there were the business trips, once a month at first, but soon there were two, or three." He swallowed past the rock in his throat. "Then came the day he told me he was leaving me." June twelfth, 2015. A day burned into his memory.

"Aw crap. Did he say why?"

Dean sagged against the cushions. "Initially? He blamed me. He said I was stifling him. He felt… imprisoned. Stuck. Trapped." He could still hear Lyle's voice. "I asked what I could do to make things better. To make him not want to leave. He told me his mind was made up." He shivered. "I wasn't proud. I begged. Finally, he admitted he'd met someone else."

"What a bastard. He put you through all that, and he was cheating on you?"

"Oh, it gets better. Her name was Erin."

"Jesus."

Dean nodded. "She worked for one of the companies he represented. They'd 'connected' during their business meetings." He hooked his fingers in the air. "All those trips? They were to see her. Then came the real killer blow. He said I'd been an experiment. We'd started talking that first day in the gallery, and he'd found me attractive, sexy... Things he'd never felt for a guy before, and he wanted to see where they led."

Aaron gaped at him. "He started a relationship through *curiosity*?"

Dean shrugged. "He had an itch. I scratched it. Except I thought he loved me. God knows I loved him." *Christ, how I loved him.*

"So he left."

"And took with him any inclination I felt to pick up a brush. I didn't go outside my apartment for a month. Everything got delivered. I didn't answer mail. After two weeks, the gallery owner started calling, but I didn't respond. For the first time in my life, I didn't want to paint. My parents kept calling, my brother too, but I just crawled into a hole and hid."

"He really did a number on you, didn't he?"

Dean said nothing for a moment. At last he inhaled a long, slow breath. "You know, if it had only been sex, I could've coped with that. I wasn't looking for romance. I wasn't looking to fall in love. I was happy as I was, for God's sake. And then he rolled in there, and suddenly I was happier than I'd ever been, more inspired, and in love for the first time. If I'd known the truth, I'd have run a mile to get out of his path. But to tie my heart up in knots, to mess with my head, to let me think we were going to be together—and then blame me because I'd somehow trapped *him*?" Cold rage bubbled through him. "Jesus. Ash was right. Why the fuck did I let this go on so long? Why did I allow the memory of what he did to have such a tight grip on my life?"

Aaron got up from the couch and walked into

the kitchen, returning with two glasses of water. He handed one to Dean, and retook his seat. "How long did you hide for?"

Dean took a long drink from his glass. "Two years. By then, every painting I'd done was sold, and suddenly there was no more income."

"What did you do for two years?"

"Read. Watched movies. Gained thirty pounds." Dean patted his stomach. "Which was harder to take off than to put on, let me tell you. Then I got a job."

"Doing what?"

"Book illustrations. Not under my own name, of course. I couldn't do that. But it was a living. I found a cheaper apartment, moved again... And always in this direction, toward Maine."

"Something must have changed. I mean, you started painting again."

"My dad came into some money, and he split it between him, me, and Ash. He said he didn't believe in making us wait for him to croak—not if it would help us in the here and now—and besides, he was worried I was about to go under. And then last fall, I got the idea I needed to come back to Maine, to the state that inspired me in the first place. I came here on a visit, and damn it, it really was like coming home. I found a place to live, packed up my stuff— and that included my painting equipment that had been gathering dust in a closet. I was going to take it slow, start by sketching again, getting a feel for the place..." And hoping he'd find himself back on the right path again.

"So that's why there are no exhibitions looming. You're starting all over again."

Dean nodded. "I did contact a couple of gallery owners, just to let them know I wasn't dead." He chuckled. "They got all excited about the idea of more paintings."

"Are you really gonna put the past behind you?" Aaron's eyes were kind.

Dean sighed. "Ash gave me a stiff talking to, but really, it was stuff I'd been telling myself for about three months. I knew it was time to move on."

"I'm glad you did," Aaron said warmly. He cocked his head. "Were you serious about wanting to go on a hike tomorrow?"

"Yeah. I was painting right up until I took a shower and then came here. I painted all day yesterday, apart from when I stopped to make a lasagna. Part of painting is knowing when to take a break." Dean smiled. "I was going to ask you for some pointers. Are there any good trails you can recommend?"

"That depends. Are we talking energetic, gentle, scenic…?"

Dean grinned. "I think I'd better start off easy. That hike down to the water at the lighthouse showed me I need to work on my fitness levels."

Aaron nodded. "Okay, gentle it is. To start with, at least." He bit his lip. "How would you feel if the trail came with a guide?" Dean frowned, and Aaron held up his hands. "Feel free to say no, but tomorrow is my day off. The laundry is done, I bought groceries too. And if you prefer your own company, you only have to say so."

Dean stroked his sparsely bearded chin. "I'll make you a deal. You come on a hike with me, and I'll go to the Wyeth exhibition with you."

Aaron's face lit up. "Deal. I'll even pack a lunch for us. And tomorrow, I'll swing by your place and pick you up. Well, I will as soon as you give me an address."

Dean couldn't resist. "This is all some ploy, isn't it?" When Aaron froze, he added, "You just want to see the painting."

Aaron relaxed. "Sure. Let's go with that."

It wasn't until Dean was finally out of the door and on his way home that he realized it had been an odd response. Then he dismissed it. He was looking forward to spending more time with Aaron. The prospect sent a frisson of anticipation through him, and he quickly pushed down hard on his burgeoning excitement.

Don't let yourself fall into the same trap.

Except it wasn't the same. Aaron wasn't about to make a move on him, was he? If anything, Dean was the more interested party, much as he fought the attraction.

An attraction he couldn't deny any longer.

Chapter Ten

Monday, April 5

Aaron killed the engine and got out of the car. Dean's house was nestled among tall trees, and the only sounds were creaking branches swaying in the breeze and the chirping of birds. Two Adirondack chairs sat on the wraparound porch, and Aaron imagined sitting out there on long summer evenings, a tall glass of something cold beside him. Then he smiled to himself. *Sure. Right before the mosquitoes have their banquet.*

Dean appeared at the door, a rag in his hand. "Great timing. I just stopped. I've been up since dawn." He waited as Aaron climbed the steps. "Before you see the painting, I have to tell you... we're talking early stages, so it may not look like much."

Aaron chuckled. "I'm not here to critique it." He gave Dean an up and down glance. "You're not going like that, are you?" Dean wore a pair of tattered jeans and a tee that had seen better days. Smears of paint decorated it. His feet were bare. And then Aaron had to smile. "You have paint in your hair."

It made for an adorable picture.

Dean groaned. "I do this every time. I step away from the painting, push my hair back... I really should tie it up."

"Or cut it all off," Aaron suggested with a grin. Not that he was serious—Dean's long hair suited him. Aaron had always had a thing for girls with hair long enough to wind his fingers through silken locks during sex, and Dean's hair looked soft, touchable…The smell of clean hair was always a turn-on.

Jesus. I really do need to get laid soon.

Dean stared at him aghast. "I can't do that. It'd be like Samson, losing all his strength."

Aaron laughed. "I don't think you'd suddenly lose the ability to paint."

Dean brought his hand to his chest. "And I'm not about to test that theory." He led Aaron into the house. The main area was one large open space, the kitchen and living room separated by a partition wall. Two couches sat on the right, in front of them was a coffee table, and a fat stove in the corner. A warm rug in autumn shades lay on the floor between the couches. Beyond them was a table and four chairs.

Dean headed toward a door at the rear that opened into a hall. He walked through one door into a room that captured the best of the morning sun. An easel stood beside the window, but it wasn't the one Aaron had seen at the lighthouse. This one was sturdier, with three solid feet, and the canvas sitting on it had to be at least fifty inches across.

The painting already took his breath away. The Bass Harbor Light stood on top of the cliff, against a backdrop of dark green trees, and below it was an expanse of pink-tinged rock, huge slabs of it morphing into gray and then green-ish black as they neared the water's edge. The blue sky beyond was devoid of clouds, and the only thing in it was a circling bird of prey, its wings majestic as it caught the thermals.

"It's going to be awesome," he murmured.

"I have to tell you, I'm kind of excited," Dean admitted. "It's the biggest thing I've ever done. That was part of the challenge I set myself, to push the envelope." He cleared his throat. "Okay, I'll leave you here while I go get changed. I figured jeans, a sweater, boots—and a warm coat."

Aaron laughed. "Maybe a tee under the sweater, because... layers." The previous week, he'd spied a couple of tourists in shorts. *Some people really do leave their brains at home when they go on vacation.* The temperature was barely into the forties, although it promised to improve toward the end of the week.

"Do we have time for me to grab a shower? I want to get the paint out."

"Sure. It's not a long hike—maybe a little over three miles—and it could take one to two hours, depending on our pace."

Dean beamed. "Thanks." He dashed out of the room, and a moment later, Aaron caught the sound of running water. He took the opportunity to leaf through the pile of sketches sitting on the table. Most were of the lighthouse, but there were others. He recognized the view from the porch, a drawing of the house, and one that was obviously a self-portrait, a head and shoulders view. What struck him was Dean's pensive expression.

I suppose when you're concentrating, that's how you look. Aaron couldn't draw to save his life. His teachers in elementary school had made kind noises, and Mom had dutifully pinned his work to the fridge door, but he knew he wasn't about to win any art prizes.

She stared at that painting I did of an angel and said, 'What is it?' I mean, come on…

He took a step closer to the painting, leaning in for a better look. He could barely see the brushwork.

"Any closer, and you'll get paint on your nose."

Aaron jumped and spun around. Dean stood in the doorway, clothed in a dark blue towel that hugged his hips. "That had to be the fastest shower ever."

Dean strolled into the room. "What were you staring at?"

For some reason, having Dean so close to him, the smell of clean skin and hair invading Aaron's nostrils, was disconcerting, and Aaron couldn't account for it. He pointed to the canvas's surface. "Why can't I see any marks made by your brushes?"

"Because when you start a painting, the first layers are thin. Oil painting is usually fat over lean. The paint gets thicker as you near completion." Dean stretched his hand toward a shelf, grabbed a small square glass bottle, and handed it to Aaron. "I mix the paint with this. It's a drying medium. If I had to let the paint dry completely before adding another layer, it would take so much longer. This allows it to dry faster, and prevents it from yellowing." Dean glanced at his body. "And now I'd better put some clothes on." He strolled out of the room, affording Aaron a view of his smooth back and an ass Seb would probably have killed for.

For God's sake. His ass? Why the hell am I looking at his ass?

Hanging out with his friends was obviously

having an effect on him.

Dean stared at the calm water, framed by gentle, rolling hills and dark green woods. "This is familiar…" It stirred something deep in his mind. "I think I might've visited this place when I was a kid." Memories of Ash running ahead, and his dad yelling at him to slow down…

"My mom used to bring me here a lot when I was little. It was one of my favorite walks." Aaron pointed to the right. "We'll go counter-clockwise. The first section is the easiest—it's a gravel path along the eastern shores of the pond. Farther north, the terrain gets a little trickier, but nothing heavy. I've seen families with little kids walk this trail many times."

Dean adjusted his pack so it lay snug against his back. "Then let's get started." The sky was a sea of blue, and the sunlight sparkled on the water. He was glad he'd brought his coat though. The air was chilled.

They maintained a gentle pace, strolling beneath canopies of stark branches not yet in leaf, the pine needle-strewn path surrounded on both sides by trees in varying shades of green. Now and then, there were glimpses of the pond, before the path plunged deep into the trees once more. Ahead of them, Dean spotted a couple of hikers.

"You mentioned your mom," he said as they

ambled along. "What about your dad? Didn't he like hiking?"

"I wouldn't know," Aaron said in a matter-of-fact tone. "He died when I was four. Then it was just me and Mom."

"I'm sorry. He must not have been that old."

"He wasn't. He was born with a congenital heart disease. Mom said he always knew he was living on borrowed time." Aaron sighed. "It ran out when he was twenty-six. I think it was amazing he got to live as long as he did."

"He knew he had it, and yet—"

"I know what you're gonna say," Aaron interjected. "Why did he get married and have a kid, if he knew he could drop down dead at any minute? Mom says when he asked her to marry him, she said no. In fact, she turned him down flat the next five times he asked." He smiled. "I guess he wore her down, because the seventh time, she said yes. She told me she wanted to make him happy, even though she knew it could all end in heartache."

"And were they happy?"

Aaron nodded. "You should see the photos from when they were first married. I don't think there's a single one where Mom isn't smiling. They didn't plan on having me, so I guess something went wrong somewhere. Either way, when Dad found out, he was happy. He was also praying I didn't inherit his disorder." He glanced at Dean. "I didn't, by the way."

"Did she marry again?" Dean imagined it had to be tough, bringing up a little boy on her own.

"Nope. I remember a few boyfriends, but no one stuck around. Maybe she was picky. I don't know. There was one guy who I liked. He used to sit with me when I read my Spider-Man comics."

"I guess you and your mom are really close."

Aaron chuckled. "Yeah. I lucked out with her. When I hear stories from the guys about their families… Levi never knew his mom, Seb's mom sounds like a real bitch, Shaun lost his mom to cancer when he was in high school, Dylan's parents seem like they're complete dicks… One story after another. So yeah, I thank God for my mom."

Just then, the path opened out, emerging from shade into sunlight, with the water lapping at the rocks lining the pond's shore. Ahead of them, Dean could see two hills. "Do they have names?

"Sure. They're the Bubble Mountains."

"Seriously?"

"Sure. That's North Bubble, and that one's South." Aaron pointed across the pond to an even larger mountain. "And that's Penobscot Mountain."

Dean came to a halt, staring at the placid surface of the pond, its waters so clear he could see the rocks lying beneath. "This is so beautiful. I saw photos of it that made me want to paint it, but now I see it in real life…"

Aaron stood beside him. "This place always makes me feel calm. Whenever I need to clear my head, or think, this is where I come." He stepped over rocks to a couple of large boulders, and hoisted himself onto one of them. "Wanna sit for a while? We're not in any rush."

That sounded perfect.

Dean clambered onto the other boulder and leaned back, his weight on his hands. "You are so lucky, to have all this on your doorstep."

"It's on your doorstep too, isn't it?"

Dean inhaled, drawing the crisp clean air into his lungs. "For now. Who knows where I'll end up?" Except he didn't want to think about leaving Mount Desert, not yet.

"How long is your lease?"

"A year, with an option to renew after that. I might put down roots in Maine, I might not." That would depend on a lot of things.

"Roots are good." Aaron sighed. "You remember Noah? The one with the glasses?" Dean nodded. "He moved out of his parents' place, and he's living in a vacation rental unit. It's only temporary. I think he's feeling a little lost right now."

"Is Noah the superstitious one?"

Aaron snorted. "If there is such a thing as super superstitious, that would be Noah to a T. When he was going for his driving test, we went to so much trouble to bring him good luck. He ended up with eight rabbits' feet, eight ladybug charms, eight horseshoe charms…"

"Why eight?"

"Because eight is a lucky number." Aaron grinned. "It must've all worked, because he passed. But the stuff he does to avoid bad luck… He knocks on wood all the time. Watching Noah eat M&Ms is… interesting. He'll only eat them in pairs, by color. He won't take a shower in a thunderstorm, because his grandmother once told him that was how you got struck by lightning."

"Actually? That's not superstition, that's plumbing," Dean quipped.

"If he looks at his phone and it's 11.11, he makes a wish. He said he never washes clothes on New Year's Day, because someone once told him if he did, someone close to him would die that year."

Dean blinked. "Wow. He really is superstitious." There was something else he'd been meaning to ask since Aaron's Easter gathering. "When you first mentioned Ben and Wade, you said something about history."

Aaron nodded. "When Ben was in high school, he was bullied."

"It happens, right?"

"Sure, but Wade was the guy bullying him."

He gaped. "You're kidding. But... they're dating. And they look—"

"So close? Yeah, they do. Those two are meant to be."

"And what about you?" Dean was more than a little curious about Aaron. *Why are you alone?* He was sexy as fuck, and he obviously had his shit together.

"What about me?"

For a moment he hesitated. *It's none of my business.* Then he reconsidered. He'd laid his heart bare after the party. He wasn't asking Aaron to do the same.

"Don't you ever think about finding someone, settling down...?"

Aaron shrugged. "I've had my share of relationships. Okay, none of them lasted longer than a month, but maybe they weren't meant to be." He gave a wry smile. "Except if you asked my mom why I was still single, she'd give you a different story."

"What's her theory?"

"She thinks I'm too picky."

"And are you?"

Aaron turned his face up toward the sun, and the light caught in his beard, giving it a soft, warm glow. "Maybe?"

Dean didn't respond. He was drinking in the sight. Aaron's long legs were stretched out in front of him, and Dean couldn't help but notice how the denim clung to his firm, muscular thighs. His coat sleeves were tight around his upper arms, and for a few seconds, Dean allowed himself to imagine being enfolded in those arms, caged between those thighs, Aaron's beard rasping his as warm lips pressed against his mouth. *Any girl would be lucky to have you.*

Aaron turned his head slowly in Dean's direction, his eyes sparkling, and Dean realized he'd spoken out loud.

"Thank you for the compliment."

Dean felt as if his face was about to burn up.

Aaron eased himself off the boulder, landing lightly on his feet. "Ready for more?"

Dean followed suit. "I'm ready."

Talk about a distraction.

Farther north, they crossed several artistically-constructed wooden bridges, built to span a couple of streams feeding into the pond. There was even a shingle-covered beach of sorts, and they skimmed stones, bouncing them over the pristine water. As they stood there, a large cormorant landed on a nearby boulder, and Dean watched as it pulled in its impressive wings. It sat there for a moment, then took to the sky once more in graceful flight.

Aaron removed his backpack. "Time to eat." He opened it and removed a couple of wrapped sandwiches. "Hope you don't mind yesterday's meatloaf. There was some left over."

Dean smiled. "Sounds like heaven." He peered at the pack. "I don't suppose you've got the chocolate fountain tucked away in there."

Aaron cackled. "You don't want much, do you? How about a bag of M&Ms?"

"Only if I can eat them in pairs." They both laughed.

They sat on the large boulder vacated by the cormorant, and the water trickling over the rocks was the perfect soundtrack to their meal. The sun was high, so bright on the water that Dean wished he'd brought his sunglasses. He complimented Aaron on the sandwiches, especially when he tasted mayonnaise.

Perfect.

Once they finished eating, Aaron packed away the wrap, the empty candy bags, and the bottle of water, and they continued to follow the trail. The path plunged into the woods, and they lost sight of the pond. When they finally stepped out of the cool shade into the sunlight once again, Dean was dismayed to see ahead of them the blue walls of Jordan Pond House, their starting point, and behind that, the parking lot where they'd left Aaron's truck.

I don't want this day to end.

That was enough to spur him to a decision. "We should do this again. Maybe on a trail where we're close to the ocean."

"There's the Ocean Path," Aaron remarked. "That's a longer hike, because it's a two-mile trek one way, before you turn around and reverse your steps."

"I like the sound of that. Could we make this a regular thing?" As soon as he'd uttered the words, Dean realized what he was asking for. "I'm sorry. You have enough to do on your days off without being saddled with me. I'm capable of walking by myself."

"Hey, hold on a minute." Aaron put his hands on his hips. "For one thing, I would never consider myself *saddled* with you. I like your company. If I didn't, I wouldn't have agreed to do this. For another, of course you're capable, but did you ever stop to think I might *want* to show you these trails?"

"I just don't want to impose, that's all."

Aaron narrowed his gaze. "If you're ever an imposition, I'll be sure to let you know, okay? And right now, I was thinking about that coffee shop across the street from my house… and their apple coffee cake." His eyes twinkled. "That's if you don't think I'd be *imposing* if I asked you to join me."

All Dean had heard was that his perfect day wasn't about to end just yet.

"That sounds awesome. But only if I buy. You bought last time."

Aaron rolled his eyes. "Oh, if you must." Then he grinned, and Dean swore his heart gave a little flutter.

Oh baby, it's a good thing you can't read minds.

Chapter Eleven

Wednesday, April 7
If I hear one more joke about Thunder Hole...
Aaron regularly passed tourists standing next to the road sign for a photo, all wearing the same inane grin as they pointed to it. It was a fact of life, and it wasn't about to change. Every year, they came to take pictures and whoop and holler when water rose sometimes as high as forty feet into the air, spraying everyone.
Anyone out there today is an idiot.
Weather-wise, it was not a calm day, and Aaron had been keeping an eye on that part of Ocean Path. He'd seen a few visitors heading toward the observation platform, and he'd managed to dissuade them, but he was sure there would be more of them before the day was over.
He poured himself some coffee from his Thermos, and was about to drink when his phone vibrated in his pocket. He read Dean's text:
Have you spoken with Levi yet?
Damn. He'd meant to do that the previous night, but it had slipped his mind. His thumbs slid over the screen. *Doing it now.* Then he speed-dialed Levi. When Levi didn't pick up, Aaron knew he had to be busy: Levi usually answered within three rings. Aaron sipped his coffee and gazed out at the sky. The

dark gray clouds appeared to be shifting, and that was fine by him. *Now if the wind will just die down…*

His phone rang. "Hey, sorry I didn't answer right away. I was out in the yard, helping Grammy. The sapling she planted last month needed staking. It was in danger of being blown over. All fixed now though. What's up?"

"Can Grammy hear you?"

"What? Oh. Yeah. Let me take this into my room." There was a pause. "Okay. We're alone. Why all the subterfuge?"

"I've got an idea for Grammy's birthday, but I need your help." Aaron caught sight of a guy in shorts and a thin jacket, heading toward the platform. He watched for a moment as the guy approached the metal swing gate with its clearly written sign stating the path was closed. Then the tourist tried to climb over it.

Jesus, some people don't have the brains they were born with.

He held his phone against his chest and yelled, "Excuse me? Sir? Not a good idea right now. The weather the way it is, you're likely to get swept out into the ocean, if the rocks don't get you first. And it does say the path is closed, right?"

The man gave a nod and turned back.

Aaron growled. "Sorry about that. I had to stop some Masshole from doing something stupid."

"You can tell where he's from just by looking at him? Damn, you're good. And did anyone ever tell you you'd be great in public relations? Now, what do you need?"

"I've asked Dean to paint Grammy's portrait

for her birthday."

Levi's breathing hitched. "Oh wow. That's awesome. I take it he agreed?"

"Yes, and he'll do it from photos."

"Ah, I see where you're coming from. You want me to go through Grammy's photos to find something suitable? Lord knows she has enough of them."

"Not exactly. Dean thinks it would be better if he had a hand in the photos. It makes sense. He knows what he's looking for. He can set up suitable poses. *And* it turns out he's into photography. So... *You're* going to tell Grammy you're helping out Aaron's new friend who's just started his photo business."

"Ah. And Dean turns up to take lots of photos. Sneaky. Very sneaky."

"Yup. To make it more plausible, he'll take photos of both of you. You know, family portraits? The idea is that he's adding them to his portfolio. She'd be helping him get off to a good start. That's the line you'll feed her, at least."

"She'll buy that. Do you think Dean would let me have one of the photos after? We don't have any of me and Grammy, which is shocking when you think about it."

"Oh, I think we could do that." Aaron would make sure there were copies. "We'll tell her he's doing this with all the gang." That meant letting them in on the secret, in case Grammy mentioned it.

"Makes sense. When do you want to do this?"

"ASAP. The sooner he has the photos, the sooner he can start."

"What about this Saturday? Could he manage

that?"

God bless Levi. "Let me talk to Dean and I'll let you know. You sure that's okay?"

"Yeah. All Grammy has planned is baking. And let's face it, she bakes every day. Are we telling Grammy who Dean is?"

"No. That'll be part of the surprise." Aaron couldn't wait to see Levi's face when the portrait was unveiled.

"I think he's a nice guy, by the way."

Aaron thought Dean was way more than that. "I've been looking at his latest painting. He's so good." It broke Aaron's heart that Lyle's departure had had such a devastating effect on Dean's art. *I hope wherever Lyle is, he's in a lot of pain.* The vehemence of the thought took him by surprise. Aaron didn't think he had a vindictive bone in his body, but Lyle's betrayal made him sick to his stomach. *How could he treat Dean like that?*

"I'm just glad you have a new friend."

Levi's remark snapped him back into the present. "Did I need a new one?" He had plenty of friends.

"I know you have us, but… You have to admit, times are changing."

Aaron stilled. "What do you mean?"

"We're all still friends, but—"

"But now there are more of us. And some of us have gone from being single, to half of a couple." Levi was right, of course. The last year had changed everything. What eased his mind was how readily all these new relationships had been accepted. *No one has turned up with an asshole in tow. At least, not so far.* His friends all had excellent taste in men, thank God.

"This is where I apologize again." Levi hesitated. "I didn't mean to say all that stuff on New Year's Eve. I really am happy for Finn and Joel. And I've been doing a lot of thinking lately."

"To quote Seb, did it hurt?" The conversation had taken a new direction, and Aaron's chest grew a little tighter.

"I'm being serious here." Another pause. "Maybe I should stop holding onto a dream that's never gonna come true."

Aaron's stomach clenched. *Oh Levi. Just tell him.*

"I look at my life, and what does it amount to? I have my work, and Grammy. And occasionally, my friends, although we have yet to see how things'll pan out. There has to be more to life than that."

"What do you want out of life?"

"Someone to share it with. I love Grammy with all my heart, but let's be honest here. She could last another twenty to thirty years. If I'm still living here, some lonely old bachelor when she's ready to pop off, I think she'll haunt me."

Aaron chuckled. "I think she will too. But you're *not* going to be alone, you hear me?" He couldn't hold back any longer. "That dream of yours... Why don't you tell Noah how you feel?"

"What the hell for? So he can tell me he doesn't feel the same way? So he can rip my heart from my chest, tear it into tiny little pieces..."

"Noah would *never* do that to you. He's like your brother, for Christ's sake."

"Intentionally, no, he wouldn't. That is why he is never *ever* going to know how I feel about him. You got that?"

K.C. WELLS

"I've got it. I think you're wrong, but I've got it." It was a surreal conversation to be having. Aaron stood above the observation platform, one eye on the weather, another on the foolhardy tourists in danger of losing life and limb, and one ear to his dearest friend, who was obviously going through a crisis. He wished he could do something to help Levi, but he didn't have a clue.

"You know what? I already know the first thing that needs to change. It's about time I got my cherry popped. I mean, who's still a freakin' virgin at twenty-seven?"

It was then that the truth of the situation finally hit home. Levi had truly given up waiting for Noah. *You wanted him to be your first.* Jesus, that made his heart ache. "Hey, it's not a big deal, okay? I lost mine when I was still in high school."

Except he knew in Levi's mind, his virginity *was* a big deal.

"So maybe I should take a leaf out of Seb's old book, go to a bar, dance the night away, and end up in somebody's bed. End of story."

Aaron huffed. "I've been thinking the same thing. Maybe we should both head for that bar."

There was a moment's hesitation. "I don't think the place I have in mind is your style."

"What do you mean?"

"Well, I was thinking of going to that gay bar in Ogunquit. You know, Seb's former hangout?"

Aaron suddenly got where he was going with this. "Hell, I'm all for new experiences." His heartbeat quickened.

Crickets.

"Levi?"

"Are you serious?"

"Why not? I don't have a hang-up about going to bed with a man." The words came out easy, but his pulse quickened.

"Since when?"

"Hey, you know me. I'm a laid-back, fluid kinda guy."

"Sure, but *that* fluid?"

His heart pounded. "It's just sex, right? Only, the plumbing's a little different. And it's not as if it would be a *totally* new experience. I've dated a few intrepid girls in my time."

"What does that—oh. Okay, that's TMI, dude. I did *not* need to know that." Levi paused. "You'd really have sex with a guy?"

"Sure. Maybe it's time I found out what the appeal is. I mean, most of my friends are over on the other side of the church. They've gotta be sitting there for a *reason*, right?"

There was silence, and then Levi burst into laughter. "You… you're awesome, dude. Just when I think I know all there is to know about you, you show me a whole new side."

"I like to keep you on your toes." He'd said all that to entertain, but when he thought about it, Aaron realized there was more than a grain of truth in his words. Some part of him didn't balk at the idea of getting intimate with a guy.

The shocker? Some part of him *really* liked that idea.

"Okay. If I ever get up the nerve to go to a gay bar, you're coming with me. For moral support, if nothing else. And now that I think about it… Yeah, having you with me is a great idea. You'll attract a lot of attention."

Aaron sighed. "Levi… so will you. You're a gorgeous guy, inside *and* out. I'm telling you now, you'll have to fight them off." He caught Grammy's shout in the background. "Uh-oh. Looks like you're wanted. I'll talk to Dean, and let you know about Saturday, okay?"

"Fine. Thank you for thinking of her. And thank you for the most illuminating conversation." Levi disconnected.

Aaron pocketed his phone. He *thinks it was illuminating? Not half as illuminating as it was for me.* He had no clue where all that had come from, and he wasn't sure what to do about it, now it was out in the open. What he liked most was Levi's reaction. It had that we've-been-best-friends-forever-and-new-and/or-unexpected-information-is-accepted-at-face-value-and-not-judged kinda vibe.

But do I have the nerve?

Then he saw three people heading his way, and groaned.

Work time. Fantasies would have to wait.

Dean covered the pot and raised the heat to a rolling boil. His phone juddered on the countertop, and he grabbed it before it could vibrate its way off the edge and onto the floor. He smiled when he saw it was Aaron. "Hey."

"You painting?"

"No, I'm done for the day."

"Can I stop by on the way home?"

Dean gave the kitchen a glance. "Sure. Just ignore the mess. I've been cooking."

"See you soon." Aaron hung up.

He went to work on cleaning up after himself, and all the while, the delicious aroma intensified. By the time all the countertops had been wiped down, and the dishwasher loaded, he caught the sound of an engine outside. Dean dried his hands on a towel, and went to open the door.

Aaron locked the car and walked toward the house. *Damn it, he's not wearing the Stetson. Does he have any idea how delicious he is in that uniform?* Part of Dean's anatomy certainly appreciated the sight, and he hurriedly lowered the towel.

"Come on in. Help yourself to a soda. I'm almost done." He went back into the kitchen just as the oven pinged.

Aaron strolled across the hardwood floor. "Something smells good. No, wait—scratch that. Something smells amazing. Is that fresh bread?"

Dean opened the oven and removed the tray with the rolls. "Yup. I thought I'd try my hand at making it." Aaron reached for one, and Dean smacked his fingers with his free hand. "Uh-uh. Too hot. And if you tried to eat it now, you'd give yourself indigestion." He placed the hot tray on a trivet.

Aaron wandered over to the countertop where the bowl containing the shucked clams sat. "Oh dear Lord. You're making clam chowder." He lifted the lid on the pot and bent to sniff.

"Do I have to ban you from my kitchen?" Dean grabbed a wooden spoon from the drawer and held it out at arm's length.

"And what are you going to do with that?" Aaron said with a smirk.

"Keep messing with my cooking, and you'll find out." He put the spoon down. "This is the first time I ever made clam chowder, and I'm a little nervous, okay? I soaked the clams overnight. I made sure I got all the shell. And when the potatoes are tender, I'll add the meat and the milk."

"It'll be great," Aaron told him. "If it tastes half as good as it smells, it'll be delicious."

"Did you talk to Levi?"

"Yes. He said Saturday's free."

"*This* Saturday? That's great. So what excuse did you come up with for him to give Grammy?"

Aaron grinned. "*You* have just started your own photography business, and you're looking to expand your portfolio."

Dean beamed. "That works. I've got a tripod, camera, light meter… I'll look the part. And Levi doesn't know he'll be in the portrait too?"

"Nope. Surprises all around." Aaron's stomach growled.

That was all the excuse Dean needed. "Why don't you stay? There's plenty."

"I couldn't."

"Why not? Have you *seen* the size of that pot? And what I don't eat tonight, I'm going to freeze."

"If you're sure…"

Dean laughed. "Just don't get any of it on that pretty uniform."

Aaron arched his eyebrows. "This is pretty?"

"Hey, I'm gay, and you're in a uniform. What did you expect?"

Aaron's cheeks flushed, and he glanced down. "Maybe this is a bad idea."

Dean thought fast. "Look, dinner won't be for a half-hour. If you want to go home, grab a shower, get changed, and then come back here, you've got time."

"You sure?"

He grabbed the towel. "If you ask me that one more time, I'm gonna flick you with this. Now get into that truck and go home. I'll see you for dinner."

Aaron grinned. "Deal." And then he was gone.

Dean's evening was suddenly looking a whole lot better.

Chapter Twelve

Aaron's contented sigh told Dean all he had to know. "You liked it."

"That was delicious." Aaron dropped his spoon into the bowl and leaned back. "I mean, Grammy makes a mean clam chowder, but you'd give her a run for her money."

"That sounds like a compliment."

Aaron chuckled. "When it comes to cooking and baking? Grammy is amazing. She makes the best cookies ever, and her mackerel casserole is to die for."

Dean got up from the table and picked up the empty bowls. "Sorry there's no dessert."

Aaron gave a sheepish grin. "Actually, there is." Before Dean could inquire further, he got up from the table and went outside. When he returned, he was carrying a white box. He held it out to Dean. "Here."

Dean opened it and smiled. "Chocolate peanut butter cake. To quote Seb, you're a keeper. I'll make coffee."

"Then I'll clear the table."

Dean spooned coffee into the filter. "I'm happy with the way the chowder turned out. Not bad for a first attempt."

Aaron snorted. "And now you're fishing. I don't think I can improve on *delicious*."

Dean handed him a couple of plates. "You

can deal with the cake—I'll deal with the coffee." He hoped Aaron wasn't going to leave anytime soon. Their earlier conversation had surprised him, the easy banter, the teasing back-and-forth.

Then ask him to stay a while.

Except Dean couldn't do that, not without it sounding a little weird.

Aaron took the plates into the living room, and Dean grabbed two cups. He added the bowls and silverware to the dishwasher's load.

"Oh wow. You've got one of my favorites."

"Favorite what?" Dean called out.

"Just looking at your DVDs. You don't have many."

"That's because I only buy movies I can watch again and again. For everything else, there's Netflix. So which movie caught your eye?" He walked into the room, carrying two full cups.

Aaron smiled. "*Arrival.* I saw it when it came out. Awesome movie." He was reading the back of the DVD cover.

Perfect. "We could watch it now, if you like. Unless you're in a hurry to go home."

"I'm not in any hurry. Besides, I have to do something while I'm eating my cake, right?"

Dean placed the cups on the coffee table, then picked up the remote to open the DVD player. "Stick it in." He sat on the couch and hit the TV standby button.

Aaron dealt with the disc, then sat at the end of the couch. He frowned when Dean chose to sit on the other couch. "Something I said?"

It wasn't as if Dean could tell him the truth. *If I sit here, I get to look at the screen—and you.* Then the movie started, and there was coffee and cake to occupy them.

Dean couldn't tear his gaze away from Aaron. He loved his look of concentration, his fingers laced over his stomach, his long legs parted, bent at the knee. Dean's sketchpad was right there on the coffee table, a couple of pencils next to it.

I can't.

Why not? Aaron won't mind.

Can't I quit being an artist for one lousy night?

He leaned forward, inching his fingers closer to the sketchpad, trying to do it as surreptitiously as possible.

"I know what you're doing," Aaron murmured, his focus still on the screen.

He froze. "What?"

Aaron turned his face toward Dean. "Just pick up the goddamn pencil and draw."

"You're okay if I sketch you?"

He arched his eyebrows. "That depends. Do I need to sit still? Am I allowed to breathe?"

"Sure. As long as you can do it without moving." Aaron blinked and he chuckled. "Just kidding." He picked up the sketchpad and started to sketch Aaron's outline. Aaron watched him, and Dean pointed his pencil toward the TV. "Watch the movie."

"Yes, sir." Aaron's eyes twinkled. "It's not as if I don't know the plot. I could probably recite every line, I've seen it so many times."

"Fine. You can talk. Just don't move." Dean's pencil flew over the expanse of white paper, capturing the lines of Aaron's body.

"I know you talked a lot about Lyle, but…

was there anyone before him?"

Dean concentrated on his drawing. "Sure, but back then, things were a lot more casual, and that was fine by me. I was happy that way. I wasn't looking for anything permanent. I didn't want a relationship."

"Let me guess. A relationship would take you away from your painting."

"Exactly."

"But with Lyle…"

Dean sighed. "He didn't distract me, just the opposite. Only thing was, I wasn't looking for love."

Aaron huffed. "Which, according to Levi, is when it sneaks up on you and hits you over the head with a baseball bat."

Dean lowered his pencil. "Did no one ever sneak up on you?"

"Not so far. Not sure whether that means I've been lucky or just the opposite."

"My brother thinks I've been alone too long."

Aaron frowned. "What's 'too long'?"

"Five years."

He widened his eyes. "Wow. And I thought *I* was going through a dry patch."

Dean smiled. "I've met your friends, remember? The way things are going, I don't think that dry patch will stay dry for much longer." *And whoever gets to be with you will be one lucky girl.*

Then it hit him. He was jealous of someone who as yet didn't exist.

This is crazy. I've known him for less than two weeks. How did he crawl under my skin so goddamn fast?

"I've kinda been thinking the same thing myself. Don't get me wrong, I'm not looking for love either." Aaron grinned. "Right now I'd settle for a night of passion."

"Christ, me too." Not to mention waking up to a warm body in his arms, and a slow morning fuck that stretched into a day of not leaving the bed except when they had to.

Aaron gave the sketch pad a hard stare. "I thought you were drawing me."

"Slave driver." Dean resumed his task, and Aaron focused once more on the screen.

Dean was honest enough to admit to himself that the warm body he craved was sitting on the other couch, and that he apparently preferred women.

Unfortunately.

Dean waved at Aaron as he drove away, watching until the lights of his truck disappeared from view. He stood on the porch, drinking in the darkening sky, unspoiled by streetlights, the stars just beginning to twinkle in the heavens.

Then his phone rang, and he hurried inside to answer it. When he saw it was Ash, he answered. "Hey."

"Grab your calendar, bro. I need you to check something for me."

Dean went into the kitchen and peered at the calendar hanging on the wall. "Okay. Want to tell me what I'm checking?"

"Take a look at June. Specifically, the week beginning June seventh."

Dean lifted the sheets. "Nothing so far."

"Great. Then pencil us in."

"'Us'?"

"Me, Claire, and her BFF Jon. We're coming to Maine for a week. And before you protest, relax, dude. We won't be staying with you." Ash snorted. "Trust me, you don't have enough space for all of Claire's luggage. Jon's either, if it comes to that. I've seen how he packs, and it ain't light. Is that a gay thing?"

"What brought this on?"

"Claire got to talking about you, and then Jon started Googling. Not you, by the way—Maine. I think you're safe. He broke up with his last boyfriend, but Claire says he's going through a Daddy phase— whatever *that* means. Anyhow, she and Jon have booked motels, inns, hotels, all along the coast. I'm just gonna sit back and let them do all the organizing. But keep Saturday June twelfth free. Because guess who's coming to dinner?"

"I can do dinner."

"And if you want to even things up a little, invite a friend. Oh, I forgot—you don't have any."

"Fuck you," Dean said good-naturedly. "And yes, I'll invite a friend."

"Will it be the hunky park ranger? You always did have a thing for uniforms."

"I do not."

"Pants on fire. You remember when we all went to Disneyworld, and there were a couple of marines on our flight? Man, the work you created for the flight crew, having to clean up your drool. And you know you said me and Claire are joined at the hip? Wait till you see her and Jon."

Dean went over to the fridge, picked up the dry wipe pen, and wrote *June 7-12* on the white board next to it. "Okay. I've made a note of the date. Is that it?"

"Yup. Now that I've told you, Claire can stop reminding me."

"Great. And now I can get some sleep."

"Are you kidding? It's only ten o'clock."

"Not here it isn't. Time zones, remember? And I want to get up early and paint. Unless you don't want me to?"

"Paint, paint. I can't wait to see it. Goodnight, bro. Sweet dreams." Ash disconnected.

Dean walked to the front door and locked it. He wasn't thinking about Ash's visit. He was thinking about Saturday—and spending it with Aaron.

Aaron poured himself a glass of water, then turned off all the lights. He hadn't intended staying so late, but the combination of good food, a great movie, and even better company had made him reluctant to call it a night. It wasn't until he connected his phone to the charger on the nightstand that he saw a couple of missed calls, all from Mom. He glanced at the alarm clock. She'd still be awake. When she answered after two rings, Aaron knew he'd been correct.

"Mom? You okay?"

"Why aren't you in bed?"

"Because I'm calling you! And you called *me*, remember?"

"Oh, that was only because you didn't call last weekend. I was worried."

Aaron let out a sigh of relief. "Is that all?"

"Hey, it was your idea to have a weekly call. So how did you expect me to react when you didn't?"

He stretched out on the bed. "I'm sorry. I was with the guys."

She chuckled. "That explains it."

A fragment of his conversation with Dean came to mind. "Mom, whatever happened to all my Spider-Man comics?"

"Seriously?" Another wry chuckle. "I threw them out."

"You did what?"

"You *were* twenty-three at the time. I figured you were over your crush by then."

What the hell? "Crush? What crush?"

"Your crush on Spider-Man," Mom said in a patient tone.

Where does she get these ideas from?

"I did *not* have a crush on Spider-Man."

Mom snorted. "Excuse me? Your walls were covered in Spider-Man posters. You doodled him on your homework. You were always clamoring to watch Spider-Man cartoons. You slept with a Spider-Man comic under your pillow. I was always afraid that one day I'd pick one of those up and the pages would be... you know... stuck together?"

"Mom!" he exclaimed, his voice strangled.

"And let's not forget the time you told me you were gonna marry Spider-Man when you grew up."

"You just made that up," he accused.

"You wish."

Aaron didn't believe he was hearing this. "So if I came to visit and announced I was dating a guy, you'd be okay with that?"

Her response was instant. "Sure. There's always adoption."

"What?"

"Hey, I'm like any other mom. I like the idea of grandchildren. But I'm not picky about how they get here. So sure, bring a guy home—as long as he wants kids." Aaron sputtered, and she chuckled. "Okay, I'm just kidding. Well, sort of. I don't care as long as you're happy."

"I still say you're making all this up."

"Remember when I gave you The Talk?"

Aaron shuddered. "Oh my God. I wanted to die."

"*Such* a drama queen. You've been hanging out with Levi and the others for way too long. You're starting to sound like them."

"And how do they sound?" he demanded.

"Duh. Gay. But let me get back to my point. Think about that talk for a minute, will you?"

"Do I have to? I'm still scarred."

"You didn't notice anything about it? Anything unusual?"

"I was too busy trying not to die of embarrassment."

"So it didn't strike you as odd that I didn't use any pronouns other than they/them/their? That I didn't *once* refer to what you might do with a *girl*?"

Okay, now that she mentioned it… "Mom?"

She sighed. "I was trying to cover all bases. That Spider-Man business… Put it this way. I wouldn't have been surprised if you'd come out and said you were gay. Hell, I was still waiting for the announcement when you got into your twenties."

Aaron was lost for words.

"In high school, when you started making friends with Levi, Finn, Seb—Good Lord, that boy must've given his mother palpitations—I was glad. You weren't alone. I always figured that was why you got on so well with them. They made you feel comfortable in your own skin. Have you ever met a gay guy you *weren't* comfortable with?"

Aaron was still in quiet mode. *Dean. How long is it since we met? Almost two weeks? And look at the way we get along. As if we've known each other forever.*

"Okay, where did you go?"

If you only knew.

"I genuinely had forgotten about Spider-Man," he confessed. "And you really would be okay if I started dating guys?" *You think you know a person…*

"Something you want to tell me? Aaron… are you all right?"

"Just a lot of things coming at me right now," he said truthfully. The chat with Levi, with his mom, the way he was looking at Dean…

The way Dean was looking at him, because making comments about his pretty uniform implied a whole lot of looking.

"Do I need to come visit?"

That brought him back to earth with a bump. "No, I'm fine, honest."

"I'm curious though. What made you think of

your comics after all this time?"

"I was talking about some of the guys you dated. One of them liked to sit with me and read my comics." And hadn't that recollection made him curious too? "Mom... how come you never married again? You dated... Were none of them good enough for you?"

She chuckled. "Sweetheart, *I* wasn't the problem."

"What does that mean?"

"Every guy I ever dated, I brought home to meet you. And if you'd warmed to any of them, I'd have been in there like a shot."

"Hey, don't put the blame on me. *You'd* have been the one marrying them."

"And you were just a kid. Whoever I chose had to be a good father. I just hadn't reckoned on how picky you were."

"Picky? Me?"

"Oh, come on. *You* may not remember all the excuses you gave when you stopped dating those girlfriends of yours, but I sure do. 'She's too needy.' 'Too thin.' 'She doesn't read.' 'She's a cat-person, not a dog-person.' Do any of those ring a bell?"

Now that she mentioned it...

"I figured I'd know when you found the right one, because you'd stop seeing them with your eyes, and see them with your heart instead."

"That's way too profound for this time of night." He paused. "And you did it again, didn't you? You said 'them', not 'her'."

"So I did. Looks like I'm still covering all the bases."

"So it's my fault you stayed single?"

Mom sighed. "No, baby. But you were an important part. And who knows how much weight I'd have put on your reaction if a guy had come along and swept me off my feet? I might've said, 'Screw him, he's six. What does he know?' So maybe you're not the only one who's picky."

"I really need to get some sleep." *And kill this conversation.*

"Okay. Then we don't have to talk this weekend, seeing as we just caught up. But don't worry me like that again."

"I won't. I promise."

There was a pause. "You sure you're okay?"

He didn't know how to answer that, not without revealing the rabbit hole he'd just fallen into.

"You know what? You're right, I should let you get some sleep. Take care, sweetheart." Mom hung up.

Aaron undressed, his world in a spin. His own words danced in his head.

I'm all for new experiences.

I don't have a hang-up about going to bed with a man.

I'm a laid-back, fluid kinda guy.

It's just sex, right?

Maybe it was time to discover if all those statements were just empty words—or if they added up to something new and different, and more real than anything Aaron had previously encountered.

Chapter Thirteen

Saturday, April 10

Dean peered through the windshield at the pale blue cedar shakes-covered house. "So what's Grammy like?"

"She's seventy, but sharp as a tack. And some of the things she says I don't really understand, but that's because she's a Mainer, all the way through to her backbone." Aaron chuckled. "I've gotten to know some of her sayings, but that's only because she says them a lot."

Dean smiled. "That reminds me of when we'd visit my grandparents, before we moved to Ohio. Some of the things Grandpa would say... it was like another language." He glanced at Aaron. "So... Are you going to be my assistant this afternoon?"

"Sure. I did have one idea. Seeing as you're setting this up for a painting, you might want to think about what she's wearing."

"I don't want to put her to any trouble."

Aaron grinned. "Grammy won't mind." The front door opened and Levi stood there, arms folded. "I guess that's our cue to go in." They got out of the car, walked around to the trunk, and between them they carried Dean's photographic equipment along the front path to the door.

Levi greeted them with a smile. "Well, you

certainly look the part. Good to see you again, Dean. And thanks for doing this. Come on in."

As they stepped into the hallway, a voice rose from behind the door. "Oh Jeannie Crummel. Why won't this cussid thing start up?"

Levi rolled his eyes and hurried to the door. "What's the matter, Grammy?" he said as he opened it.

"That numb lawnmower. It won't start."

"But why are you cutting the grass now? Dean's here to take the photos. And besides, today is not a good day for mowing."

"Ayuh. You may be right. It was teemin' wicked hard last night. I'll bet the bay was all riley this morning."

Dean glanced at Aaron and whispered, "Okay. I'm lost."

Aaron chuckled. "It's all right. In this case, I speak Grammy. Cussid is cursed or obstinate. Teeming means it was raining really hard. And riley? That's the color of the ocean after a big storm."

Dean leaned in close. "You'd better stick around. I might need a translator."

The door opened wider and Grammy emerged. She was shorter than Levi, her once dark hair shot through with silver. One glance at those eyes told Dean Aaron had nailed it. Grammy was one sharp customer.

She walked toward him. "So you're the photographer?"

He extended his hand. "The name's Dean, ma'am."

Grammy snorted. "Everyone calls me Grammy. That includes you. I hear you've met the gang?"

"Yes, ma'am—I mean, Grammy."

"That Seb is a bit of a rig, ain't he?"

Even without Aaron to translate, Dean had a good idea what that meant. "He is indeed. Thank you for taking time out of your day to do this for me."

She waved a hand. "It's no bother. I tend to glob around most days." She gestured toward Levi. "This one can take care of himself— just have to keep him supplied with cookies and cake." Her eyes glittered. "You look like a cookies-and-cake kinda guy to me."

He laughed. "Guilty." He glanced at her attire. She wore a pair of cream slacks and a teal-colored blouse. A single string of pearls sat around her neck.

Grammy arched her eyebrows. "Do I pass muster?"

Dean nodded. "You look awesome. Now, where can I set up?"

She pushed the door open. "This is the living room."

Dean followed her inside, taking in the room with its paintings, ornaments, and comfy-looking couches and chairs. It was something of a shock to see his own work above the fireplace, even though he knew it would be there.

"Not much room," he admitted.

"How about in here?" Grammy slid open a pair of doors to reveal a dining room. There was less furniture in there, but it still wasn't the setting he was searching for.

"I've got an idea," Levi piped up. "Come with me."

He led Dean and Aaron to the French doors

at the end of the dining room, which opened onto a patio. Levi gestured to the back yard. "This is Grammy's realm. What do you think?"

Dean scanned the garden, his gaze alighting on a tall tree, a bench beneath it. "That's perfect." The dappled shade, the lush green of the shrubs behind the bench…

Beside him, Grammy sighed. "My husband planted that tree when we were first married. He never got to make old bones, so he never saw how beautiful it grew to be. It's also my favorite spot for sittin'."

That decided him. "If it's not too cold out here, I'd love to take photos of you on the bench, with Levi."

Grammy smiled. "Then I might just put on a sweater, if that's okay."

Dean assured her it would be fine.

"Am I dressed okay?" Levi asked. He wore jeans and a dark blue sweater.

"You'll do just fine. Now, with the help of my assistant for the day…" Dean gestured to Aaron. "I'll set up the camera while Grammy finds a sweater." He waited until Grammy and Levi had stepped back into the house before turning to Aaron. "I like her."

"Everyone does. Even if she did take a switch to some of our backsides when we were younger. Wait until you try her cookies."

Dean inclined his head toward the house. "It was weirder than I thought it would be, seeing my painting in there." He could still recall working on it in the attic, his painting space.

"And come June, there'll be another Dean Durrell painting to hang in there."

Dean aimed to make it the best portrait he had ever painted.

By the time Dean had finished, the best of the light was fading. He'd lost count of how many photos he'd taken, but he figured a real photographer would have done that. Once he had them loaded onto his laptop, he would pick one, or maybe three or four, and then choose the best elements to include in the portrait. The equipment had been packed into Aaron's trunk, and he guessed it was time to go. They had a long drive back to Mount Desert.

He went back into the house to say his goodbyes, and found Aaron and Levi deep in conversation in the living room. From Levi's expression, it was clearly a serious topic.

Grammy came out of the kitchen and walked up to him. "Those two... Thick as thieves. Always have been." She squeezed Dean's arm. "Dinner is almost ready."

"Excuse me? What dinner?"

Grammy raised her thin eyebrows. "You thought I was gonna let you drive all the way back to Bar Harbor without feedin' you first? You've been at it all afternoon."

"I couldn't impose on you like that," he protested.

"Who's imposin'? There's plenty. Besides, I made mackerel casserole. You try telling Aaron he's gonna miss out on that if he leaves now." She raised her voice. "Aaron. You 'n' Dean are stayin' for dinner."

Aaron broke off and came to the door. "Hey, we can't do that. We've taken up most of your day already."

Grammy narrowed her gaze. "Are you sayin' no to my mackerel casserole? And my homemade biscuits?"

Aaron's eyes widened. "Lady, you fight dirty."

She cackled. "Ayuh. Now go wash your hands. You have five minutes."

Dean laughed. "I may have only met you for the first time today, but even I know not to argue with you."

Grammy patted his cheek. "Smart boy." Then she went back into the kitchen.

Levi joined them. "She's already set the table for four. I didn't even see her do that. She's way too sneaky."

"Thank God tomorrow is Sunday and I'm not working," Aaron observed. "It's not so bad if we get back late."

Dean didn't mind. It had been a productive afternoon, and Aaron had proved an able assistant. He had a good eye, suggesting poses for Grammy and Levi. Grammy had talked throughout the entire process, sharing stories of Levi growing up, and the things some of his friends had gotten up to. She reminded Dean strongly of his own grandmother, now passed.

A good day, and it wasn't over yet.

It wasn't until Aaron glanced the clock on the sideboard that he realized how late it was. Dinner had been delicious, and the conversation that had followed over coffee and Grammy's chocolate cake had been entertaining. Dean appeared relaxed and content, chatting about Levi's job, and it was good to see how easily they talked.

It was no use. They had to make a move sometime. Even at this time of night, it would take them four hours at least to get back. *Why didn't I notice the time?*

That was easy. He was enjoying the company.

Now and then during dinner, Dean had caught Aaron's gaze, and they'd exchanged smiles. *What is it about his smile?* There was nothing forced about it, a genuinely happy expression that reached his eyes, and made his face glow.

Maybe he's the gorgeous redhead Grammy was talking about back in January.

Except hadn't the rest of that quote been about falling madly in love?

Then he realized Grammy was speaking. "Sorry, Grammy. What did you say?"

She huffed. "I *said*, you boys are not drivin' all that way tonight. Not when I have a guest room."

"Oh, we couldn't do that," Dean said in a

rush.

"Course you can. It'll take less than a minute to make up the bed, and if you don't wanna share, there's a foldin' bed in there too. I'll make you breakfast in the mornin', and then you can drive back."

"Grammy," Aaron began.

She jerked her head to stare at him. "You gonna argue with me, boy?"

Aaron bit his lip. "No, Grammy."

She gave a sweet smile. "Good boy. Now, I know you weren't expectin' an overnight stay, so I'll find you toothbrushes. I keep a stack of 'em in the cabinet in the bathroom. I know Aaron here is an early bird, but don't you feel you have to be up at the crack of dawn. You get up when you feel like it."

"This is very kind of you," Dean murmured.

She smiled at him. "I do this a lot. Levi's been havin' people stay over since he was in eighth grade." Then her shoulders sagged, as if all her energy had drained away.

Levi got up from his chair and went over to her, his hand on her shoulder. "Okay, lady, now it's *my* turn to talk. You've had a full day, and you're tired. So forget about the dishes, cleaning the kitchen… You go get into bed and I'll bring you your warm milk and your tablets. I'll take care of these two. You've done enough for one day."

Grammy reached up and curved her hand around his cheek. "You are one sweet child. And one day you'll make someone a wonderful husband." She got up from her chair, and Levi walked with her toward the door. She paused at the threshold and smiled at them. "Goodnight, boys. Thank you for the company." She gazed at Dean. "I'm awful glad to have met you."

"The feeling is mutual, Grammy."

The door closed behind them, and it was then Aaron realized he was about to share a room with Dean.

"Is the guest bed big enough for two?" Dean asked.

Aaron nodded. "I've shared it before now with one of the guys when we stayed over. You sure you don't wanna fold out the bed?" His pulse quickened.

"We don't need to if there's enough space."

Aaron cocked his head. "Are you a wriggler? Do you snore?"

"No to the first, and I don't think so to the second."

Why the hell am I nervous about this? Jesus, he'd slept with most of the guys at one point or other, and hadn't thought twice about it.

Except this was different. This was Dean, and there was definitely something going on in Aaron's head when it came to him.

"If I'd known we were gonna stay the night, I'd have brought my pajamas," Aaron quipped. Thankfully, the words came out firm, and considering the mess his thoughts were in, that was nothing short of amazing.

"That would have been difficult," Dean remarked. Aaron gave him an inquiring glance and he smiled. "I don't own a pair. I usually don't sleep in anything. But for you, I'll make an exception."

Christ.

The guest bedroom contained a queen-size bed, an overstuffed armchair, and a chest of drawers in oak. Round, fat little lamps sat on the nightstands on either side of the bed, casting a warm glow around the room.

An ordinary room.

Then why is my heart beating so goddamn fast?

The reason for Dean's rapid pulse was currently stripping down to his briefs, and Dean was doing his damnedest not to stare. Aaron was lean and muscular, his waist narrow, his shoulders broad, his thighs firm and toned.

Dear God, Dean wanted to *touch*. Then Aaron turned around, and he ached to trail his fingers over Aaron's wide chest, to tease those nipples that stood proud with his fingertips and his tongue. He wanted to lick a path from Aaron's collarbones to his navel, and then just carry on going until he reached the soft bulge of his white briefs.

Touching was out, and he knew it. But there was an alternative.

Dean went over to where he'd laid his sketchpad on the chest of drawers, and picked it up.

"Do you sleep with that thing?" Aaron teased.

"Of course. You never know when inspiration will strike."

"What do you do, draw in your sleep?" Aaron

climbed into the bed beneath the sheets. "And what are you planning on drawing?"

Dean stilled. "You, if you'll let me."

Aaron blinked, then gave a shrug. "Sure. How do you want me?"

He walked over to the nightstand and tilted the lampshade. "Lie on your back, one arm behind your head." The light cast shadows over Aaron's body.

Aaron complied. "Like this?"

Dean sat at the foot of the bed, his pencil flying over the paper. "It's been a while since I did this." He completed a series of rapid sketches, getting Aaron to change position every five or so minutes. "There's a word for this kind of lighting. It's called *chiaroscuro*."

"Sounds Italian."

Dean smiled. "That's because it is. It's an artistic term that literally means light-dark, the use of strong, bold contrasts between the two." He paused. "Push the sheets lower, will you?"

Aaron said nothing, but slid the sheets down until they reached the waistband of his briefs, revealing more of his taut belly. "This better?"

Dean nodded. "Arms behind your head, please." Aaron did as instructed, and the motion stretched him, making his chest appear broader, his belly even more taut. Dean resumed his sketching.

"Can I see?"

"When I'm done."

"You're mean."

"And you're moving again."

Aaron rolled his eyes. "Are you like this with all your models?"

Dean bit his lip. "I wouldn't know. This is the first time I've done this. I don't count the life drawing classes in college."

"Life drawing?"

Dean nodded, his gaze focused on the sketch. "Nude models." He paused once more. "Can I just…" He tugged at the sheets until one bare leg was revealed. "You can sit up now. Put the pillows behind your back."

Aaron sat, leaning against the headboard, his arms outstretched, resting on the wooden rail, one leg bent at the knee, the sheets forgotten. Dean sketched, taking longer to capture Aaron's pose. More than once, his gaze lingered on Aaron's briefs, until Aaron cleared his throat, and Dean jerked his head up.

Aaron smiled. "If you want me naked, just say so." His eyes gleamed in the lamplight.

Oh dear Lord. Dean swallowed. "I want you naked."

Aaron slid his thumbs under the waistband, and eased his briefs over his hips, tossing the cotton garment aside, his shaft clearly filling. "How do you want me now?"

Inside me.

Dean stared at him, noting the way Aaron's chest rose and fell, a little faster than before. "You're gorgeous."

Aaron arched his eyebrows. "Is that the artist talking?"

Dean put aside his sketch pad. "No, that's me talking."

"Is it really wrong that the only thing in my head right now is Kate Winslet saying 'Draw me like one of your French girls, Jack'?"

He was glad he wasn't drinking at that moment. "I look nothing like Leonardo DiCaprio."

Aaron narrowed his eyes. "But I make a pretty good Kate, is *that* what you're saying?" Dean's dick pushed at his boxers, and Aaron's gaze flickered lower. His breathing hitched. "Is that for me?"

Dean froze. "What if it is?"

Then Aaron's cock rose slowly, stiffening to the point that it stood at attention. It wasn't overly long, but its girth was enough to make Dean's hole tighten at the thought of it filling him, stretching him…

Aaron glanced at his own erection. "I guess this is what you call a vicious circle. It's pretty obvious seeing me naked turns you on. Seeing you get hard for me? Apparently turns *me* on. Question is, what are we going to do about it?" He slid his hand along his thick shaft, pulling gently on it.

Oh my God.

"I thought you were into women," Dean murmured

"Me too." Aaron's lips twitched. "Maybe I'm testing the waters."

"Just how much testing are you prepared to do?"

Aaron stilled. "Why don't we find out?"

Dean crawled from the foot of the bed and lay beside Aaron, his heart hammering. Without a word, he reached over and curled his fingers around Aaron's rigid cock.

Aaron shivered. "Okay, that feels way better than I imagined."

Dean stroked the warm, firm flesh, noting how Aaron's shivers multiplied with each casual tug.

"You've been imagining this?"

"Yeah."

He sped up his movements, and Aaron squirmed on the bed. "A guy giving you a handjob?"

Aaron locked gazes with him. "Not exactly." He shuddered as Dean spat on his hand and grasped his shaft with a firm grip. "*You* giving me a handjob."

What the fuck?

Then Dean pushed aside his confusion when Aaron arched his back and rolled his hips, propelling his dick through the funnel of Dean's hand. "Don't stop," Aaron begged. The sight and feel of Aaron chasing the sensation was enough to make his own shaft painfully hard, to the point where it strained against the cotton of his shorts.

"Your cock feels so good," Dean admitted.

"Not half as good as your hand," Aaron said in a strangled whisper. He didn't break eye contact as Dean worked his length, his hips speeding up, bucking, rocking, until Dean felt the shudder that rippled through Aaron, and he knew his orgasm was imminent. Aaron gasped as he shot his load, an arch of spunk decorating his chest, and Dean held on until the last drop had emerged.

Aaron was shaking. "Jesus. Okay, that was different." His breathing was shallow.

"Good different or bad different?"

"A definite good different." Aaron lowered his gaze to where Dean's own turgid dick tented his boxers. "But what about you?"

Dean fished his cock out, gave it two or three good tugs, and came on Aaron's belly, shuddering with each pulse until he was spent.

Aaron stared at his cum-spattered torso.

"Okay, that really was a first." He reached over to the nightstand and grabbed a couple of tissues from the box sitting there. He carefully wiped away all traces, then deposited the wadded tissue on the nightstand. He glanced at Dean's boxers. "If you usually sleep naked, that's okay by me."

For a second the comment took him by surprise, until he reasoned Aaron might have been embarrassed and unsure of what to say. Dean removed his briefs, then picked up his sketching pad and put it on the chest of drawers. He walked around to the other side of the bed and got in.

Aaron lay on his side. "You sure you're okay with this?"

He nodded. "It's been a while, that's all. I've gotten used to sleeping alone." He pulled the sheets up, and Aaron turned off the lamp, plunging the room into darkness. Dean lay there, his mind trying to catch up with what had just happened.

Aaron's whisper drifted across the bed. "Dean... this isn't going to make things awkward, is it?"

He'd been asking himself the same question. "No, no it's not. We're adults, for God's sake. We both wanted this, right?"

"Yeah. I do have one question, though."

Dean steeled himself. "What's that?"

"Can we do it again?"

He smiled. "Right now?"

Aaron's throaty chuckle was the perfect response. "Goodnight, Dean."

"Goodnight, Aaron." Dean closed his eyes, but Aaron was there, behind his eyelids, naked and hard, and Dean knew he really did want to do it again, and more besides.

It's not the same as before.
I made the first move.
I'm in control.

Except that last thought was a joke. Dean had never felt so out of control in his life.

Aaron knew from the sound of Dean's breathing that he was asleep. He rolled onto his back and laced his fingers behind his head.

Okay. What. The. Fuck?

That first touch of Dean's hand on him had set his heartbeat racing. He couldn't decide whether his quickening pulse was because a guy was jerking him off, or because it was Dean. He'd told the truth. A couple of times during the past week, he'd woken with his regular morning hard on, and yeah, he'd imagined Dean's slim fingers curled around his dick. Just *thinking* about it had brought him off faster than usual.

I want to do it again.
I want this.

Except that wasn't quite true.

He wanted more.

Does this make me bi?

Then he sighed. *Enough with the labels.* Noah's words resounded in his head.

Don't get stuck on labels. Go with the flow. Be open to new experiences. You might surprise yourself.

Aaron had done that, all right. And maybe there was room for more surprises.

K.C. WELLS

Chapter Fourteen

Sunday, April 11

Dean opened his eyes. Outside, he could hear birds singing, and the sunlight was doing its best to sneak into the room. For a moment, he wasn't sure where he was, until he heard Aaron's slow, even breaths beside him.

So it wasn't a dream.

He turned his head to gaze at the sleeping Aaron, and was lost in admiration. *I never knew until now that I have a thing about backs.* Because Aaron's was beautiful. Dean wasn't about to compare it to sculptured marble, but it was pretty impressive. He glanced toward the chest of drawers where his sketchpad sat, but dismissed the idea. Drawing Aaron's back while he was asleep sounded a little creepy.

Then Aaron yawned, stretched, and rolled over, his eyes still closed, and Dean had something much more interesting to look at.

Oh my God. It could be a flagpole.

Okay, it wasn't *that* big, but it managed to lift the sheets. And now that he thought about it, Dean's morning wood was just as hard. He snuck his hand under the sheets, wrapped his fingers around his shaft, and commenced to work it with slow gentle tugs.

Aaron opened his eyes, his gaze drifting lower to the movement of Dean's hand. "Good morning to you too."

Dean stilled. "Morning."

"Hey, don't stop on my account." Aaron turned onto his side facing Dean, then reached for his own erection. "You know, I'm feeling really guilty about last night."

Oh shit. "I see." Any thoughts Dean had had of playing with Aaron's delicious cock went out of the window.

Aaron nodded. "Yeah, really guilty. I mean, you did all the work."

It took a second or two for his words to register. "Wait—what?"

"Gotcha." Aaron grinned. "Had you going, didn't I?"

"Has anyone ever told you you're evil?"

He chuckled. "Not lately. But about last night... There was I, thinking a handjob was just a handjob."

"I doubt it felt all that different from your own experiences," Dean observed. "I mean, a hand is just a hand." Aaron slowly pushed the sheets lower, and they caught on his erect cock, making it slap against his belly as it bounced back. Dean licked his lips. "And a mouth is just a mouth."

Aaron's eyes were huge. His breathing quickened. "Oh God."

Dean shifted in the bed, until his lips were inches from the taut head of Aaron's dick. "Tell me you want this."

"I think you already know the answer to that," Aaron croaked. He gripped his shaft around the base, holding it steady. "For God's sake, do it."

Fuck, the way he smelled, a warm, rich man scent that went straight to Dean's cock. Then he froze when there was a knock at the door.

"Guys? I heard voices. There's coffee and breakfast if you're ready."

Aaron rolled his eyes. "I'm gonna have to talk to Levi about his timing." He raised his voice. "Be right with you."

Dean waited until he was sure Levi had gone before speaking. "Maybe it's for the best."

"Are you kidding me?"

Dean stared at him. "Have you ever had a blow job from a guy before? No? Then do you *really* want your first time to be here, with Grammy probably just down the hallway? Not to mention Levi. I thought you might want a little privacy for that. And I should have thought of that before I made a move, but damn, you were so tempting."

"And you would have been doing all the work again."

Dean blinked. "You'd be up for giving me a blow job?"

Aaron smiled. "It might surprise you what I'd be up for."

There was another knock at the door. "I thought you guys were coming."

Aaron's eyes twinkled. "Not yet," he whispered. "That might have to wait till we get home."

Dean's day had just taken a new and interesting direction.

"Unless my curiosity gets the better of me during the drive back, because if *that* happens, we're talking road head," Aaron added.

That made it more likely their day would end up in one of two places—jail, or the ER.

It wasn't until they'd passed Portland that Aaron brought up the subject he'd been dying to discuss all morning. "Is it that different?"

In the passenger seat beside him, Dean chuckled. "A frame of reference would be nice. Is what different?"

"Sex with a guy. You know, as opposed to with a woman."

"I wouldn't know. How would I? I've only ever been with guys. Though I don't suppose it's all *that* different."

Sex had occupied Aaron's thoughts since breakfast, and he knew he'd appeared distracted: Levi had given him several wry smiles. "When did you know you were gay?" Maybe that was a safer topic.

"I guess I was fifteen, sixteen. Not that I did anything with anyone until I was seventeen, and then it was only making out with a guy in my class. I never brought anyone home—Mom was strict on that subject once she realized what was going on—but then again, I wasn't happy about doing anything under their roof. I waited until college before I had sex for the first time. What about you?"

Aaron shrugged. "I was still in high school when I got laid for the first time. Her bedroom, while her parents were out visiting her grandmother. Can't say it was all that memorable. And to be honest, it was over real fast. Of course, them coming home early might've had something to do with that." What he'd never admitted to a soul was how disappointed he'd felt. The next day, he'd stared at his reflection and sighed. *Was that it?*

Dean chuckled. "Tell me about it. I can only say, things got better with practice." He laughed. "I've had my share of funny experiences though."

"Such as?"

"Well, there was this one time I was with a guy, and the condom slipped off and got stuck in my ass."

"Seriously? That can happen?"

"To be honest, it was his fault."

"Why?"

Dean snorted. "I think when he bought the condoms, he was suffering from delusions of grandeur, if you follow my drift. Not that I'm a size queen, but…"

"Aw. Poor guy. Maybe he didn't know they come in different sizes." Aaron grimaced. "I'm not a fan of condoms. I don't use them unless she insists, and it's always their call." He huffed. "Not that there have been *that* many girls. So what happened?"

"He tried to get it out with his fingers, but that sucker wasn't going to budge. Of course, it would have come out eventually, but I got into a panic. I ended up going to see a proctologist who removed it. And I'm not a fan of condoms either. Not since that episode, anyway."

"Is it the same with guys as it is with women? I mean, do they expect you to buy them dinner, flowers, chocolates? And does it take three or four dates before you score?"

Dean laughed. "Dinner features occasionally. And as for scoring, I think there was one guy who waited till the second date. The rest? Pretty much the first."

"Wow. I *have* been batting for the wrong team." They both chuckled.

"Things have changed since I first came out," Dean remarked. "For one thing, there are a ton of apps if you want to meet guys. Sex is pretty much on tap. You want a threesome? No problem. Something more kinky? Go for it. And condoms are pretty much a thing of the past too."

"How come?" This was turning out to be a fascinating conversation.

"Most of the guys I've ever been with were on PrEP. Have you heard of that?"

Aaron nodded. Seb had mentioned it once or twice, and Aaron had been curious enough to Google it afterward.

"You get into a habit of asking a guy for his status." Dean sighed. "Not that I've had to do that for a while."

"Status?"

"Yeah, his HIV status, the results of his last test…"

Aaron frowned. "How often do you get tested? And tested for what?"

"HIV, STDs…And as for how often, that depends. When I was active, every three months. It's a habit a lot of guys get into. I mean, if you're on

PrEP, you have to get tested, but… There was this one time I went out with an older guy. He said regular testing was a thing even before PrEP."

Aaron shook his head. "It's like a whole different world."

"What do you mean?"

"I have an annual physical, okay? But I don't think it tests for STDs. I wouldn't even *consider* getting tested for those, unless I had symptoms, or I got a call from someone I'd dated recently, telling me something was wrong. I just assumed the physical would pick up stuff like that."

Dean's responsible attitude put him to shame.

They lapsed into silence, and Aaron concentrated on the road ahead. It wasn't long, however, before his thoughts veered back onto their original course. "I've watched gay porn. So I'm not a complete novice."

"Was that research?"

Now that he thought about it, maybe that was exactly what it had been.

"Do Levi and the others know that?"

"Nope. I mean, I tell them I watch porn—it's not as if that's something to be ashamed of, right? I just don't go into specifics."

"And what did you think?"

He'd gone this far. "I thought it was kinda hot." He'd told himself at the time his reaction was due to a lack of sex.

I was kidding myself, wasn't I?

"The hottest sex I ever had could've been right out of a porn scene," Dean admitted.

"What happened?"

"It was 2009. I had an exhibition at a gallery in

Chicago, and I'd traveled there for the opening night. I was a little nervous, because I'd done a ton of work for it, and news flash—I still get nervous on opening nights."

Aaron thought that was cute.

"Anyhow, I was talking with my brother on the phone, and he recommended I get a massage. He'd had his first one and was raving about it. So… I went to a men's spa."

Aaron grinned. "Okay, *now* it's beginning to sound like a porn scene."

"Hey, I went there with only one thought in my head—a massage. So I turned up, and the masseur was this ripped guy maybe in his late thirties. Totally sexy dude. God, what he could do with his hands… And yes, I'm talking about the massage."

Aaron chuckled. "Of course you are. Get back to the story."

"I was lying on his table, my face poking through a hole at the end, wearing nothing but a towel draped over my ass. Anyway, at some point I noticed the towel had slipped right off, and he was working almost exclusively on that area. We're talking slick fingers in my crack and over my hole. I'd never had a massage before, so what did I know? I have to admit, it felt amazing, so I spread my legs to give him more room to work his magic, because yeah, talk about magic fingers. Then I finally got up the nerve to lift my head and take a peek at him."

"He was naked, wasn't he?" Aaron glanced in Dean's direction.

Dean grinned. "You've seen this one before. Yeah, he was naked, and hard as a rock. He glanced down at his dick, and all I could do was nod. He told me to roll onto my back, and when I did, he climbed up onto the table, lifted my legs onto his shoulders, gloved up, and slid right in there. Easiest penetration *ever*, because by then I was a limp rag thanks to his massage. He spent twenty minutes pounding my ass, and I came without even touching my cock. That load sailed right over my head. Then he grabbed my dick and jerked me while he carried on fucking me, and I came again. When he was done, he shot his load onto my stomach, then wiped me down with a hot towel. He pointed me in the direction of the shower, told me it had been fun, and then he was out of there."

Aaron squirmed, his cock pressing against his zipper. "Okay, that beats anything *I've* ever experienced." He was starting to think he'd missed out, big time.

"So… Are we talking about sex because…"

"I'm curious, okay?"

"Just curious?"

Aaron was past hiding. "This morning I was all set for you to suck my dick. I think you already know the answer to that."

"Does this mean, at some point you want us to take up from where we left off?"

Yes, please. The sight of Dean's mouth *right fucking there*, close enough that if he'd stuck out his tongue, he could have lapped the pre-cum from Aaron's slit, had gotten Aaron harder than he'd ever been in his life.

Damn it, Levi. A couple more minutes… was it too much to ask?

"You've gone quiet."

"As long as it's something you want too." When Dean fell silent for a moment, Aaron's heart quaked. "Hey, you have to be honest with me, okay?"

"About last night…"

Shit. Shit. He steeled himself for whatever was to come.

"You told me you'd thought about me giving you a handjob. Maybe I should be as honest with you."

"Okay," Aaron replied in a cautious tone.

"The moment I saw your cock? I knew where I wanted it. And it wasn't in my mouth."

Holy fuck. Hallelujah. And let's throw in Merry Christmas. Aaron gripped the steering wheel. "Great. Now I get to drive with a hard on. Talk about something else."

"Actually, there *was* something I wanted to talk to you about. All those drawings I did of you last night—"

"Which you have yet to show me," Aaron interjected.

"When we get to my place, I'll show you. Because that's kind of what I want to talk about." There was a pause. "Would you let me paint you?"

Okay, he hadn't expected that. "We talking in the nude?"

"Yes, we are."

"And what kind of pose would you want me in? What would you want to do with it when it was finished? Would you hang it in a gallery? Is everyone gonna see it's me?"

Dean laughed. "Whoa there. Slow down with the questions. I already know how I want to pose you. I'd like to do a back view, maybe with you sitting on a stool, your head turned away, so no one would see your face."

"My back?"

"Hey, I like your back, okay?"

"So you don't wanna paint my dick? Not sure if I should be insulted here."

Dean snorted. "I can do a frontal view, if you'd prefer that."

"No, I actually like the idea of a back view. Would you want me to sit for you?"

"If you wouldn't mind. I'd make sure you were warm enough. Can't have you getting a chill, right?"

Aaron cackled. "I think I'd be more concerned about the temperature if you were painting my cock. When would you want to start?"

"Well, it wouldn't be right away. You see, there's this portrait I need to get working on. It's an important commission for a friend."

Warmth spread through him. "Is he a good friend?"

"Seeing as I jerked him off last night, I'd say that was a big yes. But we need to change the subject, because apparently this friend can't drive with a hard on."

Aaron laughed. "How about we discuss the next hike we're gonna do?"

Much safer terrain.

Aaron stopped the truck on Dean's driveway and turned off the engine.

Dean met his gaze. "Do you want to come in?"

Aaron wasn't sure what he wanted. The logical part of his brain had kicked in once they crossed over onto Mount Desert. "I should really get home. There's stuff I need to do before tomorrow, you know, like laundry, shopping…"

Dean studied him. "Having second thoughts?"

"A little, maybe?" Talking about sex was a whole lot easier than actually doing anything about it.

"We don't have to do anything," Dean said in a low voice.

"No, I want to," Aaron remonstrated. "I guess I've wanted to for a while. There *is* one thing I'd like to know though." His pulse quickened.

"What's that?"

His heart hammered. "Do you kiss?"

Dean blinked. "Sure, I kiss."

Aaron wasn't sure why it was such a big deal. He only knew it was something that had slipped into his head sometime in the middle of the night. "I'm asking because you gave me a handjob, but… you haven't kissed me. And I know guys do kiss, because I've seen them. I mean, even in porn they kiss. Sometimes, the kissing can take up half of the scene, so I'm guessing there's not a lot of difference there. But maybe that's not something you like to do, so—"

"Aaron…" Dean's hand was on his face. "Stop talking so I can kiss you."

Aaron froze, and Dean moved in. His lips were warm and soft, his beard was kinda scratchy, and

Aaron didn't mind that one bit. He stroked Dean's neck, deepening the kiss, not wanting it to end.

Except he knew if he let it go on, he'd still be there at midnight.

Aaron broke the kiss. "Okay. I really do need to go."

Dean's eyes locked on his. "But you *are* coming back."

"Yeah, I'm coming back." He smiled. "And yes, you can paint me. Whenever you're ready, just give me a call."

"And if I'm not ready to start painting you, but I just want to see you… that'd be okay?"

This time Aaron was the one to lean in. He kissed Dean lightly on the lips. "More than okay," he murmured.

"Good to know," Dean whispered. He straightened. "Then I guess I should let you go do laundry and shopping."

Aaron chuckled. "Now that's a great way to kill a hard on." He popped the trunk. "Can I help you with your stuff?"

"No, I can manage." Dean got out of the truck and walked around to the rear. Aaron waited until he was at the front door before starting the engine. Dean gave him a wave, and Aaron pulled out of the driveway.

He smiled as he drove along Bar Harbor Road.

Dean is way cuter than Spider-Man ever was. Sexier too.

Dean went into the house and closed the door behind him. He put his equipment on the floor and went over to the couch.

What have I started?

He sat, opened the sketchpad, and spread his drawings out over the coffee table. Except all that did was bring back the way Aaron's dick had felt in his hand, the sounds he'd made when he came…

Didn't you learn your lesson the last time?

His stomach clenched. *It's not the same as before.* Aaron hadn't made the first moves, *he* had. The circumstances were totally different. It was just sex—well, it *would* be sex when they finally got around to it—there'd be no strings, and that was the way they both wanted it.

Then why am I still leery? He analyzed the situation. *Aaron doesn't want a partner.* He wanted the experience. *He's just curious.* And Dean didn't mind satisfying that curiosity.

What intrigued him was how much satisfaction Aaron would require.

Chapter Fifteen

Thursday, April 15

By Thursday, Aaron hadn't heard from Dean and it was starting to worry him. Not that he thought anything had happened to Dean—it was more a case that he'd expected a call.

I haven't called him *though, have I?*

Of course he hadn't. That would have been weird. What could he have said? *Hi, I was just wondering if I could come over so we can continue my… education?* Yeah, that was corny as fuck. And a little obsessive. Plus, it made it sound as though all Aaron was interested in was sex. Which he wasn't. He totally wasn't.

Who was he kidding? Of course he was. He'd passed horny four days ago.

So far that week, he'd made his rounds, given advice on which trails to take, gotten a few tourists to put out fires that had threatened to set the place alight—okay, maybe that was a slight exaggeration, but really?—and generally got on with his life.

When his brain would let him.

It was just a hand job, for fuck's sake.

Except the way Dean had looked at him, *stared* at him, while his hand had been busy… *Jesus, that was hot.* And the conversation on the way home had done nothing to dampen Aaron's need. He'd been *this* close to offering to help Dean indoors with his equipment, on the off-chance events might have taken a different route, and he'd have ended up with Dean's mouth on his dick, something he'd been thinking about non-stop ever since Levi had knocked on the freaking door.

He'd gotten into bed a few nights and lain there, unable to get to sleep, unable to stop thinking about Dean. Then it hit him. What was that he'd said to Levi during their punch-fueled conversation, when Aaron had told him no girl was about to materialize and sweep him off his feet?

I'm not gonna be lying awake nights, 'cause I can't get her out of my head.

Jesus, the irony…

One part of the conversation during the ride home had stuck with him. Dean had talked about a guy's status. This was clearly a big deal. That had been enough to send Aaron to his laptop, to research where someone might get tested in Maine. He could have called one of the guys, but that would have opened up a can of worms Aaron was happy to leave sealed for the moment.

Talk about a rabbit hole. There were private clinics, STD clinics, Planned Parenthood… Eventually, he found a sexual health clinic in Ellsworth, and that was perfect, close enough that he could get there when the day job finished. He phoned and made an appointment, allowing himself enough time to go home first and change out of his uniform. The whole notion of being tested just for the purposes of sex was a new one. Everyone who worked in the park got a yearly physical, but this was different. This was so he could say to Dean, *I'm okay. We don't need condoms.*

Except it was more than that. Dean's attitude to testing had made him reassess his history. And the clincher? He didn't want to do anything that put Dean at risk.

It didn't matter that he'd been having sex for about ten years. Not a whole lot of sex, but enough. No, this was an adventure he couldn't wait to get started on.

Aaron turned into Long Lane, and scanned the buildings for the clinic's sign. It didn't look any different to the houses around it. He turned off the engine, got out of the truck, and strolled toward his destination. As he neared the door, it opened—and Dean came out.

He gaped at Aaron. "What are you doing here?"

Aaron smirked. "Same thing as you, I suspect."

"First time in a while for me. To be honest, there seemed little point getting tested—until now."

That send a trickle of anticipation down Aaron's spine, all the way to his dick. Then he recalled the lack of contact. "Are you okay? I was beginning to worry."

"I've been MIA since Sunday, I know." Dean flushed. "I'm sorry. When I really get into a painting, I lose track of everything."

"You remember to eat, don't you?"

That flush deepened. "Sometimes. Do crackers with the occasional smattering of paint on them count?"

Aaron groaned. "Never mind Seb saying you're a keeper—you *need* a keeper."

Dean's eyes gleamed. "Are you volunteering?"

Hell yeah. Dean needed looking after. "Tonight, I am. Go home, and I'll be there once I finished here—and I've been shopping." When Dean frowned, he smiled. "For once, I'm gonna feed *you.* I won't say I'm a brilliant cook, but it'll be edible and all you have to do is eat it."

"Sounds like a win-win to me."

Aaron inclined his head toward the building. "Does this take long?"

Dean peered at Aaron. "Is this the first time you've done one of these?"

"Outside of my yearly physical? Yup."

"And you're doing this because of me?"

Aaron bit back a smile. "So you're saying you're not here because of me?"

Dean's eyes twinkled. "Okay, you got me. And thank-you."

"Hey, no biggie. This is important to you. So tell me what I have to look forward to." He glanced at his phone. "In about three minutes."

"It usually takes about ten to fifteen minutes. They'll start with a sexual history: you know, number of partners—"

"How far back are we talking? Because if they mean recently, that'll be a quick answer."

"They also ask whether you're a top or a bottom." Dean's lips twitched. "Although I don't suppose that applies to you."

That didn't mean Aaron hadn't been thinking about it. What surprised him was that he'd considered both options. *If I'm gonna do this, I wanna experience everything.*

"They can also do a full STD panel at the same time, drawing blood to test for syphilis, a urine test for gonorrhea, swabs for chlamydia…"

"This all sounds wonderful," Aaron quipped.

"Hey, not that it's anything to be proud of, but most gay guys, if they're active, will pick up an STD every once in a while, usually chlamydia or gonorrhea—they're pretty common." Dean glanced toward the door. "Not that I had anything like *that* to worry about."

Aaron was about to be late. "I'd better get in there." He wanted to ask if Dean would wait, but that sounded all kinds of needy, and definitely not him. *What the fuck is wrong with me? It's just a test.* Besides, Dean had transportation, right? "I'll see you back at your place."

"Good luck." Dean headed for his truck.

Aaron paused at the door. "Why would I need luck? Is there something you're not telling me?"

"I didn't specify *where* they'd swab for chlamydia, did I?" Dean chuckled.

Aaron let out another groan. *Great. They're gonna stick something up my ass.* As if the annual prostate check wasn't bad enough.

Brave new world.

Dean took a last look at the living room. It was tidy, not that he expected it to be anything different. He'd hardly been in there the past four

K.C. WELLS

days. He was glad he'd run into Aaron, and even happier that Aaron was on his way.

I've missed him.

It hadn't been until that morning when he made the appointment at the clinic, that it occurred to him Aaron hadn't been in touch. *I'm just as bad.* His mom used to complain that they could drop the bomb and Dean wouldn't notice if he was painting.

He went to get tested. Aaron was obviously a responsible guy, not that Dean had expected him to be anything else. Then the implication hit home, and he realized his dry spell was about to end. *I want this.*

More importantly, he wanted this with Aaron.

The next moment, he was running into the bedroom. *Tell me I'm not about to run out of lube. Because that would really suck.* He yanked the nightstand drawer open, and heaved a sigh of relief. Sometimes, being anal and buying three bottles at a time paid off.

He caught the sound of an engine outside, and went to open the door. Aaron got out of the truck, carrying a flat cardboard box in one hand, and a brown paper bag in the other.

Dean took one look at the lid and burst out laughing. "When you said you were making dinner…"

Aaron gave him a hard stare. "You telling me you *don't* want pizza? Because that just means more for me."

Dean narrowed his gaze. "You know there's a lot riding on this, right?"

"You mean my choice of pizza might make us incompatible?" Aaron climbed the steps to the front door. The smell emanating from the box was heavenly.

"You're doing well so far." Dean took the box

into the kitchen, set it on the countertop, and opened it. He grinned when he saw Jordan's chicken-bacon-ranch. "You just passed with flying colors. Let's eat while it's hot."

Aaron removed the sides from the paper bag. "I was tempted to buy two pizzas, but instead I settled for these."

Dean eyed the onion rings and fries. "I approve." He sniffed. "Oh dear Lord, you brought cheese and garlic knots. I love those." He arched his eyebrows. "So you didn't come here with plans for after dinner?"

Aaron frowned for a second, then his eyes widened. "Christ, what was I thinking? Garlic?"

"Hey, it's okay. We just have to make sure we both eat them. And I'm certain I have a new toothbrush somewhere."

And there it was, out in the open, the implicit understanding that they were going to fuck. There was no mistaking the change in Aaron's breathing, the way his pupils grew larger, the sharp bob of his Adam's apple.

Dean didn't hesitate. He moved in closer, cupped Aaron's nape, and drew him down into a gentle kiss. "Nervous?"

Aaron chuckled. "Nope. Horny. Not to mention hard as a nail." He grabbed Dean's other hand and brought it to his crotch, holding it there.

Dean gave the bulge a leisurely rub. The low moan tumbling from Aaron's mouth mingled with his own—

Then his stomach growled, and Dean realized he hadn't eaten since breakfast.

"Pizza," he murmured against Aaron's lips.

"Hmm?"

"Pizza. You know, food? Sustenance?"

Aaron flushed, and his beard seemed redder than usual. "Good thinking."

They brought all the food to the dining table, and Dean grabbed a couple of sheets of paper towel. The pizza was delicious, and it wasn't long before every slice had disappeared, along with all the sides.

Aaron chuckled. "Have you eaten today?"

"I refer you to my previous comment about crackers." Dean tilted his head. "Would you like to see the portrait so far?"

"You're damn straight." Aaron grinned. "Oops. My bad." Dean didn't hold back on the eye roll. He led Aaron to the guest room/studio, and opened the door.

The catch in Aaron's breathing was gratifying. He stood a few feet away from the easel. "When did you start this?"

"Sunday. When we got back from Wells."

"But you must have been working on it day and night."

"Pretty much, yeah." Dean had been up with the dawn every day, stopping only when his body protested it was time to quit for the night.

"Her birthday isn't until June thirteenth. You have plenty of time."

"It doesn't work like that," Dean informed him. "Once the painting is finished, you have to let dry out completely, so the paint hardens. Once that happens, then it needs varnishing. You can't just finish it the day before."

"I know nothing about painting," Aaron admitted. He stared at the canvas. "I'm just..." He sighed. "It's awesome. You've really captured them."

It was still in its early stages, but it lightened Dean's heart to hear the words. "I'm glad you're happy. In fact, I'm glad you're here. I needed a break."

Aaron turned slowly to look at him. "I see. So *that's* why I'm here?" There was a mischievous twinkle in his eyes.

"It's not the only reason. How did the test go?"

"They said the results for the blood test would be in a day or so, not that I'm worried anything is gonna show up. My last physical was in January, and I haven't been with anyone since. As for the rest, they told me there and then. I had no idea instant results were a thing."

"No surprises?"

Aaron beamed. "No surprises."

"Same here." Dean took a step toward him. "So I guess that means…"

"It means I go to the bathroom and find that toothbrush you mentioned."

"I'll help."

"Fuck, you can kiss," Aaron murmured. Kissing was as far as they'd gotten, and that was just fine by Aaron. Their clothing was on the floor, except for their briefs, and they knelt on the bed, their arms around each other. His hand was on Dean's nape and his eyes were closed, not to shut out the knowledge that he was kissing a guy, but rather to lose himself to his other senses. Dean's body was warm, with a citrus fragrance that clung to him, invading Aaron's nostrils. The sighs falling from Dean's mouth were a sensual soundtrack, and there was still a hint of mint on his lips.

"Says you." Dean stroked him, slow passes up and down his spine. Aaron slid his hand into the back of Dean's briefs and gently squeezed his ass cheeks. They were firm and round, covered in a soft down. Aaron cupped them, spreading them a little.

"Touch it. Please."

Aaron opened his eyes to find Dean's gaze locked on his face. He rubbed a fingertip over Dean's hole, loving the shiver that rippled through him. "So warm and soft." Aaron buried his face in Dean's neck, kissing him there as he continued to rub and tap Dean's pucker, aware of the change in Dean's breathing.

Heat built between them in a lazy spiral, and each new noise from Dean's lips only served to heighten Aaron's desire, ramping up his need.

Dean broke the kiss. "Let me look at you." He arched his back, his hands on Aaron's shoulders as he looked him up and down. "So gorgeous."

Aaron tugged gently on Dean's soft, silky hair, tilting his head back before leaning in to claim his mouth in a fervent kiss. "Look who's talking." He reached down, both hands on Dean's covered ass.

Dean flicked Aaron's nipples with his thumbs, and Aaron shuddered. Dean grinned. "Oh. Are these sensitive?"

"A little—Christ!" Aaron shivered as Dean's mouth closed over one nipple, his fingers tweaking the other until it stood proud. "Okay, I didn't know they were *that* sensitive." Dean flicked Aaron's nipple with his tongue, moving higher, until his face was buried in Aaron's pit and he was kissing him there. "No one ever did that before. Wow."

Dean pulled back. "Is that a good wow?"

Aaron smiled. "*Definitely* a good wow." Then it was back to kissing, Dean's body pressed to his, undulating, grinding, his hard shaft meeting Aaron's equally erect dick.

Dean glanced lower. "Something is trying to get my attention." He reached into Aaron's briefs and fished out his shaft. "Damn." Dean worked Aaron's dick with a leisurely hand. "So thick. Such a beautiful cock."

Aaron stilled. "Can cocks be beautiful?" It had always struck him as an odd-looking appendage, something of an afterthought, as if God had stuck it there at the last minute.

Dean smiled. "There are all kinds of cocks in the world. Small ones, big ones, long ones, fat ones, slim ones,…" His eyes glittered. "Tasty ones." Then he bent low to take the head of Aaron's dick into his warm mouth.

Jesus.

Aaron leaned back, his weight on one hand, and stroked Dean's shoulder with the other. "Been a while. I've missed this." He laid his hand on Dean's nape, exerting gentle pressure. A groan poured out of him when Dean swallowed him to the root. "Fuck." The pressure on his shaft was exquisite. He straightened, both hands on Dean's head, keeping him there, loving how Dean worked his cock with lips and tongue.

When Dean pulled free, Aaron tugged him up into a kiss, before lowering him onto his back on the bed. Dean's arms were around his neck, his knees wide, and Aaron rocked against him, his waistband caught under his balls. "Love your mouth," he murmured.

Dean stroked his nape. "And if I want to know how *your* mouth feels?"

Aaron was more than ready for a new experience.

He laid a trail of kisses down Dean's body until he reached his briefs. Dean's cock strained against the cotton, and Aaron kissed the bulge. Dean's breathing hitched and Aaron didn't hesitate. He lowered the waistband just enough to free the top half of Dean's shaft, trapping it against his fuzzy belly. Then he bent over, licked a path up to the head, and took it into his mouth. Dean let out a low cry, and Aaron gave a hard suck, his heartbeat racing at the noises pouring from Dean.

He's waited five years for this.

"Oh God." Dean shuddered. "Take 'em off." Aaron slid the briefs over Dean's hips and tossed them onto the floor. Dean drew his knees up, his legs wide apart, his dick rising, stiff and glistening.

Aaron gazed at the pretty pink cock, its root nestled in a mound of ginger pubes. "I stand corrected. Dicks *can* be beautiful." He curled his fingers around its base, and resumed his sucking, working the shaft, his hand in harmony with his mouth.

Dean rocked his hips. "For a first-timer, you're a natural." Aaron's hand rested on Dean's stomach, and Dean covered it with his own. "Want to try something new?"

Aaron paused. "What did you have in mind?"

Dean drew his knees toward his chest. "Kiss my balls? My taint?"

"Are you sure that's what you want?" Aaron pressed a chaste kiss to Dean's sac, then another to his taint. "You sure you didn't have another destination in mind?" Dean's pucker was right there, tight and pink. Aaron blew gently on it, watching it contract even more.

"You don't have to."

Aaron chuckled. "I hate to break it to you, but you're not my first rim job." He leaned in and kissed Dean's hole.

Multiple shivers rippled through Dean. "Oh yeah."

Aaron grinned. "You like that." He grabbed Dean's ass cheeks and spread them. "Look at that." He leaned in again and planted another kiss, only this time he followed it with a lingering lick, aware of the quiver that resulted.

"Kiss me," Dean demanded. Dean's arms held him tightly, his legs wrapped around him, his heels resting on Aaron's ass, a position that wasn't new to Aaron, and yet it was. Then Dean's hands were inside his briefs, on his ass. "These need to come off too."

Aaron wasn't about to disagree.

He stood on the bed, balancing as he removed his briefs, conscious of Dean's gaze locked onto his cock as it bounced up. Aaron knelt, shuffling forward until his thighs were hooked under Dean's knees.

Dean reached down to wrap his hand around both dicks. "Lord, I can barely make it." He inclined his head toward the nightstand. "There's lube in the drawer."

Aaron stretched to retrieve it, his heart pounding. He squeezed some onto his fingers, then rubbed them over Dean's hole before sliding a single finger into him. Dean's body gripped it, sucking it in, and he couldn't wait to feel that tightness around his dick.

Dean shivered. "You've done this before." He did it again when Aaron added a second finger. "More lube. It's been a while."

"I'm not gonna rush this," Aaron murmured. "I won't do anything that could hurt you." He withdrew his fingers and squeezed more lube onto them. His own cock was like steel.

Dean stroked Aaron's thigh. "I want you. Please, don't make me wait."

Aaron slicked up his shaft, and shifted closer to guide it to Dean's hole. He gave a gentle push, and Dean groaned when the head entered him. Aaron held still, letting Dean adjust, ignoring the urge to thrust until he was balls-deep. "Fuck, it's so tight."

Dean gave his own cock a tug. "Does it feel good?"

Aaron smiled. "It feels fantastic." He leaned forward to kiss Dean, loving the feel of Dean's arms around him as Aaron inched his way into his body.

"You feel amazing." Dean's breathing synchronized with Aaron's leisurely thrusts. "You don't have to hold back now." He moaned as Aaron picked up the pace. "Yeah, like that."

Aaron pumped his hips. "If I keep this up, I'm gonna come real fast." He took Dean's mouth in a long kiss. "Put your arms around my neck." When Dean complied, Aaron lifted him, his cock still inside him. "Now hold on." His hands were on Dean's slim hips as Dean bounced on his dick, his feet on the mattress, arms locked around Aaron's neck, and their gazes locked on each other.

Fuck, that was hella *hot*. They kissed, feeding each other moans and sighs as Aaron brought Dean down hard on his rigid cock.

Aaron pushed Dean onto his back, then continued to fuck him with slow thrusts. Dean nodded. "Rotate your hips a little. Do a slow grind." Aaron did as instructed, and Dean's eyes widened. "Oh yeah, just like that."

"You feel so good." Then he gasped as Dean's body tightened around his cock. "What the fuck was that?"

"You feel me squeezing?"

Aaron groaned. "Fuck yeah."

"Do you like it?"

"Hell no, I fucking *love* it." Then Dean tweaked Aaron's nipples, and he shuddered. "Can't last much longer." He pumped his hips, thrusting harder, faster, settling into a rhythm. "I'm gonna come."

"Then come inside me," Dean panted.

Aaron drove his cock home, stiffening as he shot his load. Dean pulled him down into a kiss, clinging to him until he was totally spent.

"Oh shit, I feel that." Dean tugged on his dick, and seconds later, spunk coated his abs. Aaron kissed him, unwilling to let go of the moment.

K.C. WELLS

"That was one hell of a way to end a dry spell." Dean cupped his cheek. "Still no regrets?"

"None whatsoever." Aaron glanced at their damp bodies. "I guess I need to move, huh?" He eased his now limp dick out of Dean, and flopped onto his back. He ached, but in a good way.

"I wore you out." Dean sounded kind of pleased with himself. He rolled onto his side and kissed Aaron, a sweet kiss that sent warmth trickling through him. "But then, you did the same to me."

Can I do it again?

"Does this mean, I get to come back?"

Dean blinked. "After you suffered the torture of getting your ass swabbed? You think I'd let you go through all that and then say *that's it, no more*?"

"Yeah, well, when you put it like that…" They laughed.

"Besides, I like this. You in my bed. It's on a par with you in my ass."

"About that…"

"Whatever it is you're thinking, say it. No secrets here."

Aaron bit his lip. "They did ask whether I was a top or a bottom, you know. At the clinic."

"What did you tell them?"

He grinned. "I said I was gonna try both options before I committed myself. So… what did *you* tell them?"

Dean's eyes sparkled. "Is this your not-so-subtle way of asking if I top? More specifically, if I want to fuck you?"

Aaron stilled. "You see right through me, don't you?" And after what they'd just done, it seemed selfish to be asking if Dean would return the favor.

Dean's eyes were warm. "And I like what I see. So to answer your question…" He pressed his lips to Aaron's in another lingering kiss. "Yes, I want to fuck you. If you're *sure* that's what you want."

"I'm sure."

"But not right now. Because right *now*, I have something very different in mind."

"What's that?" Aaron's mind boggled.

"I was going to take a shower. And I wanted you to join me because… I need protecting in the bathroom."

Aaron tried not to laugh. "From what?"

"Spiders," Dean said in a solemn voice. "Huge ones. They hide in corners and then run out at me."

Aaron stared at him. "Seriously?"

"Cross my heart."

"And if I *wasn't* here to protect you from the big bad spiders, what would you do?"

Dean rolled his eyes. "Duh. Burn the house down."

Aaron laughed. "Then isn't it a good thing I'm here? I'm great with nature. It's my job." He held out his hand. "Let's go show those spiders they can't frighten us."

Anything to make the evening last a little longer.

Chapter Sixteen

Dean sat on the edge of the bed, listening to Aaron pee. It was almost ten o'clock, and Aaron had been making I-have-to-go noises for the last fifteen minutes. Dean knew he'd be up early for work the next day.

Is it selfish that I want him to stay?

He couldn't shake off the irrational fear that once Aaron stepped out onto Dean's porch, the last few glorious hours would somehow disappear. *He knows I want us to do this again.* It wasn't as if it was going to be a one-night thing. And holding onto those hours wasn't wrong. What had surprised him was Aaron's level of comfort.

He knew what he was doing. The fact that he'd been doing it with a guy hadn't seemed to faze him in the slightest. There was no angst, no guilt…

Maybe that comes later, when I'm not around.

Yeah, he was being *really* irrational.

The bathroom door opened, and Aaron clicked off the light. "So…" He leaned against the door frame. "Where do we go from here?"

Dean cleared his throat. "Where do you want it to go?" Aaron stared at him, but said nothing, and Dean wondered if he had Aaron all wrong, if he wasn't as laid-back as he appeared to be. He patted the bed next to him. "Come here." Aaron walked over to him and sat, and Dean laid his hand on Aaron's thigh. "Aaron… if you don't tell me what's on your mind, I'm going to have to kill you."

His words had the desired effect. Aaron snorted.

Dean stroked his leg. "We're friends, aren't we?"

"Yes, we are."

"And we're going to stay friends, right?"

Aaron's eyes met his. "Yeah, we are."

"Doing stuff together, like you said. More hikes… I'm going to paint you…" That got him a nod. "Then why not be friends with benefits?"

Aaron blinked. "You'd be okay with that?"

Dean suddenly got it. He smiled. "Aaron, I hate to tell you this. You're pretty hot in the sack, but your dick doesn't work miracles. One night with you does *not* mean I'm about to declare undying love." Aaron cackled. "So yes, I'd be fine with that." He grinned. "Just so long as you're not here every night for those *benefits*." He hooked his fingers in the air. "Or suddenly it's just benefits and the other stuff disappears. Not that I think that's likely," he added. "We were friends first."

Aaron smiled. "You really wanna do more hikes?"

"I said so, didn't I? And maybe there are other activities we could do too."

"Okay, now I'm intrigued."

Dean sighed. "You're good for me, you know that?" Aaron frowned, and Dean squeezed his thigh. "You were right. I do need a keeper. I'm not saying I need one twenty-four-seven, but occasionally, yes, to make sure I take a break now and then."

"And eat?"

He laughed. "Yes, and eat. All that matters is that we're clear from the outset what we both want out of this."

"So we're talking friendship, sex—and no strings."

Dean beamed. "Exactly. Now, does that work for you?"

Aaron nodded. "Perfectly. I don't want there to be any awkwardness between us. But maybe there's something else we need to be clear on."

"Okay."

Aaron leaned back on his hands. "This is not a one-sided thing. If I call you and say *hey, what about tonight?* and you don't feel the same, you say so. And vice versa."

Dean nodded. "I like that." His heartbeat raced. "And if I ask you to stay the night?"

Aaron stilled. "Is that something you might do?"

This was a time for honesty. "If you're here and it's late, I'm not going to kick you out of bed—not if you don't want to be kicked out. And every time you come over doesn't have to end up in bed."

Aaron arched his eyebrows. "So if I come over because I really need you to suck my dick, that'd be okay? If that's all we did?"

"Sure. Why not? A blow job is sex, right?"

Aaron chuckled. "Sorry. I'm having a hard time getting my head around this. If I'd arranged a date with one of my exes, and told her all I wanted was a blow job, I think she'd have left me on the spot. And maybe cut my balls off for good measure."

Dean shrugged. "Maybe some men are

content with very little."

Aaron cocked his head. "Can you swim?"

"Excuse me?" Talk about out of left field.

"It's a simple enough question."

"Yes, I can swim."

"Ever surfed? Or done any water sports?"

Dean bit back a smile. "The only water sports I've participated in might not be your thing. Where are you going with this?"

Aaron looked him up and down. "My spare wetsuit would be too big. We'll rent one. And I've got a couple of boards."

"You want to take me surfing?"

"Not exactly. The newest craze around here is stand-up paddle boarding. How would you like to try it? I haven't had a go yet, but I was planning on trying it. So I wondered if you'd like to try it with me?"

Dean liked that idea a whole lot. "Deal."

Then Aaron gaped at him. "Oh my God. I just realized what you meant by water sports. I came across that once on a gay porn site." He grimaced. "That is *so* not my thing."

Dean chuckled. "I'll let you into a secret." He leaned closer and whispered, "It wasn't my thing either." He smiled. "We're good?"

"Yeah, we're good. And about me staying the night sometimes…" Aaron's smile reached his eyes. "I'd like that. I'd like that a *lot*." His brow furrowed. "Just not tonight."

"I know, you have a long day ahead of you tomorrow. But then it's the weekend."

"Sundays are usually good. Maybe we should keep Sundays as our day to do stuff." Aaron got to his feet, and his air of reluctance was apparent.

Dean rose too. "Thank you for this evening." He cupped the back of Aaron's head and drew him down into a long, tender kiss.

"You really like kissing, don't you?" Aaron murmured, his hands on Dean's face and neck.

"What gave it away?" Finally, he broke the kiss. "I know, I need to let you go."

"And if I came back tomorrow night?"

Dean smiled. "That sounds great. I'll cook."

The warmth generated by Aaron's kiss still lingered even as Aaron was pulling out of Dean's driveway.

He's coming back.

Their conversation had washed away Dean's fears. They both knew where they stood, what they wanted out of this. No surprises.

Except Dean knew *nothing* in life was ever *that* cut-and-dried. That was the thing about surprises— no one saw them coming.

So what's waiting for us right around the corner?

Aaron locked his front door and went into the kitchen. He hadn't stopped smiling all the way home. What filled him with delight wasn't the prospect of sex, but his recollections of the evening. He paused at the fridge door, his eyes closed as he remembered the sight of Dean on his back, Aaron sliding into him, a sheen of sweat coating Dean's chest…

Fuck. It was so good. One glance at Dean's face had been enough to make Aaron yearn to know how it felt to be on the receiving end, and the knowledge that he was going to find out sent a thrill through him.

His phone vibrated in his pocket. Aaron peered at the screen. It was a text from Dylan. *Are you still awake? Can we talk?*

Aaron clicked on call. "You're working the night shift, aren't you?"

"How did you know?"

"Because you never call at this hour when you're home. You're too busy doing other… things." And now that he'd had a taste, Aaron really got that. *How do any of them find time to get stuff done?* Christ, if he had a partner, they'd be forever fucking.

I could get seriously addicted to it.

"Listen, I have a huge favor to ask."

"Okay. Hit me with it." The mood Aaron was in, he'd agree to anything.

Well, within reason.

"May eighth. It's a Saturday."

"I'll take your word for it."

"You know the house Mark inherited? The one next door to Grammy's? Well, we've decided to work on the back yard. And it needs a *lot* of work. Mark and I sat down and planned out how we'd like it to be."

"We?"

"Well, it's gonna be my home too. The thing is, the room that's gonna be his massage therapy room? It has these French doors that open out onto the yard. Mark wants it to be part of the experience. A new patio, plants that smell good…"

"Sounds wonderful. What's the favor part?"

"May eighth, he's organizing a sort of a garden party. Okay, it's not *really* a garden party. It's more a come-work-on-a-garden party."

Aaron grinned. "Maybe you should have Mark call me. I might be able to understand him better."

"Oh shut up. The thing is, I'm inviting all the gang to help out."

"Oh *I* get it. Free labor."

"No," Dylan protested. "Sure, there'd be a lot of work to do, but at the end of the day there'd be a barbecue. We're not talking burgers and hot dogs, okay? More a surf 'n' turf kinda deal. Steak, chicken, lobster…"

"So an *upmarket* barbecue."

"I suppose. And as much beer as anyone can drink. Having said that, I've seen how much we drink when we get together. The alcohol might cost more than the food. And if anyone wants to stay, they'd be welcome, but they'd be sleeping on the floor, because there's no furniture yet. Well, there is, but there's only one bed, and I'm not giving up my bed for anyone."

Aaron went over to the wall to look at his calendar. "You know May ninth is Mother's Day, right?"

Dylan snorted. "Sure, but it's not as if I'll be going to visit my mom. Mark neither, if it comes to that. That's why we thought you might like to stay over. I assumed you'd be going to see your mom the next day. That's why I was calling now. In case you wanted to make plans. Please, say you'll come."

"What have the others said?"

"So far, everyone I've called is in. And if you

want to bring Dean, that's okay."

Aaron chuckled. "I don't think so. It was bad enough when I invited him to my Easter party. If we turned up together, tongues would definitely wag."

"Would they have a reason to?"

Aaron ignored the question. "Besides, he'd be busy working on his painting."

There was a pause. "Aaron…"

Of all his friends, Dylan was probably the one who could most easily relate to Aaron's situation. "Okay, I'm in. And… maybe we can talk. Just you and me."

Another pause. "Do we have something to talk about?"

"Yeah, we do."

"That's all you're gonna give me?"

"Yup."

"Christ, you're worse at teasing than Seb."

He laughed. "I'll take that as a compliment. Just don't let us turn up and find you lied to us all and it's pizza for dinner."

Dylan laughed. "Surf 'n' turf. I promise. And now I'll let you get some sleep. Just think of me, stuck behind this desk, answering stupid calls from the lady in 308."

"What does she want?"

Dylan snorted. "To get in my pants. She's not exactly subtle."

"Tell her you have a boyfriend. That might cool her heels."

"Are you kidding? That isn't something I want spreading around. Not while Dickhead is the manager, at least. Thank God he won't be for much longer. He's moving to a hotel farther up the coast.

When he leaves, we're gonna throw a party."

"Be careful. The next manager might be worse."

Another snort. "I seriously doubt that. And besides, we've met him. He seems okay. Now, sleep. And we *will* have that talk." He disconnected.

Aaron grabbed the pencil that hung from a string beside the calendar, and circled May eighth. A day working outside with his friends sounded as if it would be tiring, but a lot of fun. And no way was he taking Dean.

Seb didn't need any more bullets.

He climbed the stairs to his bedroom, pausing at the door. *When was the last time I had someone in my bed?* Not since fall. The idea of Dean staying the night sent tendrils of warmth curling through him. He hoped Dean was a snuggler. There'd been one girl who'd insisted on Aaron keeping his distance while they slept. She claimed it made her claustrophobic to have someone curled up with her.

Aaron imagined Dean in his arms, his head resting on Aaron's chest. He thought about waking up, and the delicious ways they could deal with their morning wood. Friends with benefits was the perfect solution. All itches scratched, no complications…

What could go wrong?

Chapter Seventeen

Friday, April 16

Dean put down his paint brush and glanced at his phone. It wasn't on silent, and there was plenty of battery. It was also six-thirty, and Aaron hadn't called to say when he'd be over.

Has he had a tough day? Was he taken prisoner by tourists who resented being told they couldn't schedule a mass nude swim off Sand Beach? Even now, have they stripped him, tied him to a rock, and left him to be nibbled to death by fish when the tide comes in?

Yeah, Dean needed to take a break.

His phone burst into life, and he jumped. He heaved a sigh of relief when he saw it was Aaron. "Hey. I was beginning to think you'd forgotten."

There was a pause. "Are you feeling okay?"

"I'm fine. Why wouldn't I be?"

"So no sickness, no cramps…"

He chuckled. "I think I would've noticed anything like that."

"Oh. Okay then. So it's not food poisoning."

Dean frowned. "Aaron, are you sick?"

"Since early this morning. I didn't go to work today. Woke up with stomach cramps, I threw up, and I've been dealing with diarrhea all day. I assumed it was something we ate last night, but if you're fine, that means I've picked up a bug."

"It does sound like the stomach flu. How do

you feel?"

"Like crap. Ugh. Bad choice of word. So I won't be coming over, for obvious reasons."

"Have you eaten much today?" He loaded Google and searched for gastroenteritis.

"I've been too scared to. Whatever goes in one end doesn't stay in there for long."

Dean scanned the search results. "Have you got bread in the house? Toast would be okay. But no spices. You'll irritate your stomach."

"Aw damn, and I just made a curry too."

Dean bit his lip. "That was sarcasm, right?"

Aaron chuckled. "You spotted that."

"Okay, you need to rest. Plenty of fluids, a little toast... Watch movies. Take it easy for a couple of days."

Another chuckle. "Yes, doctor. And... I'm sorry. I was going to take you on the Ocean Path trail this weekend."

Dean smiled. "I don't think it's going anywhere. It can wait. Now get some rest."

"Thanks."

"What for?"

"For being you."

"You're welcome. Who knew park rangers needed keepers too?"

"And on that note... I gotta go. Bye." Aaron disconnected.

Dean went back to his online search, grabbed a pencil, and started writing.

Aaron needed looking after, and Dean was just the man to do it.

AARON'S AWAKENING

Saturday, April 17

Aaron got out of bed and stumbled into the bathroom. He'd woken at some ungodly hour with cramps again, but they'd stopped eventually, and he'd fallen into a doze until dawn. He'd gotten up to drink a glass of water, then he'd gone back to bed.

He stared at his reflection in the bathroom mirror. *Okay, I've had enough now. This can stop.* Then he clutched his stomach as another cramp twisted his guts.

It seemed his bout of stomach flu wasn't ready to quit.

Ten minutes later, Aaron tugged on his sweats and a tee, and trudged into the kitchen. As he opened the bag containing sliced bread, he heard a car pull up outside, and he went to investigate.

Dean's truck was parked in front of the house. *What's he doing here?*

Aaron opened the door as Dean climbed the steps, a Hannaford's paper bag in his arms. "Hey. Should you be here? Didn't I read this is infectious in the early stages?"

"I've got a surgical mask and gloves in my pocket."

"Really?"

Dean rolled his eyes. "I swear, in the

dictionary under gullible, it says, *See Aaron…*" He frowned. "Wow. It's only just occurred to me I don't even know your surname."

"It's Allen." Aaron scowled. "I have no clue what possessed my parents. Who gives a kid the initials AA, for God's sake?"

"I like Aaron. It suits you. And my parents were just as bad. DD? Lord, the teasing I got in school. 'Did your mom name you for her bra size?'" Dean's eyes sparkled. "Well… can I come in, or are we going to talk on the doorstep?"

Aaron stood aside. "Come on in, but if you catch this, it's your fault, you got that?" Dean walked through the house to the kitchen, and Aaron followed. "Did we arrange to meet? I only ask, 'cause I'm kinda fuzzy right now."

"No, we didn't. I'm here to make sure you're okay, and to bring you some stuff." He placed the paper bag on the countertop.

Aaron stared as Dean removed a bunch of bananas, a bag of rice, a loaf of bread, a box of crackers, and another of green tea. Then he brought out a jar of honey and a couple of lemons. "What is all this?"

"I did some research. This is what Google recommends for gastro issues. We're going to keep your diet bland for a few days."

"'We'? Shouldn't you be painting?"

Dean smiled. "Nope. I'm taking care of you today. Now, go sit on the couch, and I'll make you some green tea with honey and lemon. Apparently it helps with gastro problems."

Aaron chuckled. "Right away, Doctor Google."

Dean speared him with a look. "You're going to be a bad patient, aren't you?"

He couldn't remember anyone taking care of him, apart from Mom, and it was kinda sweet. "I'll be good, I promise. But you don't need to spend your day taking care of me, honest."

"What if I want to? You've seen Grammy's painting. It's going well. So that means I can afford to take a day off." Dean pointed to the living room. "Couch. Now."

Aaron snorted. "Never mind about me being a bad patient—I'm gonna start calling you Nurse Ratched."

Dean winced. "Ouch."

Aaron leaned in and kissed him on the cheek. "Thank you." He straightened. "Now go find the antibac wipes in the bathroom and clean your face." He went into the living room and sat on the couch. "You're not the only one who can Google, you know," he called out. "It said this can take three to five days to clear up. You gonna do this every day?"

"No, but I'll look in on you from time to time, and I'll cook for you every night."

Aaron swallowed. "What did I do to deserve this?"

Dean poked his head around the door. "We're friends, aren't we?" Aaron nodded, and Dean smiled. "Well, this is what friends do. They take care of each other." He paused. "Hey, if Levi, Seb, Finn, or any of the others lived closer, they'd be here too, right?"

"Yeah, they would."

"So you've got me." He disappeared from view.

You have no idea how grateful I am to have you as a

friend.

"Aaron?"

"Hm?" He opened his eyes to find Dean standing beside the couch. "Hey, what happened to the movie?"

Dean chuckled. "It finished. You slept through most of it. Trust me, you didn't miss much." He held out a cup. "Here, drink this."

Aaron took it. "Have to say, this green tea does settle my stomach. Not that I could face coffee right now." He sipped at the fragrant liquid.

"Stay off the coffee for a day or two." Dean sighed. "It's late. I should go."

"Do you have to?" Then he reconsidered the impulsive question. "On second thoughts, that might not be such a good idea. Let's save it for when I'm *not* running to and from the bathroom through the night." He paused. "Will I see you tomorrow?" Aaron knew he sounded needy as fuck, but having Dean around had been wonderful. They'd binge-watched TV all day, once Dean had introduced him to a comedy series entitled *The Marvelous Mrs. Maisel.* Aaron hadn't laughed so much in ages.

"Of course." Dean's eyes twinkled. "We have season two still to come." He leaned over and kissed the top of Aaron's head. "Get some sleep. I'll be here tomorrow morning to make you tea and toast."

The intimate gesture sent warmth flooding through him. "Thank you. Again."

"And again, you're welcome. See you in the morning." Then he was gone.

Aaron sipped his tea. Another day with Dean and *Mrs. Maisel* sounded perfect.

His phone buzzed, and he glanced at the screen. Mom. He clicked Answer. "What's wrong?"

"Why should anything be wrong? Am I not allowed to call my one and only son unless there's something wrong?"

"Not at this time of night, unless you wanna give me a heart attack."

"You didn't call today."

"That's because I'm sick." Guilt spread through him. *And I was too busy enjoying Dean's company to remember to call.*

"What's the matter?"

"Stomach flu."

"Ew."

Aaron rolled his eyes. "Your sympathy is overwhelming."

"Make sure to keep your diet—"

"Bland, yeah, I got it. Look, don't worry, okay? A friend has been here today, taking care of me."

There was a moment's hesitation. "New friend?"

"What makes you say that?"

She snorted. "Because if it was one of the gang, you'd have said. So, who is this mystery friend? Anyone I need to know about?"

Christ, she could give Seb a run for his

money.

"His name's Dean, and he's a painter who moved to Bar Harbor."

"And he's been taking care of you? Sounds like a *very* good friend."

"He is. Now, if there's nothing else you wanna tell me, can I go to bed? I need my sleep." He did *not* want to talk about Dean. His mom was capable of sniffing out a secret even over the phone.

"I'm sorry you're sick, sweetheart. And I only called because I wanted to know if you were coming to see me soon."

He chuckled. "What you *really* mean is, am I planning on seeing you on Mother's Day? Have I ever missed it? Hmm?"

"So it's yes? Great. I'll cook something special." She paused. "If you want to bring a friend, that'd be okay."

"Except that assumes this *friend* wouldn't be busy visiting *his* mom."

"Oh. Damn it."

"And don't go planning anything. It's Mother's Day. Let me surprise *you*." He'd been looking at restaurants, but the rush to book tables had already begun. If the worst came to the worst, he'd buy the food and cook dinner for them.

"You're a good boy."

"Mom… twenty-seven, remember?"

"You'll always be my boy. Now get some sleep. Love you."

"Love you too."

Another pause. "And if this Dean was important, you'd tell me, wouldn't you?"

Hell no. "Yes, Mom. Goodnight, Mom." He

disconnected. One sip of his tea made him grimace, and he got up to make a fresh cup. He went in the kitchen to find all the dishes washed and put away, and the countertops cleaned and uncluttered.

God bless Dean.

Aaron heated a cup of water in the microwave, and reached into the cabinet for a teabag. He listened absently to the whirring of the oven, his mind elsewhere.

Yesterday I knew where this was going. Today? I'm not so sure.

Dean's visit had thrown him for a loop. *Friends with benefits, he said. Friendship, sex, and no strings, he said.* Okay, Aaron had said that, but Dean had agreed, right? So what was it about Dean playing doctor that had Aaron's emotions in a mess?

Aaron opened the microwave door, removed the cup, and dropped the teabag into it. He stared at the steaming liquid, trying to fit what he knew into something resembling order.

He went to the trouble of looking up how best to treat this. He shopped. He fed me, made me tea. He gave up a day's painting to take care of me, watch stuff with me. And although Dean had remarked that any of his friends would've done the same, Aaron wasn't so sure. They'd have spent an hour or two, tops, but...

He really cares.

Aaron had thought he knew what he wanted out of this arrangement.

He hadn't counted on Dean being exactly what he *needed*.

Chapter Eighteen

Tuesday, April 20

Dean took a step back from the easel. He figured another week, possibly ten days, of painting, and Grammy's portrait would be finished. He was pleased with it, and he hoped she would be too. Dean knew from experience that portraits could be problematical. *We don't see ourselves as others see us.* There'd been one client who'd taken one look at the finished work, and demanded Dean make her appear younger.

God, how he'd wanted to tell her he didn't work miracles.

Instead, he'd spent a few days staring at the photos and doing his best to smooth out her complexion, tone down the silver in her hair, and generally perform cosmetic surgery with a paintbrush. He'd thought the end result made her appear as though she'd had a face lift, but to his surprise she was delighted. And yet, there'd been other clients who had wept happy tears when they saw their likeness.

I guess people will always surprise you.

His phone rang, and he put down his brush to answer it. He smiled when he saw Aaron's number. "Hey. How was the first day back at work?"

"It was okay. I found out I wasn't the only one who'd been struck down by a stomach bug. We're still trying to work out who was patient zero.

How's your day been?"

"I missed my morning coffee with you."

"Aww. I missed that too. But I'm calling to say pencil me in for Saturday. We're doing that hike I promised you."

"Great. What time?"

"I thought morning would be good. That way, you have the afternoon free if you wanna paint."

And what if I want to spend it with you? Then he remembered their arrangement was a two-way street. *Don't push.* "Works for me."

"Are you still painting, or are you done for the day?"

Dean assessed the canvas. "You know what? I think I'm done." He needed a break, and coming back to it the following day with fresh eyes would accomplish more than continuing. Besides, he was getting hungry.

"I just got home, and I'm really not in the mood to cook."

Dean didn't hesitate. "You can come over and eat with me if you like." For a moment there was silence, and he cursed himself for his impulse. *He saw me on three consecutive days. Maybe he wants a break.*

"Actually, I had something else in mind."

Dean suppressed his sigh of disappointment. "That's okay. We can do it some other time."

"No, that wasn't what I meant. Do you like lobster?"

"Yes."

"Okay. Do you know where Clark Cove is?"

"I'm sure I can find it on a map. Why? Are you planning on catching your dinner?"

Aaron laughed. "Hell no. Remind me to tell

you about Seb's summer of working a lobster boat. Enough to put anyone off fishing. But just up the road from the cove is the Travelin' Lobster. Nothing fancy. In fact, it's just a stand, run by a local fisherman. The lobster's great. They cook it on the grill, and there are picnic tables where you can eat. All outdoors, so wear a coat. But it's a pretty varied menu. So I was thinking... wanna join me for some lobster?"

Dean couldn't remember the last time he'd eaten freshly-caught-and-cooked lobster. "That sounds awesome. But if you'd prefer to eat alone, I—"

"If I wanted that, I wouldn't be calling you, now would I? Except... shit."

"What's the matter?"

Aaron sighed. "I swear, that bug has softened my brain. They aren't open yet, not till mid-May."

"That's okay. Thanks for thinking of me."

"Hey, wait a minute, you don't get off *that* easy. There's always Geddy's on Main Street. Their Lobster Cobb salad is to die for."

"You sure you want to eat seafood after this past week?"

Aaron groaned. "Yes. If I see another bowl of rice or a banana, I think I'll scream. And I was fine all day."

"Okay then. If you're sure."

"I'm sure. Seven o'clock all right for ya?"

"That's fine."

"Great, then I'll meet you there. It's just up the street from the harbor. You can't miss it. Look for the giant lobster claw holding a cup of coffee. Or pizza. Or a steamer. They're all up there."

Dean laughed. "See you there." He disconnected. Dinner with Aaron sounded like the perfect way to end his day.

Sometimes you don't need benefits. You just need a friend.

Their table was tucked away in the corner, but Aaron didn't mind. He'd eaten there enough times to know the servers were on the ball. Dean perused the menu, and Aaron had to force himself not to stare. Dean wore a white shirt, open at the neck, and jeans, and Aaron could smell the scent of his shampoo still clinging to his hair, mingling with the smell of his citrus bodywash.

He tapped Dean's menu. "Well? What leaps out at you?"

Dean chuckled. "You had me at Bar Island Lobster Cobb salad. It sounded amazing, and now I see what's in it, it seems even better. But the lobster stew looks good too, and so does the shrimp and scallop scampi."

"Well, why don't you order the salad, I'll get the scampi, and we can share. That way, we get the best of both worlds."

Dean beamed. "Deal."

The server appeared and took their order, then reappeared with a carafe of water. Dean surveyed the pine-clad dining room, gazing at the far side where one wall was covered in street signs, paintings, and even a stuffed moose head. Then he grinned. "Hey. That's my road." He pointed to the sign for Bay View Drive.

Aaron took a long drink from his glass. "This place gets a lot of tourists. Come summer, you won't be able to get a table in here unless you reserve it."

"When does the season really get going?"

"End of May." He gestured to the other diners. "This is still pretty quiet."

"I suppose you're going to be very busy."

Aaron nodded. "The boat tours haven't started yet, but once they do…"

"Tours of where?"

"Great Harbor and Somes Sound, plus there's a visit to the museum at Islesford. Every morning for three hours, except Mondays and Saturdays."

"That's not so bad. At least you get two days off."

Aaron chuckled. "Only until June eighteenth or thereabouts, then the tours are every day."

Dean's eyes gleamed. "Maybe I should book one, and watch you in action."

Aaron had an idea that might prove a little distracting. "But you'll be busy too. There's the lighthouse to finish…"

Dean nodded. "Then I'll start work on Jordan Pond." He cocked his head. "I haven't forgotten, you know."

Aaron feigned innocence. "Forgotten what?"

"You said you'd sit for me." He smiled. "Remember?"

As if I could forget that.

Their appetizers arrived, a dish of crispy calamari with a sweet chili sauce, and all conversation was shelved while they ate.

"If you're working Sundays in June, you won't be able to go to Grammy's party," Dean observed after a moment.

Aaron smiled. "Already taken care of. I put in a request for that Sunday off. They're pretty good about things like that." And it wasn't as if he made it a regular thing. Some of his coworkers were always pleading for time off, usually for some family event, so he didn't feel guilty about his requests for those days when he got together with his friends.

They're my *family.*

"What's going through your mind right now?"

Aaron blinked. "Why do you ask?"

"You were smiling. Happy is a good look on you."

Whereas you look good every time I see you. "I was thinking about the guys."

"I'm glad I got to meet them. Did Seb really work on a lobster boat? I can't picture that."

Aaron snorted. "Neither could he, at first. Christ, he was pissed. But I'll bet he doesn't mind it so much now." Dean gave him an inquiring glance. "Marcus was staying at his parents' summer house in Cape Porpoise, where Seb was working. That's how they met." He pointed to the dish. "You want that last calamari?"

Dean laughed. "You can have it. Just don't complain when I take the last piece of scampi."

Aaron grinned. "Turnabout is fair play." He dipped it into what was left of the chili sauce.

"They all seemed happy for Finn and Joel,"

Dean remarked. "But then, weddings are usually happy things, right?"

Aaron wiped his lips with his napkin. "Finn's a good guy."

"How did they meet?"

"The way Finn tells it, he'd been watching Joel walk his dog Bramble on the beach for weeks before fate stepped in."

"What happened?"

Aaron cackled. "Bramble got loose, that's what. Finn helped Joel get him back, and the rest is history. Joel hasn't been out that long."

"Did Finn mention Joel has kids?"

He nodded. "He married, because apparently that's what some gay guys did when they couldn't come out to their families or those closest to them. He stuck it out for years, never once looking at anyone other than his wife. And when he finally stopped hiding who he was, they decided on an amicable divorce. Then he met Finn. Talk about a fairy tale ending."

The server arrived with their entrées, and Aaron was grateful for the interruption. He didn't mind talking about his friends, but more and more of them were finding their own Happily Ever After, and all that did was throw his own situation into sharp relief.

Why should I feel like this? I am happy. For God's sake, I'm happier than I've been for a long while. He was being stupid. He had nothing to complain about, and a lot to be thankful for. *Friends with benefits, remember?* They were going to go on hikes, learn to do stand-up paddle boarding... If he got an itch, and Dean was available, then it would get scratched, and that had to be an improvement on the last six months.

"You're looking awfully thoughtful," Dean remarked. He cocked his head. "Still sure you want to do this?"

Aaron shook his head with a smile. "I swear, sometimes it's as if you can read my mind. And yeah, I still want to do this." He just didn't want to talk about it in the middle of a restaurant. "By the way, I'm saving you from a grilling."

Dean arched his eyebrows. "Someone wants to cook me slowly?"

He laughed. "No, but it could amount to the same thing—torture." He told Dean about Mark's plans for the yard. "You were invited, but I already declined on your behalf."

Dean frowned. "Why would you do that without asking me first?"

He blinked, then pressed his hand to his chest. "Aw, sweetheart, are we having our first fight?"

His tone had the desired effect. Dean burst out laughing. "Yeah, that didn't come out the way it sounded in my head."

"And I didn't mention it for a couple of reasons. One, I figured you'd be working on Grammy's painting. Or the lighthouse painting. Two… well, the second was kinda selfish."

Dean's eyes twinkled. "Color me intrigued."

Aaron took a drink from his glass. "These guys know me, okay? They have super-sneaky ways of ferreting out information—stuff I might not wanna share."

Dean stuck his fork into sliced egg and avocado. "And you don't want to share a certain… arrangement with them."

"Wouldn't be my first choice, no. And it's none of their business." That didn't mean he'd changed his mind about talking with Dylan. Aaron knew he could count on him not to blab. And he had to tell someone, because damn it, this was huge.

He just wasn't sure whether *someone* included Mom.

To his relief, Dean nodded. "I get it. I mean, I saw what they were like the last time. I can understand why you'd want to keep it on the down low. And you're right. It's no one's business but ours." He rolled his eyes. "This salad is awesome."

Aaron preened. "I did good. And I promise I'll take you to the Travelin' Lobster when it opens."

"I'll hold you to that." Dean gestured to their surroundings. "I like this place. It's got a nice feel to it. When you mentioned it, I looked it up online. I found a few other places too." He smiled. "Now, tell me about Saturday's hike. Where are we going?"

Aaron described the Ocean Path trail, loving the way Dean's eyes lit up.

All of a sudden, he couldn't wait for Saturday.

K.C. WELLS

Chapter Nineteen

Saturday, April 24

Dean took his backpack off and stretched his arms above his head. "That didn't feel all *that* much longer than the walk around Jordan Pond." Not that he was tired, not in the least. The breeze off the ocean had been invigorating, and they'd indulged in frequent stops to admire the view. Although the trail went along the Park Loop Road, at regular intervals they'd encountered steps off of it, leading to bluffs where they could stand or sit, the waves pounding the rocks below them. Trees grew in the crevices between the beige-colored slabs, and the sound of the ocean attacking the shore was pretty spectacular.

"It was. Maybe four miles." Aaron smirked. "I think you spent most of the walk back talking about that puppy."

"But he was so cute!" They'd passed a couple of hikers along the way, who'd been walking with their golden retriever. They'd introduced Digby, who was a friendly, bouncy puppy, eager to meet new people.

"Yeah, he was."

Dean tossed him the keys. "You can drive." He sighed as they got into the truck. "I always wanted a dog when I was a kid."

"Your parents wouldn't let you?"

He shook his head. "Mom was allergic. Then

when I moved to Philly, I didn't feel good about the neighborhood. After that, I was always moving from place to place."

"Dogs need a lot of walking," Aaron said as he turned on the engine.

"So? I'd walk him. It's not as if there's any shortage of great walks on this island, right?"

"You've already decided, haven't you?" Aaron observed with a wry chuckle. "Do puppies and painting mix well? Why am I imagining future phone calls where you tell me your puppy knocked the easel over with his wagging tail?"

Dean snorted. "To knock over *that* easel, he'd have to have a tail the size of Godzilla's. And I wouldn't go for a dog that was too bouncy. I'd want a more laid-back breed." He grinned. "I'm a fan of laid-back."

Aaron squinted at him. "So now I've gone from being Kate Winslet to a dog? You really know how to make a guy feel good."

"Don't *you* like dogs? Or are you more a cat person?" Not that Dean was averse to having a cat, if it came to that.

"I like most animals, but it isn't fair to have a dog when I'm at work all day." He pulled out of the parking lot. Dean got his phone out and typed. Aaron glanced across at him. "What are you doing?"

Dean peered at the screen. "There's the SPCA in Hancock County."

"I know where it is. It's in Trenton, south of Ellsworth. Where we went to get tested?" He cackled. "This couldn't wait till you were home?"

Dean was barely listening. He stared at a photo. "Aw, he's adorable."

"*Who's* adorable?"

"Robby. He's a Boxer Beagle mix, and he's an older dog."

"How old?"

"Seven."

"That's not bad."

Dean scanned the dog's details. "It says he's good with cats too."

"Has he got any special needs? You gotta know that kinda thing." Aaron snorted. "Listen to me, talking like this is a done deal. Do you know all the shit you have to go through before you can adopt a dog?"

Dean read quickly. "My rental agreement doesn't specify no pets, so I'm good to go on that score. The humane society has a meet & greet, there's an application form, they want references, and there's a short waiting period." He grinned. "I think that covers everything."

Aaron laughed. "You're serious."

"Of course." He went back to his search. "And yes, under Special Needs, it says he needs frequent 'potty breaks'." He grimaced. "They couldn't just say walks?" Dean pocketed his phone. "So… will you come with me when we go there?"

"When *we* go?" Aaron let out an exaggerated sigh. "Fine. Yes. We can go check out Robby. Just don't set your heart on him in case he finds his forever home before you even lay eyes on him."

Dean let out a happy sigh. *I'm going to get a puppy.*

"So… does that make Robby a Bogle or a Beaxer?"

Dean groaned. "Let's stick with puppy,

because both those sound awful."

"Does this mean you're gonna stay put for a while?" Aaron inquired as they merged onto Bay View Drive. "I know you've got this place for a year…"

Dean had been thinking about that too. "Maybe it's time I put down some roots. I love it here on the island." *And I'm really hoping this thing we've got going works out.*

Except that wasn't the whole truth. There was a tiny part of him that hoped what they had would blossom into something more permanent, not that he'd ever say as much to Aaron.

He doesn't want more. And Dean wasn't about to scare him off. *Besides, why would you even want to go down this road again? He might be getting his itch scratched, but remember, he's into women. So forget about yearning for something more permanent, because he doesn't want that.*

Maybe if Dean told himself that enough times, he'd believe it.

Aaron pulled up in front of the house. "You're coming in, aren't you?" Dean asked. They hadn't made plans beyond the hike. "I can make us lunch. There's still clam chowder in the freezer, if you're interested." He kept his tone neutral, not wanting to push Aaron into a decision if he had things to do, places to go.

Aaron grinned. "Well, now that you mention it, I *am* a little hungry. Is there any of that bread left?"

Dean chuckled. "I froze some of that too, so yeah."

"Great. And while we eat, we can get the ball rolling." Dean frowned, and Aaron rolled his eyes. "SPCA? Application forms?"

"Oh, sure. Then you think I *should* get a dog?"

Aaron laughed. "Like I said, I think you've already decided." They got out of the truck, and Dean led the way, his mind not on lunch, but an idea for what might follow it.

Aaron loaded the bowls and plates into the dishwasher, along with the glasses and silverware. "So what are you gonna do with the rest of your Saturday?" he said to Dean in the living room.

No answer.

Aaron peered around the partition wall, but Dean wasn't there. "Dean?"

"In here."

Aaron chuckled and walked through to the hall. "In where?" He poked his head around the door to Dean's studio, and found him draping a heavy cream sheet over a stool. "What are you doing?" Then he caught sight of a couch against the wall. "Is that new? Looks comfy."

"Got it Monday from a garage sale. And yes, it's supremely comfy." Dean straightened, his eyes gleaming. "Take your clothes off."

That was all it took to send Aaron's blood heading south. "*Now* you're talking." Then he narrowed his gaze. "I've got a sneaking suspicion we're not on the same page."

Dean grinned. "We might be, but not right this second. There's something else I want to do first." He gave Aaron a pointed stare. "You're still wearing clothes."

Aaron removed his sweater with feigned reluctance. "You only want me for my body," he groused. Then he shivered when Dean walked behind him and kissed his bare back between his shoulder blades.

"I want you, all right," Dean murmured before reaching around Aaron to stroke his chest, his fingertips brushing Aaron's nipples, his touch as light as a feather. Aaron's breathing hitched as Dean slid his hands down his torso until he reached the waistband of his jeans. He popped the button and slowly lowered the zipper. Aaron moaned at the feel of Dean's warm hand on his bare cock.

Dean chuckled. "No underwear? Were you being forgetful—or hopeful?"

Aaron shuddered as Dean freed his dick and gave it three or four leisurely tugs. "Definitely hopeful." He glanced down to watch Dean's hand at work, his shaft filling. Then he stilled when Dean released him. "Hey. I was enjoying that."

"So was I. And while I'm painting you this afternoon, you get to think about how good my cock is going to feel in your ass—*when* I've finished."

Aaron gasped. "You little tease." He'd been imagining that very thing for the last few days, not without a little trepidation. The thought of Dean inside him sent alternate rushes of ice and fire spreading through him.

"Don't think of it as teasing, more… delayed gratification." Dean took a step back. "Jeans, off."

"The least you can do after making me this hard is paint the front view," Aaron grumbled. "What's the point in getting him all excited if no one gets to see him?"

Dean walked around him, glancing at Aaron's shaft as it stood to attention. "*He* does seem to be making a *point*, doesn't he? Maybe I should call this painting, *Find the Salami*." He indicated the stool. "Sit. Then I'll get you how I want you."

"I know how I want *you*," Aaron muttered, planting his ass on the stool.

"And how would that be?"

Aaron decided Dean wasn't the only one who could play dirty. He speared Dean with a hopefully smoking hot glance. "Sitting on that couch, while I ride you till you come in my tight virgin ass."

"Fuck." Dean's eyes were like saucers, his breathing ragged.

"And I do mean virgin. Not so much as a fingertip. Not even a rim job." Aaron noted the bulge at Dean's crotch. "Aw. Now you have to paint with a hard on. Too bad." He grinned. "This is fun."

Dean gaped at him. "You are pure evil."

Aaron wagged his finger. "You're burning daylight."

Dean disappeared from view. "Move your left leg out, point with your toes," Dean instructed. "Now look over to the right. That's it. Put your left hand on your left thigh. Back straight. Now stay like that."

"For how long?"

"Till I say you can move, that's how long." There was a pause. "Were you serious?"

"About what?"

"Not even a finger? No toys? Nothing?"

"Cross my heart." Aaron twisted to gaze at Dean over his shoulder. "You really do get to go where no man has gone before. No woman either, for that matter."

Dean scowled. "You moved!"

Aaron resumed his pose, trying not to shake with laughter.

This was a *lot* of fun.

"Okay, you can move now."

Aaron got up from the stool and bent over to touch his toes. "Christ, I'm stiff."

Dean snorted. "You were stiff when we started." Then he let out a chuckle when Aaron reached back to grab his cheeks, pulling them apart to reveal his pucker, and waggling his ass. "Subtle, Aaron."

He straightened, turning slowly to face Dean. "You're done for the day, right?"

Something flickered in Dean's eyes, and he reached down to his crotch to mold his fingers around his obvious erection. "Yes, I'm done." When Aaron moved toward him, he gestured to the easel. "Don't you want to see how it looks?"

"Not now. I'd prefer to wait a while." Aaron smiled. "Some things are worth waiting for." His gaze flickered down. "To quote you, Jeans, off."

"No coffee? Tea? Water?"

Aaron chuckled. "I've been sitting on that stool for three hours, and all I could think about was you fucking me. And the only thing I want from you is lube. *Lots* of lube." Then he laughed when Dean darted from the room. "You don't keep lube in every room?"

"Why would I want lube in there?" Dean hollered from his bedroom. "In case I feel the urge to jack off while I'm painting? And suppose I get it on the canvas?"

"Ew."

Dean appeared in the doorway, clutching a plastic bottle. "Now... where were we?"

Aaron walked over to him, grabbed a fistful of Dean's tee, and tugged him toward the couch. Dean sank onto it, dropping the bottle onto the seat cushion beside him, and Aaron straddled his lap, his hands on Dean's neck and nape while their lips met in a lingering kiss. Dean stroked his waist and ass, sliding to caress his thighs, his fingertips exploring Aaron's body even as his tongue explored Aaron's mouth.

"You being naked and me clothed has this whole illicit vibe to it," Dean murmured between kisses. "Sort of kinky."

Aaron kissed his neck, loving the shiver that coursed through Dean. "Trust me, this is *not* kinky. In the dictionary under kinky, it says, *See Seb Williams*."

Dean cupped Aaron's chin. "I'm curious."

"I thought that was my line," Aaron quipped. "What about?"

"Why have you never played with your ass?"

Aaron shrugged. "I guess I was too busy playing with someone else's. I figured that was more fun." He caught his breath as Dean trailed a single finger through his crack, pausing to circle his hole. Aaron swallowed. "Okay, I'm willing to admit that might have been a mistake." Dean sucked on his finger, and Aaron's heartbeat quickened. He took a couple of deep breaths when Dean slid his hand under Aaron's balls and slowly, so fucking slowly, pushed the finger into his ass, Dean's eyes locked on his. "Oh my God."

Dean stopped, his other hand curled around Aaron's thickening cock, tugging gently on it. "You're in charge, okay? You pick the pace. You say when you're ready for more."

Aaron stammered out a laugh. "Gotta say, this is kinda surreal, having a conversation with your finger up my ass." Dean's hand on his dick felt good, but having him so focused on Aaron's reactions was even hotter. "I appreciate you taking care of me."

"God, you're sexy." Dean let go of his shaft, cupped Aaron's nape, and pulled him down into a tender kiss.

Aaron groaned into his mouth when Dean withdrew his finger. "Did I say you could stop?"

Dean chuckled. "You're going to love what I have in mind." He pointed to the corner of the couch. "Kneel there, facing away from me."

Aaron got where this was leading, and his pulse raced. He grabbed cushions and stuffed them into the corner to support himself, then rested his arms on the back and arm of the couch.

"Tilt your ass nice and high, and spread your legs."

Aaron did as instructed, his heart pounding. Dean's soft kisses on his ass and lower back took him by surprise, and he sighed into a cushion. "That feels wonderful." Then he shivered when Dean licked a slow path over his hole.

"Ooh. You taste like... virgin."

Aaron snorted. "You made that up. Assholes don't come in flavors." He shuddered as Dean did it again, pausing to flick Aaron's hole with the tip of his tongue.

"I don't think you're right about that. Yours is delicious."

Aaron closed his eyes to shut out everything but Dean's tongue, the slick sounds he made, the feel of Dean's fingers pulling his ass cheeks apart, his cool breath on Aaron's hole...

Fuck, this is addictive. An irrational thought filtered through his brain. *Not one of those guys told me how fucking awesome it feels to be on the receiving end. They've been holding out on me.*

Then he froze when Dean came to a halt. "Aaron?"

"Yeah?"

Dean chuckled. "Just checking you're still breathing. You went quiet on me."

"Okay, now you know I'm alive. Stop talking and get back to licking my ass." Dean pushed his face into Aaron's crease, rubbing his bearded chin over his hole, and Aaron laughed. "That tickles." Then the urge to laugh died when Dean spread Aaron's cheeks with his fingers again, and suddenly there was a tongue in his ass. "Fuck."

"Is that a good fuck?" Dean asked, pausing.

"No, it's a don't-you-dare-stop fuck," Aaron growled. Violent shivers coursed through him as Dean tongue-fucked him, until he was rocking back, chasing the sensation, his body on fire. Then Dean kissed his cheeks, his hole, his balls, down to the head of his cock, before dragging his tongue all the way back. He settled into a rhythm, alternating between his hole and his dick, until Aaron couldn't keep still. "Dean, please…"

"Ready for more?"

"*So* ready." Aaron shifted off the couch as Dean stood to undress, his dick springing free when he shoved his jeans to his knees. Aaron helped him remove them, then gave Dean a push. Dean dropped onto the couch, and Aaron was there, kneeling between his spread thighs, Dean's shaft in his mouth.

Dean moaned, rocking his hips. "You suck cock like you've been doing it forever." He shuddered when Aaron flicked the head with his tongue.

Aaron raised his chin and grinned. "No, I suck cock like I enjoy it. This is my thing now." He loved Dean's hands on his hair, exerting light pressure, loved the way Dean's dick slid in and out of his mouth, the solid feel of it between his lips. He bobbed his head, quickening the pace.

Dean pulled free and bent to kiss him. "Ride me," he whispered against Aaron's lips.

Aaron got up from the floor and sat astride him, his heart thumping. Dean squeezed lube onto his fingers, then rubbed them over Aaron's hole before sliding one of them inside. He gazed at Aaron, his lips parted, his finger deep in Aaron's ass. "How does that feel?"

Aaron shivered as Dean moved in and out. "Feels good." He chuckled. "I imagine your dick will feel a little different."

"Yes—it'll feel better." Then Dean added

another finger, and Aaron caught his breath. "That's more of a stretch, but we won't go any further until you're ready."

Aaron gave an experimental roll of his hips, and Dean's fingers moved deeper. "Oh yeah, like that." He held out his hand. "Gimme some lube." When his palm was slick, he grabbed both their shafts and rubbed them against each other. He didn't know which sensation was better—Dean's fingers in his ass or their dicks in his hand.

Either way, he was more than ready.

Dean groaned. "I'm so hard."

"Then you need to be inside me." Aaron lifted himself up, freeing Dean's fingers, and reached behind him to guide Dean's shaft to his hole. "Now kiss me," he demanded.

Dean tugged him down into a fervent kiss, Aaron sank a little lower, moaning as the thick head popped through. "*And* there's a dick in my ass." Dean stilled, and Aaron kissed him again, grateful for the care he was taking.

Dean curved his hand around Aaron's cheek, his gaze locked on Aaron's. "You control the depth, the speed. And when you tell me you're ready, we'll switch it up a little."

Aaron inched lower still, breathing deeply. "I didn't think you were this big."

Dean's hands were on his waist, caressing him. "It won't be long before you can take all of it."

He gaped. "What do you mean? How much is in there? It's already tickling my tonsils." He shifted again. "Jesus. What have you got in there, an extendable cock?" At last, he bottomed out, Dean's stiff pubes against his ass. "That's it, right? You're not gonna slide in another couple of inches you've got hidden away somewhere?"

"This is why toys are good. I have a nice fat dildo, because sometimes, a finger just isn't enough."

Aaron snorted. "Why do I need one of those when I have the real thing?"

"Because it's fun." Dean kissed him. He put his head back against the couch. "Fuck, you're tight."

Aaron had had enough of talking. He looped his arms around Dean's neck and began to move, a slow, delicious motion, letting himself become accustomed to the feel of Dean's shaft filling him. His dick had lost some of its rigidity, but Dean stroked and played with it, his eyes locked on Aaron's face. Aaron took it slow, and when the first trickles of damn-this-feels-good spread through him, he rolled his hips a little faster, rocked a little harder, until joy bubbled up out of him at the sheer pleasure he experienced.

Dean caressed Aaron's chest. "Ready to change things up?"

Aaron nodded. "How do you want me?"

"On your side. You know what spooning is, right?"

He smiled. "Ooh, nice." He lifted himself up and off Dean's shaft, then stretched out on the couch. "Can we both fit?"

Dean chuckled. "And *now* you know why I picked a couch with deep seats." He lay on his side, tucked in behind Aaron, and Aaron shifted until his upper body rested on the cushions. Dean applied more lube to his dick, and Aaron held his breath as he slid it back in. Then Dean's arm cradled Aaron's neck, his hand was on Aaron's face, and they kissed while

Dean filled him with slow, deep thrusts. Aaron grabbed hold of Dean's hand and laced their fingers together, his moans punctuating each unhurried penetration. Dean held Aaron's thigh aloft and picked up the pace, their kisses constant.

Aaron was lost. He'd watched gay porn, he'd known what to expect—pounding, grunts, more pounding—and Dean's sensual, leisurely thrusts, gentle caresses, and lingering kisses were a world apart from Aaron's fantasies.

This was *so* much better.

Dean looked into his eyes. "You feel amazing." He moved in and out of him, his breathing shallow.

"I feel..." Aaron groaned as Dean's cock nudged his prostate. "I feel like I'm gonna come."

"Then come," Dean demanded.

Aaron gripped his dick, gave it three sharp tugs, and shot his load in an arc onto the floor. Dean kissed his lips, his neck, and his chest as his orgasm jolted him, then held him until the tremors subsided.

Aaron cupped Dean's face. "Now it's your turn."

Dean shuddered. "Thank God." He bucked his hips, clinging to Aaron, and suddenly Aaron felt a slow throbbing inside him, accompanied by an exquisite warmth.

He grabbed Dean's face and kissed him, aware of every pulse of Dean's cock. When Dean lay still, his shaft deep in Aaron's ass, Aaron stroked his hair, running his fingers through the long strands.

"So... how was it?" Dean asked.

Aaron sighed. "Awesome. Better than I thought it would be. Except for..." He clammed up.

Dean raised his head. "Except for what?"

"I wanted to do that thing you did," Aaron confessed.

"What thing?"

"You know, where you squeezed my dick with your hole. It felt so amazing when you did it, I wanted to make you feel that good too."

Dean smiled, then kissed him, a sweet kiss that warmed him. "Sweetheart, you made me feel *so* much better than good. For a first time taking a dick, you were fantastic. And how about you don't run before you can walk? There'll be other times." He winced.

Aaron stilled. "Are you okay? Did you hurt yourself?"

Dean chuckled. "This was a first for me too—sex on a couch. I think I prefer doing this in a bed." He sighed. "It must be nearly six o'clock. Almost time for dinner."

Aaron did *not* want to leave, but he knew he was being selfish. "Did you want to do some more painting?"

Dean's smile reached his eyes. "Nope. I've done enough. The only thing I plan on doing for the rest of the day is be with you." He stroked Aaron's cheek. "If you want to stay."

Aaron bit his lip. "I'd like that."

Dean grinned. "In that case… how does pizza in bed sound?"

He beamed. "Freakin' perfect." Then he chuckled. "*After* I've been to the bathroom."

Chapter Twenty

Sunday, April 25

Dean woke surrounded by warmth, and he couldn't have been happier. Aaron's chest pressed against his back, one arm draped across his waist, and—

Dear God, he's hard. Then he smiled to himself. *When is he* not *hard?* He tilted his hips, feeling the weight of Aaron's thick shaft slide through his crack.

I know where I want that. Then he moaned when a firm hand gripped his dick.

"Well, hello there." Aaron gave it a leisurely pull. "*Someone* woke up happy. I was gonna ask if you had plans for this morning, but I think I already know the answer." Aaron's soft lips and beard grazed his neck, and Dean shivered.

"I was… going to continue painting you, but…" Dean was rendered speechless when Aaron rolled his hips, making him even more aware of his erection.

Another whisper of a kiss. "But?"

"It's… it's… Christ, I can't think straight when you do that." He rocked back, wanting more.

"Hate to break it to you, but thinking straight is always gonna be a problem." Aaron nuzzled his neck, and Dean shuddered.

"What I was *trying* to say was… it's okay if you

have other plans."

"Painting works for me."

"Great. Just… no teasing me during the breaks."

Aaron's gasp was comical. "Me? Tease?"

"You know exactly what I mean." All of a sudden, Dean found himself on his back, Aaron's face inches from his.

"Then I'd better make the most of this. You know, get it out of my system."

Dean bit back a smile. "I thought you did that last night."

Aaron's eyes gleamed. "*That* was a goodnight fuck. *This* is a good morning fuck." His lips twitched. "I know. It's easy to confuse the two. But I'm sure with practice, you'll be able to differentiate."

Dean nodded. "It might take a *lot* of practice," he declared in a sage tone. "But I'm a fast learner."

"Hey, I'm all for that." They laughed. Aaron reached toward the nightstand drawer. He chuckled when he peered into it. "Either you jerk off a whole lot, or you're planning on us doing this a lot."

I'd do this every night, given half a chance. What came to mind wasn't the sex, but going to sleep in Aaron's arms.

Aaron removed the bottle, then applied some to his fingers. He stretched out at Dean's side, and their lips met in a sweet, chaste kiss.

Dean wanted time to slow down. He wanted to remember everything: the gentle way Aaron prepped him, stretching him; Aaron's arms hooked under Dean's knees as he moved in and out of him; Aaron cradling him as he filled him with languid thrusts; those moments when Aaron picked up a little speed, hips pumping; strong, deep drives into him that made Dean's toes curl; and through it all, the constant kisses that connected them, made them one.

Making love had never been this heart-stoppingly exquisite, and when he came, Aaron kissed him, holding him through his climax. It wasn't long before Aaron tumbled over the edge, only this time Dean brought him there with his mouth, loving Aaron's shivers and jolts as Dean took every drop.

Aaron pulled Dean into his arms. "That was—"

Dean stopped his words with a kiss, and Aaron sighed into it. When they parted, Dean looked him in the eyes. "No words, okay?"

Aaron smiled. "Okay." Dean laid his head on Aaron's shoulder, Aaron's arms around him.

Perfect. That was perfect.

Dean took a step back and gazed at the canvas. Aaron's portrait was coming together nicely. *Which is amazing, considering he's such a distraction.* Dean had to admit, Aaron was also a lot of fun.

"Are you happy with it so far?" Aaron asked as he buttoned his jeans.

"Yes, but why don't you want to see it for yourself?"

"Uh-uh. I prefer to see it when you're sure

you've finished it." He pulled on his sweater.

Dean grinned. "You know you want to take a peek."

Aaron scowled. "Yes, I do, and *not* looking at it is torture, but I'm gonna stick to my guns on this. Now, are you still on for Saturday?" When Dean started at him in puzzlement, Aaron rolled his eyes. "Echo Lake? Stand-up paddle boarding? We have a two-hour 'Experience' booked." He hooked his fingers. "A buddy of mine, Dolan, is one of the instructors. If we go in your truck, you'll need a National Park Pass, but I can arrange that." He cocked his head. "You do still wanna do this, don't you?"

Dean nodded. "I haven't gotten a wetsuit yet, but I'll do that this week."

"The surf shop on Main Street has everything you'll need. It's also where they run the trips from. And yeah, rent one. In the summer you could do this in shorts and a tee, but it's not warm enough for that yet."

"And I was hoping to visit the SPCA this week too," Dean informed him. "They're closed Mondays, and open till five every day except Thursdays." He smiled. "Do you still want to come with me?"

Aaron chuckled. "Wouldn't miss it. I'm keeping my fingers crossed Robby is still there."

"He is," Dean confirmed. "I checked. Are you sure you don't want to stay for dinner?"

Aaron walked toward him, stopping within a few feet of the easel. He crooked his finger. "Come out from behind there." When Dean did so, Aaron took him in his arms. "I would love to stay, but if I do, I'll be going to work tomorrow in last week's uniform." He kissed Dean on the lips, whisper-soft. "It's been an awesome weekend. I made the most of it, because once we hit the end of May, my schedule will be crazy busy. So yes, I'll come with you to the SPCA. Wednesday might be best. I'll pick you up at your place. We can decide on a time later. And after, come to my house and I'll feed you."

It wasn't until Aaron was at his truck, waving at him as he got in, that the thought struck him.

Even when we're not having sex, we're kissing, touching…

Friends with benefits, fuck buddies…Neither term encapsulated them.

And if we're like this now, where does it go from here?

Dean knew where he wanted it to go.

He closed the door, aware of the silence. Dean smiled to himself. *Most of this weekend, all I've heard in this place is us laughing.* He was going to make the most of it, because it sounded as though Aaron wouldn't be around much. He aimed to make the most of every minute they got together.

His phone's shrill tone shattered the quiet, and Dean glanced at the screen. He walked into the kitchen, connecting to Ash's call. "Hey."

"Okay, are you sitting down?"

Dean stilled. "Do I need to be?"

"I'd say that's a big fat yes."

"Hit me with it. What's happened?"

There was a pause. "I'm gonna be a dad."

Dean gasped. "Oh wow. That's awesome. I didn't even know you two were thinking of having kids."

Ash snorted. "That's 'cause we weren't. In

fact, the opposite."

"Oh. Oh wow."

"Those weren't the first words that came out when Claire told me, I'll be honest. We're still trying to figure out what happened, but as the doc says, no method is one hundred percent foolproof."

Dean hesitated before asking. "And… are you guys happy about this?"

Another pause, and his heart sank. "Now we've gotten used to the idea? Yeah, we're happy. Mom is ecstatic. She was dying to call you, but I put my foot down. I said *I* wanted to be the one to share the good news. Of course, *now* she's making you-need-to-get-married noises."

He laughed. "Well duh. And will you?" He waited for Ash's derisive snort.

"Maybe?"

That brought Dean to a halt. "Seriously? You and Claire have been together since the earth was cooling. I thought you didn't believe in marriage. 'We don't need a piece of paper,' remember?"

"Shit, you still sound just like me."

"Hey, it came in useful when we were kids."

Ash sighed. "When it was only me and Claire, a bit of paper wasn't important. But now? I have to consider the baby. So yeah, we're talking about it. If we do, it'll have to be before she gets as big as a house."

Dean chuckled. "Do yourself a favor. Don't say that while she's in earshot." A thought occurred to him. "Does this mean you're going to cancel the Maine trip?"

"Why would we do that? She's pregnant, dude, not sick."

"I was thinking about morning sickness. She might not want to be traveling right then." He remembered Mom's stories about how sick she'd been with Ash.

"We discussed this last night. Claire says she'll be fourteen weeks along by then, so morning sickness shouldn't be a factor. I looked it up. They figure it's all done and dusted by week twelve."

Dean laughed. "Have you been reading that book Mom was always telling us about? *What to Expect when You're Expecting?*"

"Oh God, I remember that, *and* the one by Dr. Spock." Ash cackled. "Remember that time you asked her if he wrote it after he left Starfleet?" He coughed. "And I *might* have bought a copy of both."

"Oh wow. My little brother grew up fast."

"You should see her and Jon, planning a baby shower. Talk about excited. Mind you, if Jon has a hand in it, I'm gonna bet there'll be rainbows and sequins *everywhere*."

It took Dean a second or two to recall who Jon was. "This is her bestie, right? The one who's coming with you to Maine?"

"Bestie, partner in crime, the gay brother she always wanted… Okay, enough about me. Tell me what you've been up to in the, what, two weeks since we last spoke."

"Not much. I haven't finished my painting of the lighthouse yet, because I've been working on a commission. Aaron—the park ranger I told you about?—asked me to do a portrait of his best friend's grandmother, for her birthday in June. Actually, it's the day after you guys come for dinner."

Plus, I got tested so Aaron and I could fuck bare.

"I went on a hike with Aaron the other day, and I've decided I'm going to get a dog. We're going to the SPCA this week to get the ball rolling."

And then there's the sex…

"Oh, and next Saturday, we're going to try stand-up paddle boarding." *And I'm painting Aaron in the nude.*

It took him a moment to realize Ash had fallen silent. "Ash? You still there?"

"Is there something you wanna tell me?"

"I just gave you the highlights. What more do you want?" He'd left out a lot, because that was none of Ash's business.

"I couldn't help noticing—"

"Noticing what?"

Ash chuckled. "Are you kidding me? It's *Aaron this* and *Aaron that*, not to mention a whole lotta sentences starting with the word 'we'. So I guess what I'm asking is…are you and this Aaron *just* friends? *Special* friends? This *is* the guy who invited you to that thing at his house, right? Will he be there when we visit? Because it's beginning to sound as though I should meet him."

Dean's heartbeat raced. *Shit.*

"Dean?"

He cleared his throat. "He's just a friend, okay?" Those moments when Dean wished Aaron would be more than that didn't count, because that particular road was full of potholes, he'd been down it before, and he wasn't going to do it again.

I'm not about to let someone break my heart a second time.

Aaron wouldn't hurt him, he knew that instinctively, but they'd set their boundaries and Dean had to abide by them. *This was all my idea, remember?*

"If you say so." Another sigh filled Dean's ears. "Bro, I just want you to be happy."

"And if I tell you that right now, I am very happy, will you believe me?"

Ash fell quiet for a moment. "Sure, I'll believe you. But… I wanna meet this friend of yours."

Dean knew he wasn't going to quit. "Fine. I'll invite him to dinner. Satisfied?"

"Yup. Jon can't wait to meet you. He's a fan of your work." Ash chuckled. "He also thinks you're hot, but then, there's no accounting for taste. Plus, he gets his seeing-eye dog next week."

"Fuck you," Dean said with a chuckle. "*Now* can I go make my dinner?"

"Are we eating alone tonight?"

Dean rolled his eyes. "Yes, *we* are. Now hang up so I can eat before my stomach thinks my throat's been cut." He paused. "Congratulations, bro. I'm happy for you. Tell Claire I said so, and give her a hug from me."

"Does Jon get a hug too?"

He laughed and disconnected. Dean put his phone down and wandered over to the fridge. His mind wasn't on food, however—it was on Aaron.

We made love this morning. I didn't imagine that, did I?

Dean was being pulled in two different directions, and it was starting to hurt.

K.C. WELLS

Chapter Twenty-One

Saturday, May 1

Dean couldn't remember the last time he'd felt so relaxed. The surface of Echo Lake was flat, its waters crystal clear. His wetsuit fended off the chill breeze, and when the sun emerged occasionally from behind the clouds, it warmed his face.

"This wasn't what I expected," he confessed to Aaron who was a few feet away on his own board. Their instructor, Dolan, had left them to it, after making sure they knew what they were doing. Dolan lay on his board near the shore, moored in the undergrowth. The only sounds were the birds, and the wind rustling the treetops.

"How did you think it would be?"

"More vigorous? I thought we'd be battling waves or something."

"Hey, if you want to go surfing, we can do that another time." Aaron chuckled.

"What's so funny?"

Aaron grinned. "Watching you paddle in circles. It was really cute."

"Okay, so it took me a while to get the hang of it. Be nice. It's my first time on a board," he declared, a hint of indignation in his voice.

Aaron sculled a little closer. "I think you did great." His eyes twinkled. "But it *was* kinda cute." He inclined his head toward the center of the lake.

K.C. WELLS

"Wanna head out there before we go home?"

Dean nodded. "I can see now why Dolan is in such good shape. This really works your upper body." He held his paddle straight up, and pulled back strongly, keeping it close to his board. Then he switched sides, Aaron keeping pace with him. Dean let out a contented sigh. "It's so peaceful out here. I could do this all day." Then the wind picked up and a thick cloud obliterated the sun. He shivered. "Then again, maybe not."

"Yeah, the forecast said to expect rain." Aaron scanned the horizon. "But that looks more like a storm coming."

"We don't have to go right now, do we?"

Aaron cocked his head. "You really do like this."

"Yeah, I do." He wasn't sure it was something he'd ever do alone though. Having Aaron there was the clincher.

They reached the center, and Dean stood still, maintaining his balance. "You want to know *why* I like this? It calms my mind."

"Does it need calming? You always seem so… at peace."

Dean sighed. "Let's just say, I'm doing a great impression of a swan. All calmness and serenity above the water line, but paddling like crazy under it."

Aaron knelt on his board, his paddle lying between his knees. "So what's on your mind? Anything you can talk about?"

You, Aaron. You're *on my mind. A* lot.

"My future, I guess." That wasn't entirely a lie.

"Specifically?"

"If I'll stay in Maine, for one thing." Lord

knew, he wanted to, but he was honest enough to admit Aaron was the driving force behind that desire. Then there were those more lucid moments when he looked at his situation, and feared the worst.

What if lightning really can strike twice?

What if Aaron turns out to be another version of Lyle?

What if his curiosity burns out, and he calls it a day?

They were the kind of thoughts that twisted his stomach into knots, and woke him in the early hours, covered in a sheen of sweat.

Christ, I'm a mess.

A rumble shattered the peaceful scene, and he gazed at the darkening sky. "I think our time has just run out. Let's go to my place before it hits," Dean suggested.

Aaron agreed, then hollered across the lake to Dolan. "We're coming in."

"Good idea," Dolan yelled back. "I was about to head back to the store. Thanks, guys. Don't forget to go online and leave us some feedback." He dropped off his board and waded to the water's edge, carrying it under his arm.

Dean held his paddle out to the side, and the board turned toward the shore. They sculled quickly, and it wasn't long before they were striding through the water to the rocky beach where they'd left their shoes. By the time they reached Aaron's truck, the first drops of rain spattered the parking lot.

Aaron grabbed his clothing from the cab, and began to unzip his wetsuit.

"What are you doing?" Dean demanded.

"I am *not* driving in my wetsuit. And there's no one around to see, except Dolan, and he's seen it

K.C. WELLS

all before." Dean blinked, and Aaron chuckled. "He's one of my surfing buddies. I don't have a problem stripping off."

"I've noticed that," Dean murmured. He glanced around the parking lot, but Aaron was right—the place was empty apart from Dolan heading for his car. Dean struggled to grab the zipper's cord, and Aaron helped. Then Aaron squirmed out of the wetsuit and into a pair of loose sweats. Dean followed suit, just as the heavens opened. They got into the truck, both of them shivering.

"I'm glad I listened to you and brought sweats too. Getting into jeans in the rain is *not* fun."

Aaron stared through the windshield. "Wow."

"It rains a lot here," Dean remarked.

Aaron snickered. "There's an old Maine joke that says when you notice it's gone from being cold, wet, and rainy, to hot, wet, and rainy, that's when you realize you've just missed spring."

Dean laughed. "Sounds like something my Dad said when he found out I was moving back here. 'Son, I just want to remind you there are only three seasons in Maine—snow, mud, and flies.'"

Aaron cackled, then shifted in his seat.

Dean glanced at Aaron's crotch and chuckled. "Problem?"

"Nothing that can't wait till I get someplace dry." He smirked. "Unless you wanna deal with it now."

A tremor rippled through Dean. "Why not? It *was* you who mentioned road head, wasn't it?" His heart pounded. "Or does it not count if the car isn't moving?"

"I was joking." Aaron's eyes widened.

"Pity, because I wasn't." And before Aaron could say something that might cause Dean to regret his wicked impulse, he leaned over, his head between Aaron's belly and the steering wheel, grabbed the waistband of Aaron's sweats, and tugged them over Aaron's hips. His cock sprang free, rigid and wanting, and Dean didn't hesitate. He enclosed the taut shiny head with his mouth, and gave it a good hard suck.

Aaron's only response was to reach down and slide his seat farther back, giving Dean greater access. "Jesus." He shuddered. Then his hand was on Dean's head, forcing him lower. "Aw fuck, that's hot."

Dean swallowed as much of Aaron's dick as he was able, his head bobbing as he worked the thick shaft with lips and tongue. Aaron's shudders multiplied, and suddenly both hands were holding Dean's head in place while Aaron thrust up, rocking his hips.

"Fuck, Dean."

He pulled free and raised his head. "What? Am I doing it wrong or something?"

Aaron glared. "Get back down there. It was just an exclamation."

Dean went back to his delicious task of making Aaron come. The illicitness of the situation had his own dick tenting his sweats.

"Dean!"

He pulled free once more. "What?" Aaron's shaft was slick with his spit.

"There are cars coming into the parking lot." Aaron sounded a little panicked.

"Then hush, and try not to look like someone is sucking your cock." Dean went back to it, sliding his lips down Aaron's shaft, loving the way his mouth stretched around its girth.

"Dean!" Aaron croaked.

"For fuck's sake," Dean groaned as he paused once again. "You've got me going up and down more times than a bride's nightgown on her wedding night."

"What the—where do you get shit like that from?"

"It was something Grandma used to say. But she *was* English, so—"

"Can we get back to the part where you were sucking me off? And go faster," Aaron urged.

"I would, but you keep stopping me." He took Aaron into his mouth, and Aaron rolled his hips again before freezing a moment later. "Christ, now what?" Dean went to raise his head, but Aaron held him down.

"Dolan isn't leaving. He's walking this way." And before Dean could react, Aaron turned on the engine and shifted the gear into reverse.

"What are you doing?"

"Getting us the fuck out of here before he has a chance to work out what's going on."

"Want me to stop?" Dean whispered.

"Fuck no," Aaron groaned. "I'm so fucking close."

Dean concentrated on Aaron's dick, and the air in the cab filled with Aaron's soft cries and harsh breathing. Now and then he'd bark out their location.

"We just came off 102."

"We're on Knox Road."

Dean almost choked at one point, and Aaron groaned. "Fucking potholes."

He paused. "How much farther?"

"Less than a mile, so keep sucking."

"Surely I should slow down, unless you *want* to shoot while you're driving."

"Don't you fucking dare," Aaron gasped. He put his foot down, and the back of Dean's head collided with the steering wheel.

"Careful!"

"God, I'm sorry, I just need to come so badly." Then the brakes screeched, the engine died, and Aaron's hands were on his head and shoulder. "Yeah, like that." Aaron's hips pumped. "Oh fuck. Fuck." He stiffened, and warmth coated Dean's tongue. Dean took all of it, and when Aaron's tremors had died away, he straightened, cupped Aaron's nape, and kissed him, a long, leisurely kiss, Aaron's arms around him.

Aaron broke the kiss and sagged into the seat. "Well that was a first."

"For me too," Dean confessed. He winced. "And judging by the way my back feels right now, it might be the last time I ever do that too."

"Then let's get inside and I'll give you a massage."

Dean blinked. "Really?"

Aaron nodded. "After that performance, it's the least I can do." His eyes sparkled. "There might even be a happy ending in there for you."

Dean gave him a mock glare. "After all that, there'd better be." He glanced through the windshield. "Hey, it's stopped raining."

"Has it?" Aaron's face glowed. "I hadn't noticed."

As they got out of the truck and walked toward the porch steps, a thought struck Dean.

Despite his fears, he couldn't remember ever being this happy.

Then he shivered. *Yeah, I can—right before Lyle brought my world to a standstill.*

Aaron paused at the door. "Are you okay?"

"Why do you ask?"

"Not sure. Just a feeling." Aaron studied him. "Do you want me to stay a while?"

Dean's chest grew tight, and a sensation of heaviness pervaded him. Yes, he wanted Aaron to stay. What worried him was how badly he wanted it.

Fuck it. Life was too short for all this analysis.

"Stay till tomorrow?"

Aaron stared at him in silence, and Dean's heart sank. Then he smiled. "I'd like that."

The sun chose that moment to pierce the clouds, and Dean's spirits lightened too. "Then let's get inside so I can find out if you have magic hands."

Aaron grinned. "Sure I have. To match my magic dick." He chuckled. "See? It's already hard again."

Dean laughed as he opened the front door. "Sweetheart, the number of times your dick *isn't* hard can be written on a pin head." It wasn't until they were inside the house that he realized the endearment had slipped out. Aaron didn't appear to have noticed, for which Dean was thankful. Friends with benefits did *not* call each other sweetheart.

Except Aaron was way past being a friend with benefits.

So what is he?

"I think I saw massage oil in the bathroom cabinet. I'll go grab it," Aaron called out, heading toward the doorway.

Dean took advantage of his absence to pull some air into his lungs. He already knew *exactly* what Aaron was, and there seemed little point in denying it any longer.

He's the man I'm falling in love with.

Chapter Twenty-Two

Saturday, May 8

Mark's back yard had been a hive of activity since early morning.

Once everyone had arrived, Mark had shown them the plans, along with the new plants and shrubs standing against the back wall of the house. Aaron soon understood why he'd roped them all in to help. The garden was a large space, so badly overgrown that it was impossible to see the rear fence. The morning task was to clear away all the dead trees and shrubs, pull up the carpets of weeds and dead grass, and prepare the soil for planting in the afternoon. Grammy had made a mountain of sandwiches for lunchtime, which were boxed up in Mark's fridge. Mark had written a list of jobs to be done, and all the friends had thrown themselves into the work without grumbling.

At ten-thirty, Mark yelled for everyone to take a break. They sat on low stone walls and sacks of compost, until Grammy peered over the fence and called for Levi and Noah. Soon after, chairs appeared, followed by Grammy carrying two large boxes.

She gazed at the seated men with a smile. "Okay, I'm ready. Give me a shovel."

Mark blinked. "Grammy, don't think we don't appreciate the offer, but—"

Grammy cackled. "Had you goin', didn't I? I only came over to bring these cookies. Baked 'em this mornin'."

Mark took the boxes from her. "Wow. That's a lot of cookies."

Grammy bit her lip. "Aw, bless you, you're still new to this gang. They can eat their way through two boxes of cookies faster 'n a swarm of locusts." She peered at the new plants. "You plannin' on puttin' those in today?"

"Yes." Mark frowned. "Why?"

She squinted at him. "Ever done much gardenin'?"

"Not really, no."

Grammy clucked. "Yeah, I figured. It's the wrong time of year to be plantin'. So make sure you give 'em plenty of water. I've got some bone meal you can have too."

Dylan wrinkled his nose. "Bone meal?"

"You sprinkle it in a plantin' hole before you put something in there. It's a sort of fertilizer." Grammy rolled her eyes. "Jeannie Crummel, why didn't you ask me before you started plannin'?" She sighed. "I'll give the sack of bone meal to Levi. Then when you're ready to start plantin', holler an' I'll come on over. Just to supervise, all right?"

Mark smiled. "Thanks, Grammy. I really appreciate that."

She patted his cheek. "You're welcome—neighbor." Then she peered at the plants. "Oh, you've got honeysuckle. That'll smell wonderful." She waved at them as she made her way back to her house, disappearing through the gap in the fence where Levi had removed a panel.

"I'll make coffee," Dylan offered, and went into the house.

Aaron sat on a chair next to Finn and Joel. "Did you manage to cut down that old apple tree?" he asked them.

"Eventually," Joel said with a sigh. Grammy had told Mark it had been years since she'd seen any fruit on its branches. "When was the last time anyone did any maintenance on this garden?"

"The place has been empty for a while," Mark admitted. "There used to be a gardener, but apparently he retired, and there was no one to replace him."

"And you *still* think we'll get it all done in one day?" Ben demanded.

Beside him, Wade chuckled. "With thirteen of us? If we can't, there's something very wrong."

"Of course, we *could've* been fourteen, if Aaron had brought Dean along," Seb commented with a gleam in his eyes.

Aaron shook his head. "Well, *that* took longer than I thought it would." When Seb frowned, he grinned. "I figured you'd have brought up his name way before this. You must be slipping. And as for Dean, I texted him last night before I left, and he said he was planning to be up at dawn, painting."

Shaun glanced toward Grammy's house. "I heard about Grammy's portrait," he said in a low voice. "How's it coming along?"

"He finished that last week. He's working on two different landscapes at the moment. And as for the portrait… well, you'll see it at Grammy's party."

"And he's coming?"

Aaron nodded. The gleam in Seb's eyes was

still evident, so Aaron decided to steer the conversation in a new direction. "I've been thinking… Remember when we all went camping?"

"Was that the time Finn got poison ivy on his ass?" Ben cackled.

"Yes, it was, and thank you for reminding me," Finn said with a growl. "So if you're about to suggest we do it again, I can give you my answer in two words—hell no."

Joel leaned over and kissed him. "Poor baby."

Aaron chuckled. "I wasn't gonna suggest camping, but maybe something a little more… sophisticated."

"Like what?" Levi demanded.

"How about we rent some log cabins? Maybe near water, or in woodland."

"With hot tubs?" Ben's eyes lit up. "Ooh, count me in."

"I love the idea too," Wade remarked, "but the chances of finding something available for the summer are pretty slim. Places like that get booked up fast."

"Who said anything about the summer?" Aaron commented. "I was thinking more along the lines of fall. And sure, hot tubs sound great, but so do log fires."

"Oh wow, I like the sound of that." Nathan smiled. "Plus, I can't tell you the last time I took a vacation."

Shaun squeezed his hand. "Then we need to change that."

"Where would we go?" Mark asked.

"Wherever we want," Aaron replied. "I'll find out what options are available, then we can choose."

"You gonna organize this shindig?" Seb grinned. "And will you be alone, or are you gonna invite a guest?"

To Aaron's surprise, Marcus squeezed Seb's thigh. "Okay, that's enough. Let it go." His voice was kind but firm.

Seb blinked. "Okay." He stood. "I'll go help Dylan bring out the coffee." He headed for the house.

Aaron arched his eyebrows. "Color me impressed."

Marcus smiled. "He just needs someone to keep him in check now and then. Seb tends to speak first and think after."

Ben chuckled. "Tell us something we don't know." His eyes sparkled. "Marcus, the Seb-whisperer. Who knew such a person existed?"

Aaron caught Marcus's eye and mouthed *thank you*. Marcus responded with a nod.

"Coffee and cookies time," Dylan announced as he and Seb walked toward them with a tray of cups, and two pots of coffee. "If you want creamer, milk, or sugar, they're in the kitchen." He speared Mark with a glance. "Make yourself useful and hand out the cookies."

Mark laughed. "Yes, sir."

Finn turned to Aaron. "Okay, you've sold me on the idea of log cabins. I'd be interested."

Joel coughed. "*We'd* be interested. Or didn't you plan on taking your new husband with you?"

Finn flushed. "'Husband'. Damn, that sounds good."

Aaron sipped his coffee. Seb's candid question had gotten him thinking. *How will things be between me and Dean by the time fall gets here? Will we still be friends with benefits?*

Perhaps the more pertinent question was whether he *wanted* them to be as they were now—or whether he wanted them to evolve.

Evolution was looking more and more attractive.

Aaron stretched, arching his back. "I can't believe we've filled three of these bags." He and Dylan had cleared a wide area in front of the rear fence, digging up tree stumps and cutting down dead shrubs. The next task after lunch would be to plant the cypress trees Mark had bought.

"It looks so much better," Dylan observed. He reached into his pocket, and pulled out four cookies wrapped in a napkin. "I think we deserve these, don't you?"

Aaron chuckled. "You are one sneaky dude."

Dylan snorted. "You think I was gonna leave them with the others?" He stood with his back to the fence, surveying the yard. "It's really coming together."

"I think we'll have earned that barbecue by tonight."

Dylan widened his eyes. "Oh shit. I *knew* there was something I had to do." Then he grinned. "I'm yanking your chain. We've got steaks, chicken, lobster… Enough to feed an army."

Aaron gestured to the men engaged in all kinds of labor. "Which is exactly what you have." He bit into the oatmeal raisin cookie.

"Okay, it's just us. What did you want to talk about?" Dylan's eyes lit up. "It wouldn't concern a certain artist, would it?" he said in a teasing tone.

A crumb decided to go down the wrong way, and Aaron erupted into a fit of coughing.

Dylan gaped. "Oh my God. I'm right, aren't I?"

"It's not what you think, okay?" Aaron wiped his lips.

"Then tell me how it is."

He swallowed. "It's just sex, all right?"

Dylan raised his eyebrows. "You're *fucking* him?"

"Hey, keep your voice down," Aaron whispered. "And it's a two-way street, if you must know."

Dylan said nothing for a moment. Then his eyes twinkled. "Feels good, doesn't it?"

Aaron groaned. "It feels *amazing*."

"So how does this work?"

"We're friends with benefits. That's all." Except that *wasn't* all, and Aaron knew it.

"And is that what you want?"

The question shocked him into stillness. "Why do you ask?" Aaron glanced at him, and Dylan averted his gaze. He tugged on his ear lobe, his lips pressed together. Then he opened his mouth, but quickly closed it.

Aaron narrowed his gaze. "What's up?"

Because it was clear *something* was up.

Dylan smiled, but it didn't reach his eyes. "It's nothing."

He blinked. "You wanna try that again?"

Dylan sighed. "It's none of my business, okay?"

Aaron snorted. "Considering the topic of conversation, do you really think *anything* is off the table? If you have something to say, I wanna hear it." Aaron's stomach roiled.

"You don't have to tell me anything, you know. Everyone's allowed to have *some* secrets," Dylan protested.

"What does that mean?"

Dylan bit his lip. "I asked if this is what you want, because… because of something I saw that last time we came to your place."

"And what was that?" Aaron was confused as fuck.

"Finn and Joel were talking about their wedding, Ben and Wade were sharing about their house, I was telling everyone about moving in with Mark… It was good news all round, wasn't it? And while this was going on, I… I was looking at you."

Oh Christ. What the hell did he see?

"And you seemed… I don't know… as if you envied them. Us." Dylan held his hands up. "To be honest, I wasn't sure what your look meant. *Was* it envy? Or was it sadness because everything is changing so fast? All I can tell you is, that was not the look of a happy man. And yes, I could've read you all wrong, but…" He swallowed. "I've thought about it since… that look… and maybe I wasn't so far off the mark after all."

And maybe you saw more than any of the others did.

Aaron stared at the ground. "You know, on New Year's Eve, Levi and I had our usual put-the-world-to-rights conversation, fueled by Grammy's punch. We got to talking about relationships. I told Levi I wasn't looking. Except I think I said it because that was always my line. I was the unattached hetero, the laid-back, take-things-as-they-come one of the gang."

Dylan cocked his head. "And now that line has changed?"

"Maybe?"

Dylan smiled. "I don't think we'd be having this conversation if it was just a 'maybe'."

"There's nothing wrong with the way things are," Aaron protested.

"Unless how they are is not how you want them to be," Dylan countered. "You're watching all your friends find love. Don't you want your *own* fairy tale ending?"

Aaron sighed. "I'm not sure I believe in fairy tales. I like what we have, okay?"

"Yeah, you keep right on telling yourself that. One day you might even talk it into existence."

"I'm not gonna ask for more." He couldn't.

"Fine. Maybe that's how you feel now. But if you change your mind, if the day ever comes when what you and Dean have is not enough, you tell him. You got that? You don't hide it from him."

"Why? It's not like we're in—"

"A relationship?" Dylan shook his head. "I hate to burst your bubble, but you pretty much are. And that means you need to be honest with each other." His eyes were warm. "You're gonna have to talk to Dean eventually."

Aaron's stomach clenched. "I thought I had a handle on this. The physical side? No problem. But what trips me up again and again is the emotional side."

Dylan gazed at him with such compassion that Aaron's throat tightened.

"Okay, then maybe it's time for best- and worst-case scenarios. What's the worst that could happen if you decide you want more than a friends with benefits arrangement?"

It wasn't something Aaron had given much thought to.

"It's like one of those choose-your-own-adventure books we used to read as kids," Dylan said in a patient voice. "So let's think about it. You tell Dean, and he says, 'But I don't want more.' Book says Turn to page six—which is where you break up. Is it *worth* the pain of breaking up? The alternative? Book says Turn to page nine—which is where you continue with things as they are, but you're not happy." He paused. "But there *is* another scenario. You tell Dean you want more, and he looks at you like you just hung the moon, and says, 'Thank God. I was trying to figure out how to tell you the same thing.'"

"*And* we're back to fairy tales again."

"Hey, eventually the story has to come to an end, whether it's a satisfying ending or not." Dylan smiled. "I know which ending I'll be rooting for." His eyes twinkled. "*You* may not believe in fairy tale endings, but *I* do."

"Hey, you two. Quit chatting and come eat," Mark hollered.

On impulse, Aaron seized Dylan in a hug.

"Thanks for listening," he said quietly.

"Anytime." Dylan returned the hug. "This is just between us, okay?"

He nodded. "Now let's get over there before they eat all the sandwiches." As they headed across the yard to join the others, Aaron replayed the conversation in his head. There was one thing he knew for certain.

He didn't want this story to end.

Chapter Twenty-Three

Sunday, May 9

Mom handed Aaron a cup of coffee. "Want to sit outside? It's not too bad out there."

Aaron snorted. "Nice try, Mom."

She gazed at him with wide eyes, and he had to admit, her innocent act beat Seb's hands down. "What do you mean?"

"I know exactly what would happen. We'd sit on the patio, you'd point to some feature or other, you'd tell me what you plan to do to it, then you'd turn those puppy dog eyes on me, and say '*Aaaaaron*', that way you do when you want something."

Mom let out a mock gasp. "Isn't there a law about not sassing your mother on Mother's Day?" She brought her hand to her chest. "I'm shocked." Aaron said nothing but stared at her, and eventually her lips twitched and she laughed. "Okay, you got me. I had some slabs delivered. You know that bit at the top of the garden, in the corner? The part that always catches the late afternoon sun? I'm going to put down a little patio, big enough for a couple of chairs and a small table."

Aaron looked her in the eye. "*You're* gonna put down a patio?"

She coughed. "Okay, I figured I'd let you do it."

"*Let* me?" Aaron shook his head. "Not sure if

you're aware of the concept, but nowadays there are these people called builders. You pay them money, and they'll do most anything for you."

Mom's eyebrows shot up. "Why pay someone when I've got a son who'll do it for free?" She cackled. "It's okay, I'm pulling your chain. Besides, I know how it is. You're gonna have your hands full with work soon." She opened the back door and Aaron followed her onto the patio. Mom sat on the rattan sofa, settling back against the cushions, and he sat on one of the chairs. "I guess your friend went to see his mom after all."

Aaron glanced at his phone. "Not bad, Mom. You almost made it to ten minutes without bringing him up."

To his surprise, she didn't react with a smile. "That's how long it took me to realize something is up."

Aaron took a drink. "Bullshit."

She shook her head. "A mother knows."

"Nothing *to* know," he protested, his heartbeat quickening.

Mom gave him a pointed stare. "To quote you—bullshit. So let's assume you've just told me you've got a thing for this artist friend."

He gaped at her. "That's one hell of an assumption."

She ignored him. "So… my next question is… is it serious?"

He couldn't fight her. "I have no idea."

Mom widened her eyes. "How can you not know that?"

"Because it's… complicated."

"Complicated?"

He sighed. "It's not what I was expecting."

"Okay, what *were* you expecting?"

He shrugged. "I don't know."

"Then figure it out," she fired back. Then she smacked the back of his head.

"Ouch. What the hell was that for?" Aaron rubbed it.

"For making me dizzy trying to follow this conversation. For God's sake, just *tell* me."

Aaron drank some more. "Dean and me… we have this… arrangement, okay?"

Mom stared at him for a moment, her brow furrowed. Then her eyes went wide again. "Oh. *Oh.* I see." She sipped her coffee. "Okay, so why is it complicated?"

"It just is, all right?"

She rolled her eyes. "Oh, for Christ's sake. So what if you're fuck buddies?"

"Mom!" He almost choked on his coffee.

She gave him a blank gaze. "What? I know all the current words. Hell, I even know what a cougar is." She preened.

Hell had officially opened up and swallowed him whole.

Mom patted the seat cushion beside him. "Come sit here. Please, Aaron." He did so with reluctance, and she squeezed his knee. "It's Mother's Day, so how about we pretend that on *this* day, you have to tell your mom the truth." She cupped his beard. "And I am *not* gonna judge you, you know that, right?" She locked gazes with him.

Aaron drew in a deep breath. "It's just sex, Mom."

She cocked her head. "You mean, that was

how it started, but along the way, something changed." She covered Aaron's hand with hers. "Hey, if you have feelings for the guy, there's nothing wrong with that." She paused. "You do have feelings for him, don't you?"

"Maybe?"

This time she squeezed his hand. "Hey," she said in a soft voice. "The fact that we're even *having* this conversation is pretty awesome."

"We talk all the time," he remonstrated.

"Sure, but not about personal stuff. Because I think this is the most you've ever shared about *that* in, like, forever."

Aaron stared at their joined hands. "I knew what I wanted, going in. Having sex with a guy? It wasn't a big deal. At least, that's what I told myself. And yeah, I'll admit, you threw me with the whole you-had-a-crush-on-Spider-Man thing, but once I thought about it, I figured okay, this has always been a part of me—it's just a part I ignored."

"So what went wrong?" Mom's eyes were warm. "What's gotten you into such a tangled mess?"

"The more time I spend with him, the more I realize this is not what I want—it's what I *need*. And I guess I'm trying to figure out what it all means."

"How far have you gotten with that?"

Aaron tapped his temple. "There's a lot going on in here. Dylan says I'm *processing*. He says that's what you do with the stuff you *can* control, stuff you *can* do something about. And I need to resolve this mess before anything can happen."

"What do you want to happen?" The softness in her voice was a balm.

His throat tightened, and he drank a mouthful

of coffee. "Mom… what if all I want is him?"

"There's nothing wrong with that."

"There is if he doesn't want *me*. And he's the one who came up with this arrangement."

Mom released his hand and sagged against the seat cushions. "All I can tell you is… be open and honest with him. And that means discussing it with him."

Aaron's heart quaked. *Not sure I'm ready for that.* "Maybe I'm making too much of all this. After all, I only met him at the end of March." Christ, it sounded like such a poor excuse.

She frowned. "What does that have to do with anything? I'd been dating your father for three weeks when he asked me to marry him."

He gaped at her. "You never told me that."

"Well, I'm telling you now. I thought he was being impulsive. I also thought he wasn't thinking things through. But when he kept on asking, I realized he knew what he was doing. And I couldn't say no any longer." She smiled. "Kind of glad about that. Now… tell me about Dean. What's he like?"

Aaron rested his head against the sofa. "He's so funny, Mom. I've never known anyone who makes me laugh as much as he does. He makes me smile. He's a kind, sweet, generous guy. And he… I guess the best way to describe it is that he… fits." He laced his fingers together. "We've got something. We *work* together. Maybe that's what convinces me this whole thing isn't so crazy after all."

"Sounds to me like this isn't totally one-sided." She narrowed her gaze. "And maybe if the two of you sit down and actually talk about it, you'll—"

"I'm not ready for that," Aaron blurted out. "I'll figure it out, I know I will, but… I need more time. This… this is too important to screw it up by rushing in."

She sighed. "I guess you know your own mind. You've got, what, two weeks before the season really gets going? If you're *not* going to talk about this right now, my advice would be… spend as much time with him as you can. See if you still feel the same way. But if you do…"

"I know, I know, I got the message." Just thinking about how Dean might respond made his stomach clench.

"When do you see him again?"

"Tomorrow. We're going to pick up his puppy." Aaron smiled. "Mom, you should see him. He is so excited about this. When he got the call to say the adoption was a go, he went out and bought everything a puppy could possibly need. Robby is gonna be one spoiled pooch."

"You like dogs," Mom remarked. When Aaron narrowed his gaze, she widened her eyes. "Well, it's true." Her expression softened. "Never mind about me seeing Dean—you should see yourself right now."

"Why? Do I have something on my face?"

"Yeah." Her eyes sparkled. "This really sweet look when you talk about Dean."

"Mom…"

She shrugged. "I'm just telling it like it is. But I *will* say one more thing."

"I doubt you'll stick at one, but hey, you can dream."

She smacked him on the arm. "There you go

again, sassing your mother. I was *going* to say… All the girls you've dated since high school? I never once saw you look like that when you talked about them. Not once."

That stopped him in his tracks. "Seriously?"

Mom blinked. "You think I'd miss something like that? A mother notices these things. I kept looking for a sign that one of them might end up being my daughter-in-law." She smiled. "I should've gone with my instincts and realized none of them were right for you, That's okay. I'm good with having a son-in-law."

Aaron gaped. "You don't think maybe you're jumping the gun just a tad?"

She grinned. "Nope. Just hoping. Now, let's change the subject. Where are you taking me for dinner?"

"I managed to get us a table at Angelina's in Ogunquit."

Her eyes widened. "Really? That's a pretty fancy place."

"Nothing but the best for my mom. And I know you love Italian." He peered toward the top of the garden. "So how about you show me what you want me to do up there?"

"You don't have to—"

"Yes, I do. And after all the stuff I did yesterday? A patio will be child's play. Is there a pile of gravel and sand up there too?"

Mom stilled. "I need those? I just thought I needed slabs."

"Sure, but they have to sit on something. Unless you *want* them to sink into the earth." He cocked his head. "Didn't you ask what you'd need when you ordered them?"

She bit her lip. "It was sort of an impulse."

"Mm-hmm. Okay then, Mrs. Impulsive, how about I come back this week with the rest of the gear, and I'll get to work."

She beamed. "I take it all back. You're a wonderful son. Even if you do sass me."

He leaned over and kissed her cheek. "Happy Mother's Day, Mom."

Her face glowed. "Thank you, sweetheart. And maybe later, you can tell me some more about—"

"Mom! You said one more thing, remember?"

There was a wicked gleam in her eyes. "Newsflash. I lied."

Aaron shook his head. It looked as if it would be the longest Mother's Day ever.

And tomorrow I get to spend time with Dean—and his new puppy.

Who was he kidding? He'd be there to see Dean.

Chapter Twenty-Four

Monday, May 10

Dean figured Robby had sniffed out every inch of the house, performing a thorough investigation the moment he'd gotten through the front door. And when he went back there and sat beside the doormat, giving a cute little whine, Dean got the message and took him outside. The need to pee was overtaken by the need to chase a squirrel, but Robby soon gave up and relieved himself. Then it was back inside to continue the investigation.

"He's inquisitive," Aaron commented as Robby trotted around the living room, carrying out more important sniffing. "Are you gonna change his name?"

"I don't think so. He looks like a Robby." Dean placed the dog bed next to the stove. "Here's a good spot, don't you think?"

Aaron snorted. "You really think that's where he's gonna sleep? I give it five minutes before he's next to your bed, whining to climb onto it."

"No, he's going to sleep in here," Dean declared.

Aaron's smirk told him he wasn't buying it.

They spent the evening on the couch, Robby sitting between them after it became obvious he wasn't about to stay in his bed. Dean stroked his soft ears. "The guy at the humane society did say he needs a lot of love. He'd been there for a while."

"How come? He's adorable."

"They said most people wanting to adopt go for younger dogs. Seven's not so old. And he's such a sweet puppy."

Aaron stroked Robby's back. "You *are*, aren't you? You are such a sweet boy." When he straightened, Dean smiled, and Aaron gave him an inquiring glance. "What?"

"I guess you like dogs after all."

Aaron rolled his eyes. "What gave it away?" He yawned. "Maybe it's time I was out of here."

"Do you have to go? I mean, have you got an early start tomorrow?" It was always the same. Aaron would make I-need-to-go noises, and Dean would ask him to stay the night.

The best thing? Aaron usually stayed.

Aaron shook his head. "Not really, no. And we're both early risers. So yes, I'd love to stay." His eyes twinkled. "Besides, I wanna see what happens when you get into bed."

"Robby is *not* sleeping with us, okay?"

"Sure. Keep telling yourself that—right up to the point where he curls up at your feet." He yawned again.

"I think that's our cue to get some sleep." Dean stood, and Robby was off the couch in a heartbeat.

"I'll grab a shower, if that's okay."

"Of course." He waited until Aaron had left the room, then went to the front door, where Robby sat. Dean smiled. "I know what you want." He took the puppy outside, shivering a little in the cold night air, and wishing he'd put on his coat. Robby inspected a couple of bushes before selecting one, did his business, and then bounded up the front porch steps. It seemed he didn't want to linger in the cold either.

Dean pointed to the dog bed. "In you go, Robby.

Robby stared at him, head tilted to one side.

"Bed, boy."

This time Robby let out a soft whine, and Dean had a good idea what that meant. *Aw Daddy, do I have to?* He crouched beside the dog bed and patted it inside. "Come on, puppy. I know you've slept in one of these before. I saw it at the center. So quit stalling and get in."

Robby's whine grew in volume, and Dean sighed. *I guess I know where's he's sleeping tonight.*

He locked the door, turned off the light, and walked to his bedroom, Robby's claws making little clicking sounds on the wooden floor as he trotted beside him. Aaron was in the shower, and Dean undressed quickly. By the time the water had stopped running, Robby was already lying on top of the comforter, his nose resting on his front paws. The bathroom door opened, and Aaron walked out in nothing but a towel.

He glanced at the bed and chuckled. "Gee, what a surprise."

"Do you mind?" Dean inquired.

Aaron frowned. "Hey, it's your bed."

"But I'm still asking. Do you mind?"

"Not in the slightest." Aaron paused at the foot of the bed. "D'you think he'll stay there?"

"We'll soon find out." Dean threw back the sheets, and Aaron dropped the towel. He chuckled. "I guess we're not going to sleep right away." He lay in the center of the bed.

Aaron straddled Dean's hips, his shaft warm against Dean's belly. He glanced over his shoulder, but Robby didn't move. "Good puppy. You stay there while I ride your daddy."

"How vigorous a ride are you planning on taking?" Dean moaned when Aaron rocked back and forth slowly.

"I'm in the mood for a gentle canter." Aaron leaned forward and kissed him. "I'm in no hurry," he murmured against Dean's lips.

"My kind of pace."

A low rumble pierced the quiet, and they turned to stare at the snoring puppy.

Dean stifled his laughter. "And tonight's mission is… make love without waking the dog."

Without a word, Aaron reached for the lube, slicked up his palm, then curled his hand around Dean's cock. He squeezed some onto Dean's fingers, and let out a sigh as Dean slid them into his body. It wasn't long before fingers gave way to Dean's hard shaft, and it was Dean's turn to sigh when he was buried to the hilt in tight, warm flesh.

Aaron bent over and kissed him. "Make love to me."

Dean cupped Aaron's nape, their foreheads touching. "With pleasure."

Saturday, May 15

Dean put his brush down and gave the canvas a critical stare. *That's it. No more.* Robby lay curled up on the couch, and he raised his head and let out a soft *woof.*

"Yes, it's finished," Dean said with a smile as he dropped the brush into the jar of turpentine, then wiped his hands. Robby had been his constant companion while he painted, and several times throughout the day Dean took short breaks to make sure Robby got to relieve himself. What amused him was the way he'd taken to talking to Robby about the painting.

Aaron's portrait stood against the wall, and now and then Dean would pause and stare at it. "I'll get to you soon, I promise."

Robby clambered off the couch and ambled over to where Dean stood. Dean reached down and stroked his ears. "I think it's time we went for a walk, don't you, boy?"

Robby's woof became a sharp bark, and he dashed out of the room. Dean knew he'd find the puppy sitting by the front door, staring expectantly at the leash hanging there. As Dean walked into the living room, he caught the sound of an engine, and he grinned.

"Who's here, puppy?" He hurried across the

floor and opened the door, not caring a flying leap about the big goofy grin that was certain to be plastered over his face.

Robby thudded down the steps and over to Aaron, who made a fuss of him until Robby was running around him, panting, his tongue hanging out, his eyes bright. Aaron straightened, grinning. "Someone's happy to see me."

"You're talking about the puppy, right?"

Aaron climbed the steps to where Dean stood in the doorway, and a heartbeat later, Aaron's arms were around his neck, Aaron's lips met his, and they were kissing as though they hadn't seen each other for weeks. When they parted, Aaron's eyes sparkled. "Wow. I don't get that kinda reception very often."

"I've missed you." The words were out before Dean could stop them.

Aaron's forehead met his, and the intimacy of the gesture told Dean he wasn't the only one. "It's been four days." Before Dean could respond, Aaron claimed his mouth in a long, fervent kiss. When he broke it, Aaron whispered, "Missed you too."

"Are you staying for dinner?"

Aaron smiled. "As long as dinner is in an hour or so."

"I take it you have an activity in mind?" Not that Dean couldn't guess what Aaron had planned.

"Uh-huh. It involves you, me, a bed, no clothes, and a whole lotta snuggling under the covers."

Warmth barreled through him at the unexpected request. "I like the sound of that. But I was about to take Robby for a walk. He's been cooped up with me all day."

"Then let's head for a coastal path. He'll love that."

Dean blinked. "He would." He grabbed his coat from the hook, his mind in a whirl.

He wants to cuddle.

He's happy to walk the dog.

When Dean had suggested a friends with benefits arrangement, such scenarios had been far from his mind. This wasn't sex with no strings.

This was starting to look remarkably like a relationship.

And if this is how it appears to me, how does Aaron see it?

Sunday May 23

It was their second stroll around Jordan Pond, only this time Robby pulled ahead of them on his leash, and Dean talked animatedly about his paintings. Aaron loved to hear the excitement in his voice. A gallery owner in Augusta had contacted Dean, with a view to exhibiting his landscapes, and the prospect had propelled Dean into a painting fervor. He'd taken masses of photos all over Mount Desert, and had already decided on his next eight paintings.

Aaron was happy for him. He couldn't help but be so when he saw the light in Dean's eyes, the spring in his step, the enthusiasm bubbling up out of him whenever he spoke about his work. And every time they were together, the idea of following Mom's advice and sharing how he felt slipped further and further into the background.

He's fired up. He's on a roll. He's freakin' happy.

Aaron did *not* want to be the one to shove an obstacle in Dean's path, not after seeing the effect Lyle's bombshell had had on Dean's life. Okay, so Aaron wasn't about to dump him—quite the opposite—but he'd learned a lot about Dean the past few months, enough to know it wouldn't take much to take him off course. Right then, Dean was painting night and day, and it was some of the best painting Aaron had ever seen.

I'm not gonna be the one to throw a monkey wrench into the works.

Besides, they were fine as they were. Because if Dean was painting up a storm, then it stood to reason everything was right with his world.

It didn't matter if everything was not right with Aaron's. After the shit Dean had gone through, he deserved to be happy, and Aaron was going to make sure Dean got all the happiness he could handle.

Sunday June 6
Dean was miserable as fuck, and he knew it.

He'd been on his own a lot the past couple of weeks, what with Aaron working more hours, and it was all too easy for his mind to wander while he was painting. Those moments when he was at his lowest ebb, he'd stare at Aaron's portrait. When Aaron did visit, Dean made the most of every precious minute, although it was a battle not to have too much emotion on show. The only thing that eased his aching heart was painting, and he poured his heart, soul, and frustration into his work.

Not seeing him as often is really starting to bite.

His one consolation was that the coming week might bring visits from Ash, Claire, and Jon. They were driving to Maine early on Monday, and Ash had promised not to drop by unannounced, but Dean didn't care about that. It wasn't that he was lonely, more a case that Ash's visit would provide a welcome distraction.

God, I miss Aaron.

Maybe it was time to concede that this whole friends with benefits arrangement wasn't going to work out. How could it, when he was falling for his friend?

This wasn't supposed to happen.

I didn't want this to happen.

Dean tried to ignore the quiet voice in his head that whispered to him, *Yes, you did. And yes, it's happened. So what are you going to do about it?*

He snorted, and said out loud, "I don't have a freakin' clue."

K.C. WELLS

Chapter Twenty-Five

Monday, June 7

Dean stopped at ten-thirty to grab a cup of coffee and let Robby out. He shivered in the morning air. "Christ, why can't this freakin' weather make its mind up?" The previous day had been a far more comfortable temperature, and a couple of days before that, Dean would have sworn it had actually gotten warm.

He watched as Robby investigated his terrain, showing no inclination to head out farther. Now that Dean thought about it, Robby never ventured far from his side.

He just needed someone to love him. Dean smiled. *I guess we all need that.*

From inside the house, he caught his phone's ring tone, and he yelled, "Robby! You're done. Get in here." The dog bounced over to him and up the steps. Dean chuckled. "You still have a lot of puppy left in you, don't you, boy?" He closed the front door and went into the kitchen where he'd left his phone. He smiled when he saw it was Ash. "Good morning."

"Hey. I'm not disturbing you, am I?" In the background Dean heard the noise of traffic.

"Not at all. I'm taking a coffee break. Where are you? And you shouldn't be on the phone if you're driving."

"Yes, *Mom.* You're on speaker. We just

crossed over from New Hampshire, and Claire wants to visit York Beach. Less than a mile into Maine, and she already wants to go sightseeing."

"Hey, Dean. How are you?" Claire called out.

"I'm good. How's the morning sickness?"

"A thing of the past, thank God. Until the next one, of course."

"There's gonna be a next one?" Ash exclaimed with a gasp.

Dean laughed. "You guys didn't drive here, did you?"

She laughed. "Hell no. We flew into Boston and rented a car at the airport. Jon, say hi."

"Hi, Dean. Can't wait to finally meet you." Jon's voice rang out clear.

"I'm flattered. Welcome to Maine."

Ash came back on. "The next place on the itinerary is Ogunquit, and—"

Dean laughed. "Am I going to get calls about every place you visit?"

Ash snorted. "No, because if I did that, we might get to your house for dinner on Saturday, and find it all locked up and you're not home. What time do you want us, by the way?"

"Four o'clock?"

"Yeah, that works. We can check into the hotel at three, so we'll freshen up and then come over to you."

"Where are you staying?"

"The Bar Harbor Grand," Claire said. "It looks amazing. It's got a pool too."

Dean laughed. "I'm happy for you, but I think you might get frostbite if you went swimming, even in June."

"Does Bar Harbor have taxis?" Jon inquired. "Or is it not big enough for that?"

Dean chuckled. "Yes, there are taxis. Not many, but I think I saw one from a company called Bar Harbor Coastal Cab & Tours. Why do you need a taxi?"

"You're not planning on serving cocktails before dinner?"

Hoo boy. "I am now, apparently." Dean made a mental note to go shopping for alcohol. "Just don't expect Manhattans or daiquiris, okay?" He smiled to himself. "You could always try our famous coffee-flavored brandy."

"Oh God. I'll take a pass on that."

"Do any of you have food allergies I need to be aware of?" Dean asked. Robby sat on his foot, leaning against his leg, and he bent to stroke his warm, sleek head.

"We're all good," Ash confirmed.

Robby pushed his head into Dean's hand. "Oh. No one is allergic to dog hair, right?"

"You got a dog?" Ash sounded delighted. "Cool."

"Ash tells me you're a fabulous cook." That was Jon again. "I can't wait to experience it for myself. May I ask what's on the menu?"

"I thought we might have clam chowder."

There was a pause before Jon spoke. "Oh my God, I'm drooling. Okay. Now I know what wine to bring."

"I can't wait to meet your friend," Ash said in a loud voice. "He *is* coming, right? I mean, you *have* invited him?"

Aw crap.

"Yeah, I did," Dean lied, "but he isn't sure. He's getting back to me."

Ash coughed. "When you finish talking to us, call him. *Then* you can invite him."

Dean stared at his phone in stunned silence. *He really does know me.* He wasn't sure if that was comforting, or scary as fuck.

Ash's snort filled his ears. "Yeah, I knew I was right. You have *got* five chairs, haven't you? I know I only saw four, but there must be another one tucked away somewhere."

"If I don't, Aaron can bring one. He has plenty."

And then it hit him. *I just committed myself to inviting Aaron.*

"Great. We'll send you pics of all the places we visit. Have a good week painting, bro."

"See you soon," Claire called out.

"Counting the hours," Jon added. The call disconnected.

Dean shook his head. He peered at Robby. "Jon sounds like he might be a handful." Robby leaned in again. "I suppose I'd better invite Aaron now." He scrolled to Aaron's number and composed a text.

Call me when you get a moment? Not urgent.

It wasn't until he was back at his canvas that the thought occurred to him.

Ash sees a lot. What if he sees too much? Dean didn't want to broadcast his and Aaron's relationship. He wasn't blind to his own emotions.

He simply didn't know how to deal with them.

Dean glanced at the landscape on the easel, and came to a decision. He lifted it carefully and stood it against the wall, then grabbed Aaron's portrait.

I don't think I'll be seeing much of you this week, so this is the next best thing. It seemed like the perfect way to spend some time—thinking about Aaron while he painted him.

I've got it bad, haven't I?

Aaron didn't call until one o'clock, but Dean knew he'd been conducting a boat trip all morning. "Hey, what's up?"

He walked over to the couch and sat. Robby shifted over to rest his nose on Dean's thigh, and Dean stroked his back. "Look, I know this is short notice, but… would you come over for dinner Saturday?"

Aaron chuckled. "Since when do I ever turn down an invitation to taste your cooking? Unless you wanna make it a pizza night…"

"Not this time, no. And I should warn you. There'll be five of us. My brother Ash, his girlfriend Claire, and Claire's best friend Jon will be here too. They're visiting Maine for the week, and Saturday is their last night."

"Oh, then you don't want me there. They'll want to see you."

Dean chuckled. "Er… you're invited pretty

much at Ash's insistence."

"This sounds like something my mom or one of the gang would do. So… do you want me to maintain a minimum safe distance at all times?"

He laughed. "And what's that? Six feet? No, but we'd better act like we're friends." *And not lovers.* Dean could be honest. *Fuck buddies* didn't remotely encapsulate their relationship. *I don't think fuck buddies cuddle as much as we do.*

"I suppose that means I can't kiss you," Aaron said with a dramatic sigh.

"Yeah, that might raise a few eyebrows. And advance warning—Jon is gay." Though why Dean should want to warn him, he wasn't entirely sure.

Aaron went quiet for a moment, and Dean wondered what had prompted the silence. "You still there?"

"Still here. And yeah, I'll come for dinner. I can't wait to meet your brother. Is he anything like you?"

"To look at? No, we're not similar. He looks like Dad, I look like Mom. Personality-wise? That's another story. But please, don't say you'll come because you feel obligated."

Aaron sighed again, but this time there was none of his previous teasing tone. "I said I'll come because I wanna see you. Okay?"

There was that slow release of warmth that always flooded through him when Aaron said stuff like that. "Okay. Thank you. They'll be here at four. You can come anytime."

"I'll do my best to arrive after them. Wouldn't want someone to jump to the right conclusion, would we?"

Dean laughed. "That's kind of like closing the barn door after the horse has bolted, don't you think? But you pretty much nailed my brother. He's great at jumping to conclusions."

"One thing. Are they staying at your house?"

"No, they'll be at the Bar Harbor Grand."

"Good. Then I might stay the night, if that's okay. Seeing as we have Grammy's party the next day."

"I'd like that. Have you got a full week?"

"Yeah, but the thought of seeing you on the weekend will give me something to look forward to."

Dean glanced toward the easel. "And I might have something to show you by then."

Aaron snorted. "You're talking about your dick, aren't you?" There was a pause. "Oops. I gotta go. No rest for the wicked."

"I wouldn't describe you as 'wicked'."

Aaron cackled, then lowered his voice. "That wasn't what you said the last time we were in your bed. That *was* you, wasn't it, saying something about my wicked tongue?"

Dean coughed. "Okay, I'm stopping this conversation right now. I refuse to paint with a hard on, especially when you're not around to… relieve the pressure."

Aaron chuckled. "Save it for Saturday night. I'll be all yours." He disconnected.

Robby raised his head, and Dean scritched him behind his ears. "And that's the problem, isn't it, boy?" he said softly. "I *want* him to be all mine."

Maybe once Ash and the others had gone to their hotel, the timing would be perfect for a heart-to-heart. Because Dean couldn't go on like this.

I know I was afraid of making the same mistake, but he's nothing like Lyle.

I know he's into women, but it feels like he's into me too. So maybe he's bi. Maybe he thinks he is too—he just hasn't said as much. Lyle didn't say as much either, and look how that turned out.

Except Aaron wasn't Lyle, goddamn it.

I know we could be happy together. Every bone, cell, and fiber told him so.

All he had to do was find the courage to say all that to Aaron.

Saturday, June 12

It took Aaron less than thirty minutes after arriving at the house to sum up his feelings about Dean's dinner guests. Ash was a warm, funny guy who reminded Aaron of Seb. His girlfriend Claire was a sweetheart, and anyone could see she and Ash were head over heels. The way they fussed over Robby was pretty cute too.

Jon was a bitch.

Okay, that was way too harsh, and he was probably a nice guy—when he wasn't flirting with Dean.

It wasn't really overt flirting, but then again, if Aaron didn't have an ounce of doubt that yeah, he was most definitely flirting his ass off, then maybe it *was* overt after all. Jon made a point of looking Dean in the eye every time they spoke. He laughed at all of Dean's jokes—hell, they all did, but Jon was the loudest. He kept inching his hand across the table, closer and closer to Dean's, until Aaron wanted to yell *Hey if you two wanna hold hands, then for God's sake, just do it.* And he fucking *monopolized* Dean throughout dinner. Aaron barely managed to get a word in.

Am I so insecure that I feel threatened by this guy? Am I really so lacking in self-confidence? Aaron didn't have to be gay to realize Jon was gorgeous. Those beautiful blue eyes, that knockout smile…

What made things worse was he couldn't work out how Dean felt about all the attention. He didn't appear to be lapping up Jon's adoration, and he made a point of trying to bring Aaron into the conversation on several occasions. But he wasn't brushing Jon off either. He wasn't fending him off with a big stick.

What it all boiled down to was, he wasn't telling Jon that what he was doing was off limits because Dean already had a boyfriend.

But I'm not *his boyfriend, am I? So why the hell do I feel so disappointed with the way Dean is reacting?* And now that he looked at the situation again, Dean seemed to be trying to redirect the conversation, to pull Aaron into it.

One thing came home to him with absolute clarity. Dean was a good-looking man, and other men were bound to be attracted to him.

Other gay men.

Not a guy who until recently had only ever been with women.

A curious guy who was discovering the joys of

gay sex.

A guy like Aaron.

What if he meets someone else? Okay, he wasn't about to ask Jon on a date, that much was obvious, but there were bound to be other guys, right?

What if he wants more than just physical? Except Aaron knew deep down what they had was more than that.

I'm just not in a good place right now.

Dylan's suggestions of best/worst case scenarios came to mind, and Aaron realized he knew exactly what the worst case would be. *He finds someone else, our agreement falls apart, and suddenly he isn't in my life anymore.*

He also knew he'd had enough of watching Jon's performance. Aaron felt sure his present mood was coloring his view of Claire's bestie, and that if he and Aaron had met under different circumstances, they'd probably have liked each other.

Probably.

Dean got up to make coffee, and Aaron followed him. "Look, if it's okay with you, I'm gonna go."

Dean blinked. "Now?"

He nodded. "I've got a headache, and it's a long drive tomorrow, so I think I'll go home and get an early night."

"You… you're not staying?"

Aaron forced a smile. "You know what? I don't think I'd be much company. You enjoy the rest of the evening with your guests, and I'll be here after breakfast to pick you up. The portrait is already wrapped up?"

"Yes, it's in the studio. I'm sorry you don't

feel well. Take some Tylenol when you get home."
Dean's gaze flickered toward the partition wall, and
Aaron knew he was about to kiss him goodnight.

"Anything I can do to help with the coffee?"
Jon sauntered into view. He leaned against the wall.
"I'm pretty handy around a kitchen, if you need a
slave to help you clean up."

I'll just bet you are. Maybe his first assessment of
Jon hadn't been all that far from the truth. Then he
gave himself a mental kick for his mean-spirited
thought.

Aaron pasted on a smile. "Dean's pretty
handy too. Sorry, but I have to leave." He raised his
voice. "It was nice meeting all of you, and
congratulations again on the baby."

The sound of chairs scraping over floorboards
filled the air, and Ash appeared. "You can't go."

"Yes, he can," Dean said firmly. He glanced at
Aaron. "I'll see you in the morning."

Aaron managed a nod, then headed for the
door, grabbing his coat from the hook. As soon as he
was outside in the cool air, he sucked in lungs full of
it, aware he was shaking.

This feels wrong. Running away wouldn't solve
anything. Only talking would do that.

Aaron turned and went back to the door.
Before he could knock, it opened, and Dean stood
there. "Hey, about this evening…"

He stopped Dean's words with his fingers.
"It'll be okay. We'll talk tomorrow, I promise."

Dean stilled. "I was about to say the same
thing."

Aaron smiled. "Who knows? Maybe we're on
the same page." *And wouldn't that be awesome?* He

inclined his head toward the living room. "Now go back in. You have guests. And we have a long day tomorrow."

Dean cupped his cheek briefly. "I'm glad you came back."

"Me too." Aaron took hold of Dean's hand and gave it a squeeze. "Thanks for dinner. It was delicious." And then he was walking toward his truck, pulling his coat around him.

Yeah, they really needed to talk. And they'd be in the truck for over four hours.

Plenty of time.

Dean closed the door and walked back into the kitchen where Ash and Jon stood, deep in conversation. They turned to face him as he approached, and Jon smiled.

"Claire's in the bathroom. I'll pour the coffee and let you guys talk."

Wait—what? Every trace of the coquettish display Dean had been subjected to had vanished. Jon could have been a different man.

He glared at the two. "Okay, I'm confused as hell right now—and I've also got a sneaking suspicion I should be angry." He gave Jon a pointed stare. "That *was* you coming on pretty strong, wasn't it? And yet now you perform a complete one-eighty?

What is going on?"

Jon's smile grew sheepish. "Yeah, about that… I think you're really cute, but you're not my type."

"That wasn't the impression you've been giving me all night. And what exactly is your type?"

Jon's eyes gleamed. "I prefer guys who aren't already in a relationship."

"Then why the—" He stilled. "Who says I am?"

"Oh honey, come *on*. Even if Ash hadn't told me about the two of you, I would've spotted it. Plain as the little freckled nose on your face. And both of you redheads too. How cute is that?"

Dean struggled to follow. "So you could see something was going on between me and Aaron, but you *still* flirted with me as though I was the last man on earth? Why would you do a thing like that?"

Jon gestured to Ash. "Because he asked me to," he said in a matter-of-fact tone. Dean glared at Jon, who held up his hands. "Hey, don't shoot the messenger, okay? I was following instructions." He cleared his throat. "And on *that* note, I'm going to take Robby for a walk, because he's standing next to the door with his legs crossed, and I think he's getting a little desperate." Jon hurried over to the hook where Robby's leash hung. "Hey, boy. Let's go for a walk, what do you say?"

"I wouldn't be in the least bit surprised if he replied. This night couldn't get any weirder." Dean waited until Jon had stepped outside, then turned to face his brother, his arms folded. "Wanna take it from the top—*bro?*"

At that moment, Claire appeared. "I told

you," she said to Ash with a sigh. "Didn't I tell you not to do this?"

Dean gave Ash a hard stare. "I'm waiting."

"I just wanted to see how you really felt about Aaron. The first time I saw the two of you together, I knew there had to be more to it than just friends. So… I gave Jon the signal."

"'Signal'?"

Ash nodded. "I'd shared my suspicions on the way here, and I told him that if I thought you were… hiding something, I'd give him a signal to start flirting with you. I wanted to see how you both reacted." He bit his lip. "I guess I got my answer."

"So what if Dean finds Aaron attractive?" Claire demanded.

"I just wanted to give him a push in the right direction, that's all," Ash retorted. "You know, in case he was on the fence and didn't wanna make a move, because of…"

Dean narrowed his gaze. "Because of what?"

Ash sighed. "I wondered if you thought he was another Lyle. And I can really appreciate where you're coming from, if that was the case. But dude… they're *not* the same. In hindsight, there were a *lot* of red flags when it came to Lyle, but Aaron? The guy doesn't have a duplicitous bone in his body."

"I agree, one hundred percent."

Ash blinked. "You do?"

Dean nodded. "And before you crashed in here with your stupid plan, I was going to talk to Aaron about where things might be headed. Until he left, because he probably felt as awkward and uncomfortable as I did." He frowned. "I mean, who does something like that? And my own *brother*, for

Christ's sake."

Ash's face fell. "I'm sorry, dude. Claire was right, it was a dumb plan."

Dean leaned in and kissed Claire on the cheek. "Let's hope he develops a few more smarts before the baby arrives."

She chuckled. "We can only hope." She glanced toward the door. "Are you going to go after him?"

"No. We'll talk tomorrow, and I need to think carefully about what I'm going to say."

"Then as soon as Jon gets back from walking the pooch, I'll call a taxi, and we'll get out of your hair." Ash gazed at Dean, his brow furrowed. "Are we okay?"

Dean rolled his eyes. "Come here, you big lummox." He gave Ash a hug. "Just don't do it again, all right?"

"I won't, I swear," Ash whispered against his cheek.

The door opened, and Jon came in. "God, it's cold out there. Never mind a morning swim tomorrow—the water is likely to freeze my nipples solid, and they'll break off." His eyes sparkled. "Something else might break off too, and we can't have that." He glanced at Ash. "He hasn't killed you then."

"He's earned a reprieve," Dean told him.

"And now we're going to the hotel," Claire added. "Where I'm going to get into that hot tub, and Ash is going to bring me several glasses of something cold, sparkling—and non-alcoholic." She hugged Dean. "I like Aaron," she said in a quiet voice. "Don't lose him."

"I don't intend to." Dean wanted Aaron to be around for a long, long time.

Please, God, let him want the same thing too.

Chapter Twenty-Six

Sunday, June 13

Aaron closed the front door and headed to his truck. His phone vibrated in his pocket, and he smiled when he saw Seb's number. "You're up early for a Sunday."

"Still in bed. Marcus is in the bathroom, so you've got me till he comes back."

"Why are you calling me? You're gonna see me in a few hours."

"I was just wondering if there were gonna be any surprise announcements, that's all. Because based on our last four get-togethers—"

"No announcements, okay? And there will be no heavy hints, teasing, or matchmaking from *you*, you got that?"

"Matchmaking? Me?"

Aaron snorted. "And I quote. 'Hey, Aaron? This one's a keeper.'"

"Dean *is* coming, isn't he? I mean, he has to be there when you give Grammy her present."

"Yes, he's coming. I was about to get in the truck and go pick him up when you called."

"Then stop talking to me and go pick up lover boy." Seb cackled. "Oops. My bad. He's just a friend, right? And hel-*lo*, handsome."

Aaron chuckled. "Marcus just came out of the

bathroom, didn't he?"

"Hell yeah, and he's ready to—okay, see you later." He disconnected.

Yeah, it didn't take a genius to work out what was about to happen in Seb's morning. *And it could've been happening in mine—if I'd stayed.*

The previous night he'd slept badly. He'd thought about what he wanted to say to Dean, going over and over the words in his head until he really did have a headache. But now that he was so close to saying them, he was having second thoughts.

Dean wants to talk too. Maybe I'll wait and let him speak first.

Because if all indicators were that Dean was happy to continue with the way things were, Aaron was going to keep his mouth shut.

No sense in rocking the boat, right?

Even if it wasn't what Aaron wanted.

Dean twisted to look at Robby on the back seat, curled up asleep on a blanket. "You're sure Grammy will be okay with me bringing Robby?" He couldn't have left the puppy at home.

"She won't mind. And he can sniff around her yard. The squirrels will probably have heart attacks though."

Dean peered through the windshield at the

quaint little town they were passing through. "This is pretty. It looks familiar too. I think we came here when I was little."

"We drove through it going to Grammy's. This is Camden." Aaron pointed to a store on the left. "That's where Ben works. Wade's family owns it. And Ben lives farther up this road."

They'd been driving for just over an hour and a half, and so far the conversation had been strictly small talk. Aaron hadn't said a word about the previous night. Dean had gotten close to baring his soul a few times, but had chickened out at the last minute.

For God's sake, what's the worst that can happen?

This was getting him nowhere. If Aaron wasn't going to make the first move, then it was up to Dean to get the ball rolling.

"Can we talk now?" There seemed to be an echo in the truck, and then he realized Aaron had uttered the exact same words. There was a moment of silence before they burst into laughter.

"Wow. Talk about timing."

Dean cleared his throat. "You go first," he said quickly.

Aaron hesitated for a second or two. "About last night…"

His heart pounded. "Look, it was all Ash's fault, okay? He thought there might be more going on between us than I was letting on, and he wanted to prove his theory, so he asked Jon to flirt with me, just to see how you reacted, and I'm really not Jon's type, and it was all an act, so—"

"Whoa there," Aaron said with a chuckle. "I thought *I* was going first?"

"I'm sorry."

Aaron glanced at him. "Hey, don't apologize. If anyone should be doing that, it's your brother. And to think I liked him. Now I feel bad about some of the words I called Jon—in my head, of course."

"Don't feel too bad," Dean advised him. "Claire thought it was a bad idea, but Jon went along with it."

"Ash arranged it all just to see my reaction? Well, I guess he got one." Aaron lapsed into silence, and Dean seized the moment.

"You said last night you wanted to talk. So did I. So I'm just going to come right out with it." His heart thudded. "This friends with benefits thing… it's not going to work."

Aaron said nothing for a couple of seconds. "Okay," he enunciated.

"And the reason it won't work is because… well… I don't think of you as a friend. Okay, I *do*, but you're more than that. You've been more than that for a while. And I like the direction we're going in. I mean, I really do, but I know this is *not* what you signed up for, and—"

"Dean."

His heart thumped. "I think I need to calm down." *And I feel as nervous as a teenager asking someone out for the first time.*

"That's a good idea. How about you take a breath, and let me get a word in?"

Dean let out a wry chuckle. "Sorry about that."

Aaron took a deep breath. "Okay. Last night I realized something. You're a good-looking guy, and—"

"It took you till last night to realize that?" he quipped.

Aaron gave him a mock glare. "Will you let me finish? I realized there would be a lot of guys who'd be interested in dating you. That was when it hit me. I don't *want* you to meet someone else. So while we might have started out with just a physical relationship, it's grown into much more than that, and…" Another intake of breath. "I want to be a part of your life, but I know that might scare the shit out of you. Hell, after all you went through with Lyle, I can totally understand why you'd feel that way. But… I'm not him. I'm not gonna suddenly decide this was all a big mistake. I know that's easy to say, but you gotta believe me, Dean. I want this. And I want it with you."

Holy shit.

"And before you say anything," Aaron continued, "there's something you should know. You might be the first guy I've ever been with, but you're not the first to steal my heart. Spider-Man got there before you."

"Spider—okay, this conversation just got really weird."

"Yeah. Mom reminded me that when I was a kid, I *may* have had a thing for Spider-Man."

Then his words sank in. "I stole your heart?" *Oh God.* The day couldn't get any better.

"I *think* that's what you did. I'm not certain, mind you, but I've never felt this way about anyone, so yeah, I'm gonna go with that. And I like the way things are going too."

Dean's heart felt as if it was dancing. "So… just so I'm clear on this… we're going to forget the friends with benefits deal, and date?"

"If you want that."

Aaron's words came across as nonchalant, but Dean detected a tremor in his voice. "Yeah, I want that."

Aaron sagged into the seat. "Thank God. I've been thinking about this for a month."

What the fuck?

"Wait—you wanted to say all this a month ago? Why the hell didn't you?"

"Too freaking scared, I guess. There was all that history with Lyle, you were the one who came up with the whole idea, I was this guy who'd only been with women… I figured with all that, you'd run a mile if I did an *Oliver Twist.*"

Dean blinked. "A what?"

Aaron chuckled. "It's this old black and white movie Mom loved to watch when I was a kid. Dickens wrote it, so that probably means it's boring as whale shit, but there's this scrawny kid who draws the short straw, walks up to this fat guy, and says, *Please sir, I want some more.*"

He laughed. "Okay, *now* I get it." He couldn't remember the last time he'd felt this light. "Damn it, I want to kiss you, but not while you're driving."

"You can kiss me when we stop, but I'm not doing that unless you need a pit stop. And don't go getting any ideas."

"Excuse me?"

"The last time I got behind the wheel, suddenly your mouth was on my dick. We are *not* getting arrested today, okay?"

Dean heaved an exaggerated sigh. "There goes my plan." They laughed.

"And about when we get there…" Aaron cleared his throat. "I don't wanna walk in there hand-in-hand and tell them all what's going on, all right? Christ, that happened the last four times, and Seb already called this morning, wanting to know if I had any news, and if he finds out about us, he is *not* gonna let me live this down."

"No one has to know," Dean assured him. "Besides, it's none of their business. Hell, we're still feeling our way through all this. We can tell them when we're ready, and not before." He sighed. "It will be a little difficult, however. I have to get through a few hours not being able to act the way I want to around you." He didn't mind all that much. He wasn't ready to be the center of attention. That place was reserved for Grammy.

"Yeah, I know. Trust me, we're definitely on the same page." Aaron shivered.

"Are you okay?"

He turned his head and smiled. "Oh yeah. It's just starting to sink in, that's all. I have a boyfriend." The morning sun lit up his face, and Dean couldn't tear his gaze away. *I love that face.*

Then lucidity returned. "Well, if you don't keep your eyes on the road, you'll have a dead one."

Aaron jerked his head forward. "Okay, okay. I should've said all this before we left your place."

Dean chuckled. "Bad idea."

"Why?"

"Because we'd have ended up kissing, and before you know it, we'd have been making love, and Grammy's party would've been the farthest thing from our minds."

"Good point." Aaron paused. "I missed you

last night," he said softly.

"Yeah, me too."

"I should've stayed."

"No, you were right to leave. I had to think. Besides, I kept myself busy."

"Well, you do have all that lube to go through."

Dean rolled his eyes. "I don't mean I was jerking off. I was putting a coat of varnish on a certain portrait."

Aaron's breathing caught. "The one of me? You finished it? Why didn't you show me when I picked you up?"

"Because I wanted the first time you saw it to be when you walked into my bedroom and found it hanging on the wall."

"Above your bed?"

Dean shook his head. "Facing it. That way, you're the first thing I see each morning when I wake."

"Ohh. That is so sweet."

"Unless it's a morning when you're already there, curled around me. Then I get the best of both worlds."

"Are you pleased with it?"

Dean smiled. "I captured you. I love it. And I think you will too."

A comfortable silence fell, and just like that, all was fine in Dean's world. They were on a good path, and when the moment was right, he'd tell Aaron just how deep his feelings went.

Aaron coughed. "So… your brother… has he always been such an asshole?"

The rest of the trip flew by, while Dean

shared stories about growing up, and Aaron talked about his mom. Now and then, he reached over and gave Aaron's knee a squeeze, and Aaron covered Dean's hand with his. Whenever the truck came to a halt, Aaron took Dean's hand and kissed it.

They were connected again, and Dean couldn't have been happier.

And the connection is only going to get better and better.

Aaron pulled up outside Grammy's house and turned off the engine. "Here we are again."

"You grew up in Wells, didn't you?"

"Uh-huh. That big brick building we passed a little while back? That was my high school. Mom still lives here." *And maybe before we drive back to Bar Harbor, I should take you to meet her.*

Then again, maybe not. He wanted to wait a while longer. *Let me get used to this first.* He loved this all-new-and-shiny feeling, the way his mind constantly veered to I-have-a-boyfriend, and warmth flooded through him.

I guess none of my previous girlfriends could match up to Spider-Man.

Dean stared at the house. "Okay. I'm ready." Behind him, Robby whined.

"Sounds like you're about to do battle," Aaron

observed. "Just remember—they don't need to know, so let's do the minimum safe distance thing."

"Can I kiss you first?" Dean's gaze locked on his. "Because I've been waiting since Camden to do that."

Aaron had spent the last three hours since Camden thinking of nothing else.

He unfastened his seatbelt and turned toward Dean, who did the same, and then Dean leaned in. Their lips met, and Aaron drew him close to deepen the kiss before gently cupping Dean's head with his hands. Dean's smell, the hint of citrus from his shampoo, and the scent of soap and cotton blended into a comforting aroma that seeped into Aaron's bones and settled there, locking Dean inside him.

This is real. Dear Lord, this is real.

"Hey you," he murmured against Dean's lips. Then he opened his eyes—and saw Grammy's front window was full of faces.

Well shit.

Then everyone scattered, so fast it was comical.

Aaron sighed. "You know that idea about *not* telling them?"

"Hmm?"

"Yeah. That ship has sailed."

Dean stiffened. "Someone saw us?"

Aaron cackled. "A whole bunch of someones. Seb must've been selling tickets." He grabbed the door handle. "No sense putting it off. We'd better get in there." He glanced at Robby with a smile. "And I know a certain puppy who probably needs to pee." Robby's tail wagged so hard, Aaron was sure it was about to come off.

"Him and me both." Dean got out and went to the back seat to ease the wrapped framed canvas from where he'd safely stowed it.

Aaron attached Robby's leash. "Come on, boy. Let's find you some grass. Just don't tell Grammy."

The front door opened, and Levi stood there, smirking. "Well, aren't you full of surprises?" He caught sight of Robby, and crouched down. "Oh my God, he's so cute. Come here, puppy." Robby almost tugged Aaron's arm out of its socket in his eagerness to get to Levi. "And what's your name, precious?"

"He's called Robby, and he's Dean's dog." Aaron chuckled as he watched Levi fussing over the dog. "How come I never get a welcome like that?"

Levi grinned. "You want me to scratch behind *your* ears too?" He straightened and held out his hand to Dean. "Hello again. You know, when Seb said you were family back at Easter, I had no idea you'd take him literally." He glanced at Aaron, then back to Dean. "Couldn't resist each other, huh?"

"Get in here," Seb yelled from inside. "Lucy, you got some 'splainin' to do."

Levi shook his head. "God, that takes me back. Grammy was always watching reruns of *I Love Lucy* when we were kids. Seb used to say that all the time. I'd forgotten, but apparently he hasn't." He stood aside to let them enter, his eyes widening when he saw the package Dean carried. "Oh wow. Is that it? I can't wait to see it. She's gonna love it."

"I hope so," Dean murmured as Levi closed the door behind them.

"It's awesome," Aaron told him, bending to take off Robby's leash. Robby went into explorer mode in a heartbeat, sniffing the rugs, his ears pricking at the sound of voices. He headed into the living room, and a chorus of "Puppy!" erupted.

"We might be able to sneak in there without them noticing, because they're too busy loving on Robby," Dean suggested with a hopeful smile.

Aaron snorted. "Yeah right." They followed Levi into the living room. Every chair was occupied, not to mention most of the floor space.

"Whose is the puppy?" Shaun demanded, sitting on a floor cushion, stroking a clearly excited Robby.

"Mine," Dean replied. "His name is Robby."

Nathan grinned. "He's cute." He glanced at Shaun. "How'd you think Cat would feel if we got a puppy?"

Shaun snorted. "He'd shit in your shoes."

"You need to come visit," Finn said. "Bramble and Robby would have a great time on the beach."

Joel chuckled. "We'd be pleased to see you too. There's only a sofa bed, but it's comfortable."

Grammy sat in her high-backed armchair by the fireplace, and she stood as they approached. "Dean, Aaron. Good to see ya." She hugged them both. "Thanks for comin'."

"Happy birthday, Grammy." Aaron bent to kiss her cheek. "I swear, you're getting shorter every time I see you."

She huffed. "Saw my doctor last week for my physical. She said I'd lost an inch in height. Told her straight she'd better find it, 'cause I want it back." She stared at the package in Dean's arms. "What's this?"

"Your birthday present, from Aaron," Dean

told her.

Aaron nudged him with his elbow. "You mean, from both of us."

Dean's flush was adorable.

Grammy retook her seat and tore at the plain brown paper. "What have you brought me? Feels like it's a—" Her mouth fell open. "Oh my Lord, would you look at that."

In the portrait, Grammy was seated on the bench beneath the tree, and Levi stood behind her, his hand on her shoulder. He hadn't been looking at the camera, but at her, and his sweet expression was what Aaron loved most about it. Dean had captured them perfectly, right down to Grammy's twinkling eyes and her smile.

Behind Aaron, Levi gasped. "I didn't know I was going to be in it too." The others crowded in to get a peek, and there were *oohs* and *ahs*.

Grammy's eyes glistened. "It's beautiful. Fellas, look at this." Then she peered at the bottom right-hand side of the portrait. "DD, 2021." She glanced at the painting above the fireplace, then back to the portrait. Her eyes widened and she gaped at Dean. "*You're* DD?"

Dean gave a short bow.

Grammy handed Aaron the portrait, stood, and seized Dean in a tight hug. "Thank you. Your painting has lit up my mornin's since the day I bought it." Then she looked at Aaron, her eyes twinkling. "So… 'my friend is startin' up a photography business.' Lord, you're a sneaky one."

"You do like it?" Aaron asked.

Grammy reached up and patted his cheek. "Dean painted me with the person I care for most in the whole world. What's not to love?" Her eyes glistened again, and she wiped them. "Okay. Enough of me blubberin'. How 'bout we get this party started? I put buckets of beer and soda on ice out on the patio, an' if any of you think it's too chilly out there, you can get the fire pit goin'. There's food too. Better get at it before the squirrels do. Little critters stole a cookie last week when I was havin' my mornin' coffee."

"Food!" Seb yelled, and everyone laughed.

"Can I take Robby out there?" Levi asked.

Dean nodded. "Sure. Just don't let him destroy any plants, or Grammy'll destroy me."

Aaron waited as they filed through the dining room, the air filled with happy voices. Then it was just him, Dean, and Grammy.

She peered at Aaron. "I take it there have been… developments since I saw you last?" Grammy glanced at Dean, and smiled. "I'll say this for ya, Aaron. You got good taste, sweetheart. And no, can't say I'm surprised." She grinned. "You *know* they're gonna have a field day with this, right?"

Aaron shrugged, affecting more casualness than he felt, his heart hammering. They were in for a grilling, and he knew it. Then Dean grasped his hand, lacing their fingers together.

"I think we can deal with whatever they throw at us, don't you?"

Aaron gave him a grateful glance. "I've got your back, if you've got mine."

Dean leaned in and kissed him. "You know it."

Grammy sighed. "Damn, that makes me happy. Only thing that would make it perfect would be if…" She glanced toward the rear of the house.

Aaron let go of Dean's hand and hugged her. "There's someone out there for Levi, you wait and see."

She bit her lip. "I kinda thought he'd already shown up, but nothin' seems to be happenin' on that score."

She sees it too.

Seb appeared in the doorway. "Grammy, get out here. It's not much of a party if the birthday girl is missing."

She cackled. "Girl. Been a while since anyone called me that." She linked her arms through Aaron's and Dean's. "Escort an old lady to her party?"

"With pleasure."

By three o'clock, everyone was sitting around the fire pit, drinking and talking. The interrogation hadn't materialized, but Aaron put that down to Grammy being out there.

He had a feeling the ceasefire wouldn't last long once she went indoors.

Grammy got to her feet. "Sorry, boys, but I need to take a nap. Just gimme an hour, okay?"

"You go rest," Levi told her. "I'll make sure everyone has plenty to eat and drink."

She kissed his cheek. "Thank you,

sweetheart." It took all of five seconds after she'd gone back inside for the interrogation to start.

"Why didn't you tell us?"

"How long has this been going on?"

"Were you together at Easter?"

"Does your mom know yet?"

"Details! We need details."

"Well, we know they've gotten as far as kissing," Seb said with a chuckle.

Aaron laughed. "Wow. It must've killed you, having to hold all this in for the last hour." He glanced at Dean sitting beside him, his legs stretched out, a bottle of beer in his hands. Dean appeared relaxed, and that went a long way to calming Aaron's last remnants of nerves. "Okay. Before we go any further… When I picked Dean up this morning, we weren't dating." He smiled at Dean. "We are now." Dean's eyes were warm.

"Aww. That's so cute." Shaun's face glowed.

"So this is literally Day One?" Ben grinned. "Okay, we won't be expecting any wedding invitations just yet." His eyes sparkled. "That'll be next week." That brought a loud burst of laughter, and Dean almost choked on his beer.

Aaron rolled his eyes. "Will you behave? *This* is why we weren't even gonna tell you guys. We wanted to get used to the idea first." Dean reached for his hand, and squeezed it. Aaron locked gazes with him. "Not that it takes much getting used to."

"Oh my God," Joel exclaimed. Aaron turned to glance at him, and Joel smiled. "If you could only see the way you two look at each other."

Finn grasped Joel's hand. "Reminds me of how you looked at me a year ago, on this very patio."

Dylan sighed. "We had no idea, did we? I mean, I certainly didn't see *this* coming." He leaned against Mark, whose arm was around his shoulders.

Shaun gazed at the circle of friends. "Our little group sure got a whole lot bigger."

Aaron couldn't miss how Levi's face tightened a little, before he schooled his features. Levi was also looking anywhere but in Noah's direction.

"You didn't answer my question," Noah said. "Does your mom know?"

"Not yet," Aaron told him. Another glance at Dean. "But I guess we'd better pay her a visit before we go home."

Dean cocked his head. "Is she going to be very surprised?"

He cackled. "Not in the slightest."

"Then I suppose I'd better let Ash and my parents know too. You *do* know Ash is going to be really smug about this, don't you?"

"Let him. I'm not sure I've forgiven him yet for that stunt he pulled."

"Hey, we're not thirteen anymore." Noah grinned. "Thanks, Dean."

Dean chuckled. "My pleasure."

Noah gazed at the group of friends. "Who knew a year could make such a difference?" he murmured.

Levi cleared his throat. "Dean, welcome to the family—again." He raised his bottle. "To friends."

Wade shook his head. "No—to love, in all its forms."

They clinked bottles, and everyone drank.

Aaron's gaze met Dean's. "To us."

Dean smiled. "To us. Because like the song

says, we've only just begun." He leaned in, Aaron met him halfway, and forgot about his friends as Dean kissed him, Dean's hand on his neck, his lips warm, Aaron's fingers in Dean's soft hair.

There were no whoops, no hollers, not even a snarky comment from Seb, just the sighs of his friends, and that made it perfect.

His heartbeat quickened as Aaron whispered the words he'd never uttered to a single soul. "Love you." Dean's breathing hitched and he pulled back, his eyes wide. Aaron nodded. "I didn't know I was gonna say that till just now, but it felt… right."

Dean smiled. "I'm glad you did. Because that means I get to say this." He stroked Aaron's neck with his fingers. "Love you too."

A rush of warmth spread through him. "And that feels even better."

"But there *is* one thing I need to know."

"Yeah?"

"This thing you've got going with Spider-Man… it's definitely over?"

Aaron grinned. "Yeah, me and Spidey? We're history." He kissed Dean once more. "You're my future."

The End

Levi's Love (Maine Men Book Seven)

Unrequited love hurts like hell
Levi Brown has loved Noah White since he was a teenager, but Noah isn't looking for a relationship. Every time Levi sees him, his heart aches for what it cannot have. Because dear *Lord*, he wants Noah, in his life, in his bed.
Especially in his bed. The only reason Levi is still a virgin is because he was waiting for Noah. Except Noah doesn't want him. Maybe it's time for Levi to finally accept the situation and move on.

Something stirs for the first time
Noah White doesn't find people unattractive – he just doesn't want to jump into bed with any of them. He and Levi have been like brothers most of their lives, and when shocking news rocks Levi's world, Noah is there for him. When their relationship intensifies, Noah is exhilarated and excited – and confused. It's kind of fitting that the first person he finds himself wanting is his best friend, but not if Levi doesn't want him that way.

How long before Levi and Noah see what's right under their noses?
Maybe it's time for an intervention…

THANK YOU

As always, a huge thank you to my beta team. Where would I be without you?

Kazy Reed, you are awesome. Thank you for being there.

Jack Parton, thank you for our trip through Maine that made me change a few details, and add even more, and for all our conversations about this book.

And a special thank you to Jason Mitchell. You still ROCK. Especially this time.

ALSO BY KC WELLS

<u>Learning to Love</u>
Michael & Sean
Evan & Daniel
Josh & Chris
Final Exam

<u>Sensual Bonds</u>
A Bond of Three
A Bond of Truth

<u>Merrychurch Mysteries</u>
Truth Will Out
Roots of Evil
A Novel Murder

<u>Love, Unexpected</u>
Debt
Burden

<u>Dreamspun Desires</u>
The Senator's Secret
Out of the Shadows
My Fair Brady
Under the Covers

<u>Lions & Tigers & Bears</u>
A Growl, a Roar, and a Purr
A Snarl, a Splash, and a Shock

Love Lessons Learned
First

Waiting for You
Step by Step
Bromantically Yours
BFF

Collars & Cuffs
An Unlocked Heart
Trusting Thomas
Someone to Keep Me (K.C. Wells & Parker Williams)
A Dance with Domination
Damian's Discipline (K.C. Wells & Parker Williams)
Make Me Soar
Dom of Ages (K.C. Wells & Parker Williams)
Endings and Beginnings (K.C. Wells & Parker Williams)

Secrets – with Parker Williams
Before You Break
An Unlocked Mind
Threepeat
On the Same Page

Personal
Making it Personal
Personal Changes
More than Personal
Personal Secrets
Strictly Personal
Personal Challenges
Personal – The complete series

AARON'S AWAKENING

Confetti, Cake & Confessions
(FREE)

Connections
Saving Jason
A Christmas Promise
The Law of Miracles
My Christmas Spirit
A Guy for Christmas
Dear Santa

Island Tales
Waiting for a Prince
September's Tide
Submitting to the Darkness
Island Tales Vol 1 (Books #1 & #2)

Lightning Tales
Teach Me
Trust Me
See Me
Love Me

A Material World
Lace
Satin
Silk
Denim

Southern Boys
Truth & Betrayal
Pride & Protection
Desire & Denial

Maine Men
Finn's Fantasy
Ben's Boss
Seb's Summer
Dylan's Dilemma
Shaun's Salvation

Kel's Keeper
Here For You
Sexting The Boss
Gay on a Train
Sunshine & Shadows
Double or Nothing
Back from the Edge
Switching it up
Out for You (FREE)
State of Mind (FREE)
No More Waiting (FREE)
Watch and Learn
My Best Friend's Brother
Princely Submission
Bears in the Woods

Anthologies

Fifty Gays of Shade
Winning Will's Heart

Come, Play
Watch and Learn

Writing as Tantalus
Damon & Pete: Playing with Fire

ABOUT THE AUTHOR

K.C. Wells lives on an island off the south coast of the UK, surrounded by natural beauty. She writes about men who love men, and can't even contemplate a life that doesn't include writing.

The rainbow rose tattoo on her back with the words 'Love is Love' and 'Love Wins' is her way of hoisting a flag. She plans to be writing about men in love - be it sweet or slow, hot or kinky - for a long while to come.

Printed in Great Britain
by Amazon

22804720R00189